Jessie Stephens is a Sydney-based author, writer and podcaster. She's an Executive Editor at Mamamia and co-host of the podcasts *Mamamia Out Loud* and *Cancelled*. She is a regular on Channel 10's *The Project* and ABC radio and television, and her work has appeared in *Body and Soul*, *Vogue*, and LitHub.

Also by Jessie Stephens

Heartsick

Something Bad is Going to Happen

Jessie Stephens

MACMILLAN
Pan Macmillan Australia

First published 2023 in Macmillan by Pan Macmillan Australia Pty Ltd
1 Market Street, Sydney, New South Wales, Australia, 2000

A catalogue record for this book is available from the National Library of Australia

Typeset in 12.5/17.5 pt by Adobe Garamond Pro Regular
by Post Pre-press Group, Brisbane

Printed by IVE

The excerpt on pages 288–289 is from 'A Sickness That Is Absolute' by Akif Kichloo, in *Falling Through Love*, Andrews Mcmeel Publishing, 2019. Reproduced with kind permission of the author.

The paper in this book is FSC® certified. FSC® promotes environmentally responsible, socially beneficial and economically viable management of the world's forests.

I dedicate this book to everyone in my life who I wish was happier.
You know who you are.

'Fiction here is likely to contain more truth than fact.'

– Virginia Woolf

1

Adella

It's New Year's Eve, and life is happening on the other side of Adella's bedside window.

The sun has not yet set, and if she looks out the window for too long the fairy floss sky will tell her she ought to be somewhere else.

The surrounding white gums dance as though there's a rhythm outdoors she can't touch from inside. Energy is carried by the wind, the brightness of the afternoon sun tickling pink shoulders and freckled noses.

She can't see any of those people from inside, of course. But she knows it. Abigail's mother came to visit an hour ago and her powdery perfume still hangs in the air. Her gold bracelets jangled excitedly, and her lipstick made her whole face look bright and festive. Before she left, she waved in Adella's direction, wishing her a Happy New Year, her eyes looking sorry.

Adella stares at the tops of a line of trees, and imagines the hordes of people gathering, the women in crisp, spotless linen, and men laughing gutturally, holding a beer to their pursed lips. She can almost hear the music. Something she knows the words to. Everyone sharing A Moment but her.

In parts of Sydney, beaches and shorelines will be overflowing with people who belong somewhere. Eyeshadow will shimmer on bright eyes and bronzed legs will interlace on picnic blankets. The wine will be cold but everything else will be warm, the fireworks marking another year of possibility.

From next door, she can hear Jia's wails. Screaming as though someone has set her skin on fire. Mitch says she enters some kind of psychotic state at three pm every day, seeing her family brutally murdered before her eyes. As far as Adella knows, Jia's family weren't murdered. She's just stuck in a world in which they were. Which, Adella supposes, is just as bad.

When Adella first arrived in Ward C, adrenaline coursed through her body, willing her to support a woman who was screaming for help. She imagines the sensation is similar to mothers who experience a physiological response when their babies cry – an innate need to soothe them. She watched, wide-eyed, as Abigail continued to draw in her notepad, as though she couldn't even hear it. She listened to an impatient nurse insist there was nothing to be afraid of before making her way back to the nurses' station and asking the male nurse if he'd been to the new Thai place on the corner of Princes Road.

Now, Adella doesn't flinch when the screaming begins. She feels irritated before she feels compassionate. How quickly we can all turn into monsters.

She turns her gaze to the wall. If how she felt was a colour, she thinks, it would be this one. Not quite white. Not quite green. Not quite grey. The colour of nothing. The colour of sick. The colour of a human brain she once saw at an exhibition, an object to marvel at, no longer functioning as a living mind.

Sometimes, lying here, she wonders if she might already be dead. Trapped inside a concrete box of madness that smells like disinfectant and box gravy. None of the doors have any locks, so she has no privacy, not even when she shits. She isn't allowed her phone, the only thing that grounds her to the world everyone else lives in. From the moment she was admitted, it was clear this wouldn't be about treatment. It would be about punishment. A prison, where your sentence is as long as it takes to *get better*.

When she was admitted, a doctor with a blister below his lip stood at the edge of her bed, flicking through a manila folder as though it contained answers. As he spoke it became clear he saw her aliveness as an indication of potential – a 'first step' in recovery. She did not know how to explain that there was a space between not wanting to live and not, entirely, wanting to die. She read once in her ancient history textbook about a form of torture the medieval Christians used to practise. It was called immure-ment: entombing someone inside a wall. That was how the space felt, between not wanting to live and not wanting to die. There was time, but there was no future. Could he understand that?

She thought of the man she'd seen stretchered in while she was in Emergency, his leg in a traction device, his face pale. He begged for more pain relief. Morphine. Fentanyl. Ketamine. He didn't care. 'More,' he kept moaning. 'More.'

That is what Adella wanted too. For the pain to go away. Anything to make the pain go away.

Today the nurses have been busy decorating. Other patients helped blow up balloons, and music played from a speaker on Cathy's desk. It all contributed to her sense that she was in some sort of day-care centre for adults. Cathy enunciated her words slowly and carefully. She spoke to patients who she knew would not speak back. To herself as she looked for whatever she had mostly recently misplaced. To family and the doctor on duty and the cleaners and the other nurses, especially when they were buried in paperwork.

'Now just because we're here doesn't mean that we can't have a party, am I right, Malik?' Malik, as far as Adella knew, had never spoken a word inside the ward. Cathy had organised pizza, which Adella suspected was more for her than the patients. She'd been repeating all day how she was a vegetarian so there would be plenty of options and 'garlic bread! Garlic bread is the best bit!' She'd clapped her hands together, like a *Play School* presenter on meth.

A few hours ago Adella had sat opposite the psychiatrist. She could feel his attempts to coax her into a shared delusion, where the world is safe and makes sense and is ultimately liveable. Surely they both know that is not true. But the subject of truth never really comes up in their sessions. What the psychiatrist wants is for her to be functional. In some respects, obedient. Easier to deal with. A contributing member of society. Something like those imagined people, on the other side of her window, who are celebrating New Year's Eve. To her they look like willing partici-pants in some kind of hypnosis.

And part of her wants that. To learn how to be alive.

But another part thinks that would be to invest in a lie. She had pretended to be one of them, hadn't she? And what good had that done?

Her maturation into adulthood had not been marked by the Big Moments that others seemed to so effortlessly collect. Her trajectory – she could see now – had been a descent into madness.

How had things gone so terribly wrong?

2

Adella

Eight years ago

The music is so loud Adella can feel it in her chest. She wonders if it might explode through her throat.

She watches a girl a few spots ahead of her in the line move her head to the rhythm, as though by accident. She seems entirely unaware she's being watched, occupying her own simple world where once there's music on, you move to it. Your body has no choice in the matter.

Adella wishes she were more like that.

Adella wishes she were a lot of things.

Living in the back of her mind is a version of herself she likes much more. This Adella knows there is room for something funny to be said, and says it. This Adella moves without the stiffness of someone being watched and reads books about clever things she effortlessly recites and doesn't have an underwear drawer full of undies with various nondescript stains in the crotch. Every night when she goes to bed, she sets early alarms and compiles heaving to-do lists, ready for this new person who possesses none of her flaws or weaknesses. She spends her last waking moments fantasising that she will be someone different tomorrow, and as she drifts off to sleep, she absolutely believes it.

She becomes aware of the silence hanging between her and Sophia, but when either tries to say anything they can barely hear each other. She wonders if Sophia is having fun yet. This would be a good moment to say something but she doesn't know what. Instead, she looks in the opposite direction, as though she's come across something very interesting.

By accident, she does. The woman whose head she was watching a moment ago has turned around and she has a face Adella recognises from some social media app. She's not famous or anything. Just a girl her age who boys at St Luke's used to talk about, with a face that makes you want to look at it for longer, from different angles. Her handle is something like '@its_bronte'. She's taller than Adella and looks how you'd expect someone to look who shares their name with an iconic beach. Thin. With Bambi eyes, the kind that look curious but perpetually disappointed in everything they happen to come across. Her height makes Adella feel short and slouched. Her clear, unmade-up eyes make Adella feel tacky. Her lilac shift dress with its high neckline makes Adella feel cheap and overexposed. The girl laughs at something and whispers to a friend to her right, and when Adella catches Sophia staring too, she wonders if Sophia would rather be here with them.

She stands up straight and imitates the energy they have.

'Is Daniel still coming?' Her tone is purposefully light.

'Yeah, the rest of the St Luke's boys are coming too. They've been at a uni party, I think . . .' Sophia pulls her phone out of her black shoulder bag, using Adella's question as permission to check if Daniel has texted her yet. Adella wonders how much time has to pass since graduating before you stop referring to groups of people by the school they went to. It's been two years.

She knows that means Nathan might be coming. That's who she was thinking about a few hours ago when she closed her eyes, letting Sophia swipe fancy colours across her eyelids. The others call him Nath but she doesn't feel like she knows him well enough to shorten his name yet. She likes to imagine she will one day. When she looks at that group of boys, she cannot understand how anyone, Sophia included, can be drawn to anyone other than him. She's met the girlfriends of the others and wonders if they, deep down, know they chose the wrong one. Do they notice Nathan when they all go out together? What happens when these people grow up? Do a group of married couples know their spouses were not created equal, with some objectively more desirable than others?

Last time she saw him there had been a series of almost invisible exchanges, so small she'd been left wondering if they really ever happened. As they'd sat around the wooden table in Daniel's backyard, she could have sworn she'd caught Nathan looking at her. When Daniel had finished with the barbecue, Nathan had brought her over a plate full of food. No one else. Just her. He

8

slipped into the chair beside her and asked: 'And what's Adella doing with herself?' There was something about how he said her name. Like he enjoyed it. But she'd thought all this before and ultimately embarrassed herself when she'd seen those same men with their tongues down other people's throats on the dark dance floor at Fonda. Her sense of things had never been something she could trust.

Once Adella and Sophia have their vodka raspberries they dance, looking at an unspecified point in the distance, pretending they're not glancing towards the entrance. Again, Adella wonders if it's possible that Sophia is genuinely enjoying this moment, while she, only centimetres away from her, is desperately uncomfortable in it.

She keeps watching the women around her, their bodies moving as though their brains have stopped speaking to them. Free. Meanwhile her mind chatters away, suggesting she dance more like that or move more like her and where should she be looking? At Sophia? Isn't that a little intense? Maybe over Sophia's shoulder. She grabs two more drinks for each of them. How much does someone need to drink before their mind falls silent?

'Oh no,' Sophia whispers into her ear while turning in the opposite direction.

'Wh–'

A man with chest hair that very nearly meets his facial hair grabs her hand while his two friends, one who is comically short, the other comically tall, laugh a few steps behind him.

'No. No,' she says, glancing at Sophia who has spat out a mouthful of her drink onto her chin.

He gyrates his hips in too-tight white jeans and just as she clocks them, Sophia leans into her ear, 'The shoes.'

How to describe them? A leather dress shoe. Maybe a loafer. The length of them competing with the length of his shin. Too big for a short man. She can't remember why but she and Sophia call them elf shoes when really they should call them clown shoes. The man could be Leonardo DiCaprio, but if he is wearing these alligator skin–looking, olive abominations then they'd agreed no further contact was allowed. A shoe tells you everything you need to know about a person, Sophia often says, because it's what people put on *last* when they've stopped *trying so hard*. A shoe will tell you the truth of their character.

'Can I get you two a drink?' the man with the fur on his chest asks, getting his wallet out of his pocket as though to prove he has access to money.

Before Adella has opened her mouth, Sophia turns around and says, 'Yes please! Two vodka raspberries would be great. What's your name?' She asks this as if she gives a shit.

'Ro–' The music cuts off the remaining syllables.

'Thank you, Ro-naaaaz,' Sophia exclaims, patting him on the shoulder for encouragement.

'You're a bitch,' Adella says. She watches Ro go to the bar with his wallet that looks like it belongs to someone twice his age.

Sophia shrugs her shoulders. 'I hope he doesn't spill our drinks when he trips over his own shoes.'

They have almost forgotten about Ro when he returns with a tray of drinks, including a shot each.

'To two beautiful . . .' he toasts, holding a shot glass in the air.

'To Ro-aallummuuula,' Adella and Sophia murmur before pouring the warm liquid down their throats, burning on the way down.

He asks them both questions they can't quite hear, something about where they live maybe, and Sophia peers at him over her nose even though he's only a few centimetres shorter than her.

They smile and nod and then Sophia announces that they both need to pee, leading Adella to the bathroom by the hand.

'Okay, but what do we do now?' Adella asks, sitting on a sticky seat while Sophia stands in the corner of the same cubicle inspecting the ingrown hairs on her knee.

'We hide.'

'I don't know, it's like . . . how much of our time are two drinks worth? Like, do we owe him ten minutes? Half an hour? He looked so proud with his stupid little tray.'

'Hurry up, I'm about to piss myself.' As they swap Sophia runs her fingers through the front of her hair.

'The man forced drinks onto us and as much as we'd like to continue hanging out, unfortunately we've lost him.' She wipes.

'He'll be where we –'

'We. Lost. Him.'

As they exit the bathroom, his white pants glow in the dark, moving to the beat of a remix of an Adele song, and it's one of the most unsexy things she thinks she might ever have seen.

'Hang on.' Sophia holds her by the shoulders, stepping onto a piece of wet toilet paper stuck to the back of her black boot.

'You know, every time I think I might be hot,' Adella says, 'I realise I have wee-soaked toilet paper attached to my fucking shoe.'

'I feel like that's a metaphor for life.' Sophia signals to their left.

They stand behind some kind of indoor hedge, where they can see white pants but white pants can't see them.

'There's Daniel,' Adella says, signalling with a nod a few seconds later, spotting him behind Nathan. They're right near the door, shoving their wallets into their back pockets. Nathan's nose and the outlines of his eyes are lit up by the screen of his phone. She wonders who he's texting.

Sophia puts down her drink and makes her way over to him, casually mouthing, 'Hey.' Adella sees her from Daniel's point of view. She smiles up at him, her thin top lip disappearing, exposing the gum above her front teeth. On anyone else, that might not be beautiful. Perhaps a different person would make an attempt to hide it. But not Sophia. On her, it is endearing. It looks like she cannot help but smile as wide as her mouth will allow.

Everything Sophia detests about her own body is what men love about it – hips and thighs and breasts she grew years before anyone else in their class. Whenever she tries to talk about how hard it was needing to wear a bra in primary school, Adella rolls her eyes. Boys – and now men – have always looked at her and seen someone simply beautiful, but women have the superpower of being able to determine exactly what makes her beautiful. It's the combination of this with that, her perfect little nose and the dimple on her left cheek. They don't just have the answer. They know exactly how they got there.

When Adella first met Sophia in Year Seven she wondered if it might be a burden to have a friend who looked like that. She had met few people who came across Sophia and didn't remark on what was so blatantly obvious. In one of their first classes in Year Seven, the English teacher had stopped mid roll call to exclaim that Sophia might have the most beautiful blue eyes she'd ever seen. Adella looked around the class, noting that Sophia was one of only a handful to have blue eyes at all, and wondered if that comment might make other kids feel bad. Like her. Who had brown eyes. 'Poo brown', according to a kid in primary school, who had laughed so hard he cried. When it got to her name on the roll, the teacher glanced up, catching her eye, before moving right along. Whenever Adella brought this memory up, Sophia pretended she couldn't remember it. They both knew she did.

The only people who didn't tend to comment on Sophia's obvious beauty were men who didn't stand a chance. Muttering that they didn't know what all the fuss was about was the only power they felt they had.

Daniel buys a tray of drinks, all vodka-somethings, and Sophia and Adella continue to dance together as though the others aren't there, even though they're right beside them. Sophia slurs something about Daniel being weird and Adella quickly dismisses her. 'He's literally watching you right now,' she whispers. Sophia smiles. Adella considers telling her how beautiful she looks. The moment passes, and she doesn't.

'Hope you enjoyed your drinks.' They both look up to see Ro turn on his too-big heel, the too-tall friend muttering 'sluts' or 'cunts' or some hybrid of the two.

'Who was that?' Nathan whispers in her ear.

'No idea,' she says, glancing at Sophia whose eyes are wet with tears of laughter.

'The weirdest thing,' she leans in towards Sophia, convinced she has stumbled across an idea that is nothing short of profound, 'is that straight men and straight women . . . passionately hate each other.' Sophia hisses 'yesss' and then starts inconspicuously doing an elf dance they learned from some viral clip last Christmas.

Nathan disappears from her peripheral vision, and she spots him sliding into one of the deep red booths in the corner, across from a friend she doesn't recognise. She shouts in Sophia's ear, 'I'm going to pee,' but walks in the opposite direction. She finds herself passing the booth he's in, his long legs taking up a seat for two.

'Adella!' he shouts over the music, leaning towards her. 'Come sit.'

He shuffles across on the sticky leather seat and then hunches himself over, directing a question about how her night has been into her ear. She tells him she was at Sophia's before. Even though she's fairly sure he can't hear her, she likes how he leans towards her when she speaks, and then angles his mouth towards her ear when he speaks. He smells like Extra peppermint gum and faintly of cigarettes. The friend stands up and gestures as if to say 'drink?'. Nathan nods.

'I'm glad you're here tonight,' he says, pushing his thick brown hair back off his face. 'Daniel said you would be.'

'Why are you glad I'm here?' She cocks her head to the side with a grin.

He shrugs.

'Just am.' He squeezes her knee closest to him.

She asks him about his trip to the Philippines, and then remembers they already had this conversation at the barbecue. She pretends they didn't and hopes he has a very bad memory.

The friend brings back drinks. They talk about uni.

'Sophia was saying you're really smart?' the other guy says, raising his eyebrows, daring her to agree.

'Don't know about that,' she mutters, bringing the short straw to her lips. It's a vodka lemonade and she can barely taste the spirits anymore. She knows the question is a trap. But she'd be lying if she said she didn't enjoy it. As much as she wishes she were more beautiful or outgoing, there is something more noble – more virtuous perhaps – about being clever. For as long as she can remember it has been her only point of difference. The extent of her value. The one thing about herself she has ever felt any gratitude for. She waits for Nathan to ask a follow-up question. Maybe about what she's studying or why Sophia would say that. He doesn't.

At some point her indoor netball team comes up. Nathan says he'd love to watch her play.

He leans in and says, 'I bet you're really good.' She smiles and shakes her head, embarrassed at the thought of him ever watching her play.

The silence between them makes her itchy so she begins telling him about the guy from before. 'You know the one who came over to us?' He nods in a way that suggests either he can't remember or can't quite hear her.

She starts laughing and attempting to explain the shoes. 'They are like these . . . elf shoes . . . and only a certain kind of guy wears them and they're just so *big*. They can step on your toes even though they're on the other side of the room . . .'

Nathan looks at her with a soft smile, and takes her hand mid-sentence, leading her to the bar. He strokes the back of her hand with his thumb, his palms soft and warm, nails curved like he cuts them rather than bites them.

The rest of the night unfolds in a series of flashes, like blurred polaroids that haven't quite developed. He kisses her at the table, his hand holding the back of her head. At one point she knocks her drink over and it spills onto her dress and thighs. She tells herself she'll go and clean herself up, but that thought disappears as quickly as it came. Sophia mouths something – maybe that she's going home. Then there's a taxi. A window wound down. Wintery air. A dark street. 'My parents are away.' The smell of rain. An unmade bed. Nathan's bed. It's like she foresaw all this. She knew it would happen. She feels like this is living.

He brings her water and they sit on the edge of his bed for a while. He shows her his computer. Apparently he makes music and there's some program up with different-coloured squiggles. It occurs to her that he is trying to impress her, show her things about himself. She tells herself to remember this in the morning. He presses play on something and she doesn't know what to do, so says it's really cool. She asks three or so questions and then runs out. Maybe she should bop her head or something but that feels embarrassing. He must sense her discomfort, because he turns it off, finding an Apple playlist and pressing play on something she recognises by Pnau. He looks at her, his eyes steady, and brings his lips to hers. She lies down. Her head spins every time she closes her eyes, so she keeps them slightly open – reminding herself of where she is.

He takes his own shirt off, and she smells his sweat no longer masked by cologne. It smells like her dad after he mows the lawn. Musky and stale.

She grinds against his erection, her bare inner thigh sensing how hard it is, while her fingers run down his chest. It's prickly, like her legs a few days after shaving. He kisses her neck as though he can't help himself, licking up towards her ear. He reaches down and undoes his belt, his mouth hanging open as he focuses. His jeans and underwear land on the hardwood floor with a clunk, and a part of her thinks how strange this is. Him completely naked. Her still clothed.

He rearranges her body like a pillow, then lays himself back on the bed, with her knees on either side of his hips. She kisses his neck, grinding harder, and he gently guides her head down the length of his stubbly torso.

She steadies herself before doing what she knows she's meant to. She flinches at the slightly sour taste. He pushes up into her throat, and she does what her high school boyfriend so patiently taught her to. She counts down in her head. *Twenty more seconds and I'll stop. Ten more seconds.* But he puts his hand on the back of her head and she thinks about the essay she needs to finish tomorrow and how she's going to get home. Her wrists hurt from holding herself up and her neck aches. She makes noises with her mouth to feign pleasure, and then she stops when she realises how ridiculous it must sound.

She doesn't know how long it goes on for. A while. She oscillates between feeling grateful she has Nathan Garcia's dick in her mouth to feeling resentful that he hasn't touched her yet. It's not even about her feeling pleasure. She probably couldn't after this many drinks anyway. It's about him wanting to look at her. Her body being marvelled at and grabbed by a person who can't help themselves. Glancing up, she sees that his eyes are closed, and when he opens them he stares at the ceiling. He speeds up, making noises. She complies. And then she feels him finish. She swallows, so as not to make him feel uncomfortable, before wiping her mouth with the back of her hand.

He sighs and looks up towards the white ceiling, blank except for a pattern around the edges, and runs both hands through his now-damp hair. She rolls into the spot between his right arm and his body, and stares up too, as though they're both watching the same blank thing. She pretends she is deep in thought, breathing heavily, but all she notices is how warm his body is compared to her cold arms and legs. After a few minutes he gets up to go to the bathroom. She hears the toilet flush. He comes back in, falls into bed, and faces the wall.

She waits to see if he will turn over, shaking a little from the cold. A window must be open and she is on top of the covers. She breathes through pursed lips and quietly rolls over to the edge of the bed. She slowly collects her bag and her jacket, and picks up the shoes she kicked off when she walked in. He doesn't stir.

As she leaves the room, she closes the door with a thud. Louder than it needs to be. She wants him to know she left.

She walks down the street, the cold running through the soles of her bare feet all the way up to her neck. A few times she glances behind her, as though he might appear and ask her back inside. Her shoulders creep up towards her ears, and her teeth chatter uncontrollably. She should put her boots on, but her toes and ankles hurt, and the cold is a distraction from what's going on in her head.

She notices that half the streetlights aren't working, and wonders if people would complain about the lack of visibility if her body was to show up, lifeless, the next morning.

Probably not, she thinks.

There would be greater emphasis placed on the fact she was walking, alone, barefoot, at four o'clock on a Sunday morning in the middle of June, basically daring a predator to jump out from behind a suburban bush. If they did, then Nathan would probably feel very guilty about not even saying goodbye. What an awful thing to think.

She sniffles and hugs her arms into her chest. It's starting to drizzle again, as though the clouds can't entirely commit to raining. As though they, along with the rest of Sydney, would just like a few more hours' sleep.

She looks up ahead and can see the lights of a main road. Finally. Once she's there, hopefully she can hail a taxi. Her stomach lurches at the thought of how much it will cost. She cannot afford to do this.

The thought of being in a car with a stranger makes her feel suddenly visible. She pulls at the skin beneath her eyes, trying to erase any smudged mascara. She hates how her body smells. Like someone else. His sweat has settled into her pores and she rubs where he licked her neck with the edge of her leather jacket. The stamp on the inside of her right wrist has turned into an inky blur. She just wants to be in the shower. A scalding-hot, quiet shower. Then bed.

Maybe in the morning there will be a message from Nathan.

She smiles at the possibility.

3

Adella

The wind tangles her hair into stringy knots as she half walks, half jogs to the cafe on the corner.

She is consumed by envy for Jake, whose weekends are blank squares on a calendar. Sometimes they're marked by birthdays or rugby league games, but never by a sickening sense that he has an assignment due on Monday, and therefore any joy he feels is stolen. Laden with guilt. A moment he should've spent with his fingers on a keyboard.

The cafe is on a main road. Outside is a big sign that says 'Cafe Luxe', which always makes them laugh because you can see where the accent has fallen from above the 'e' and the square stainless-steel tables are always sticky and unstable, a folded-up coaster lodged under one of the legs.

She finally makes it through the door and collapses into the chair opposite him, repeating, 'Sorry sorry sorry, bus was late,

I'm the worst,' trying to ignore the clock above his head that shows she was meant to be here twenty-five minutes ago.

'Nah, nah, I've got all the time in the world,' he says, a grin indicating he's annoyed but won't be for long. 'Didn't *you* say ten because you've got an assignment to finish today?'

'Yes I did, I'm so sorry. I ended up staying up last night until past five because I have work tonight . . . then my bus didn't come.' She leans back, catching her breath.

The sound of grinding coffee beans is interrupted by the commanding rev of an engine, so loud it forces everyone in close proximity to swing their heads around, brows furrowed.

'Mum says the worst injuries she sees are from motorbike accidents,' she says, nodding towards the doorway. They watch the road come alive with motorbikes, each revving their engines one after the other, before speeding down towards the highway. 'Last week she said she saw a guy whose patella had been found fifty metres away from the rest of his body.'

She doesn't know if it was fifty exactly but it sounds dramatic.

'That's messed up.' Jake takes a sip of his coffee and chocolate settles on his top lip. 'Maybe that's why depressed middle-aged men buy motorbikes. More socially acceptable to be split into pieces by a truck than to . . .' He brings his forefinger to his temple. Bang.

'Jesus.'

'It's the perfect decoy,' he says, as though concocting a plan. 'You *look* like you're taking up a new hobby and being spontaneous but really what you're saying is, "I'm indifferent to being alive". So you get on your lame little bike, between a ten-tonne

22

truck and an SUV, and maybe feel something for the first time in a decade.'

'Well, I guess that's what you have to look forward to.' She shouldn't have said that. It brings up the one thing they do not talk about.

He must clock her expression.

'Don't worry about it, it's fine.' He forgives her with a shake of the head. 'So, have you heard from that guy then?'

She taps her foot beneath the table. She does not want to talk about Nathan.

They've spoken on the phone a few times over the last fort-night and the subject of Nathan has come up, mostly because she can't help herself. She should've just pretended it never happened. By even mentioning it perhaps she jinxed it. There were some details she omitted. Others she exaggerated.

'Yeah. He messaged me on Wednesday night.' She exhales and gestures for Jake to wipe his lip. Doesn't tell him it was 10 pm and the message said 'Hey'. Certainly doesn't tell him what came next.

'When are you seeing him?'

'Not sure yet. I think he's meant to be busy this weekend and Sophia was saying he works nights at some bottle shop.'

A waitress comes over, and she orders an orange juice.

'Insane that this Nathan works seven nights a week. Must be the hardest-working guy in Sydney,' Jake says, raising his eyebrows.

'Shut up.'

'You just . . . know how to pick them.' He shakes his head. 'Remember Jono? I was thinking about him the other day.'

She laughs. 'Why? Did you ejaculate prematurely and then refuse to speak to the girl who was literally still in your bed? If so I can give you Jono's number and maybe you can create a little support group.'

'But you saw him again!' He taps the table with his palms, lightly but it still shifts, losing a serviette. 'After all that you ended up at his party, remember? And he blanked you while —'

'Don't, I can't even think about it.' She plays with the salt and pepper shakers. She hates that she told anyone any of this.

'I obviously don't know Nathan. Could be a great guy. But if it's been two weeks and he hasn't asked you out . . . then you're not a girl he wants to date.'

She swallows. 'Who said I wanted to date him?' Her voice is high-pitched.

Jake doesn't need to know she keeps checking his account. Or that Nathan followed four new girls, *two* named Olivia, at 1 am last night. Or that she attempted to stalk all of them, but only one Olivia had her account on public so she had to make do. And then found herself looking at photos from a family holiday to Rome four years ago and had to put her phone down so she didn't accidentally 'like' anything. He doesn't need to know that her manager caught her on her phone during Friday night service, and said, 'Hey, Adella?', his tone laced with irritation. She was just checking if there was anything waiting for her. A message that might change how she felt for the rest of the night.

'Sorry, I'm not trying to be brutal. You just deserve someone who's not a dick.'

If Jake and Adella were anyone else, Adella thinks, any other heterosexual man sitting across from any other heterosexual woman, telling her what she deserved, one might assume there was more to it.

Throughout high school, their friends would say they were in love, just like in the movies when the girl and the boy are best friends and suddenly realise one day they've loved each other all along. But both Jake and Adella knew that was not the case. They'd joke they got that out of the way early.

It all began in Year Eight in whatever chat room everyone was using back then.

Jake was in his living room, where a PC sat against a dark brick wall beside Darcy's birdcage, and a notification popped up that he had been added by someone named 'adella_surfs_up'.

He did not know anyone named Adella or anyone who surfed, he would always say when retelling the story to an acquaintance who was only half listening. They enjoyed their tale of meeting far more than anyone else did. At this point, Adella always added that she had never – and still has never – surfed. Immediately he typed out 'Hey'. She replied. Apparently she'd got his username off a friend at school, which made sense. He knew girls at Blackheath Public from primary school. They didn't like him very much, he'd later confess, so he thought sharing his details was a bit strange. He didn't realise that apart from an impeccably slick ponytail (no bumps) and a very specific pair of black school shoes, the ones that looked like they belonged on boats, the contacts of boys they knew was one of the only forms of social currency these girls had.

It wasn't long before Jake and Adella were talking every day after school. They'd moved past sharing weird photographs of themselves they'd taken in their bedrooms, fully clothed but with unexplainable facial expressions, and now they just talked about stuff. School. What they watched on TV. Their entirely fictionalised dating history. Playing truth or dare, which could only really be truth, and would always be some strange sexual question that made them both exhilarated and uncomfortable.

The first time they met was at Greater Union cinemas. She wore a blue t-shirt, denim shorts and skater shoes that made her legs look scrawny. Neither had made it clear whether or not this was a date, so Jake tried to pay for her movie ticket but Adella said no, her mum had given her money. Jake admitted later he was relieved because that meant he could afford McDonald's afterwards, and he hadn't had lunch yet.

When they sat down at the back, Adella said she'd seen the trailer for this movie and it looked really good. She proceeded to tell him what it was about, two scuba divers who were left out at sea by their dive group and had to try to survive, and Jake thought that actually did sound quite good. They whispered through the trailers until the woman in front of them shushed them without even turning around, and Jake's cheeks turned bright red. He wondered if Adella could tell in the dark.

Even though he liked the movie, Jake barely followed it. He promised himself never to meet a person for the first time at the movies again, because you didn't get to talk or get to know each other. You just sat weirdly close and tried not to slurp your frozen Coke too loudly in case the other person thought you were gross.

He kept wanting to bring things up from the movie that vaguely related to conversations they'd had online, but felt self-conscious because of the shushing woman. He sat deathly still until the end credits.

For a little under a week, Jake and Adella thought they might be boyfriend and girlfriend. They didn't kiss or anything, or even hold hands. But Jake sent her a message the day after their date saying 'I kinda like u' and Adella said 'same'. They added each other's names to their handles (Jake4Adella) and talked about exactly the same things they had for weeks. When they met again in the city the following weekend, Adella was acting strangely, and that night would say she actually didn't want a boyfriend at the moment. Jake scanned his body for an emotional response, but other than embarrassment, he could not find one. They decided to be good friends instead.

Adella lived – and still lives – a fifteen-minute walk from Jake. If Adella had a fight with her dad, they'd meet up on the swings in the park around the corner and talk. When Adella decided she wanted to get fit for summer, Jake would join her in that same park, and they'd try to do one hundred sit-ups before giving up and walking to the corner shop for an ice cream. Their friendship was forged over hot chips from the milk bar with extra chicken salt and a metal slippery dip that would burn their thighs in summer. When Adella's group at school would stop speaking to her for seemingly no reason, she'd unload on Jake, knowing that no matter how bad things got she always had someone. He didn't tell Adella so much about the boys in his English class who called him the 'r' word, half a dozen of them doing their own impression of someone with a severe disability, grunting and holding their hands up at awkward angles. With her, he could be someone else.

Throughout high school, when one didn't have a Valentine, which was almost always, the other would buy them a terrible gift. Adella would get Jake an extra-large nude G-string from Kmart, and he would wrap up a brick he found on the street. Still, they would buy each other cards if the day felt particularly sad.

As her orange juice arrives she promises herself not to tell him any more about Nathan. Jake hadn't seen how Nathan had looked at her that night, how he'd waited for her outside the bathroom and opened the taxi door for her when they'd arrived at his house. But most of all he didn't understand how this wasn't a matter of what she deserved, but how she felt. Her interest in Nathan wasn't just a tap she could turn off on the basis of principle.

'What happened with the girl? From Cargo Bar?'

He smiles in a way that tells Adella he likes her.

'We hung out last night. Went to some Italian place in Wahroonga and then back to hers . . .'

'What's her name again?'

'Georgette,' he says, almost mumbling.

'What kind of bullshit private school–girl name is "Georgette"?'

He smirks, rubbing at the corners of his eyes. 'Her place was insane. Tennis court. Pool. What do you call it when you have a gate at the top of your driveway?'

'Oh wow.' She doesn't know what you call it.

'Hedges. Entertainment room.' He starts counting on his fingers. 'Intercom system. She had, like, a PIN to get in and then there was a buzz and the door opened. I looked away because I thought otherwise she'd worry about me coming back later to rob her house.'

She shrugs as if to say 'fair enough', noticing the crucifix hanging from his neck on a silver chain which always looks at odds with his biceps, which stretch any t-shirt he finds himself in. He still looks like some sort of professional athlete, his chest broad and hard, his right ear the wrong shape. For most people their age, their dreams, their ambitions, are just beginning. For Jake, though, for anyone who spent the majority of their adolescence training, they have reached an end. She has never asked him about it, how that felt. He must have believed first grade footy was a possibility up until the last few years, when injury had proved him wrong.

'So when are you going to show her around your neighbourhood? Take her out to Hungry Jacks for a nice cultural meal? You could even bring a white tablecloth and ask Vili if he can bring a menu to the table –'

He cuts her off. 'She told me she hasn't gone down this direction on the freeway for a decade.'

She gasps in mock horror.

'Her loss. Doesn't know what she's missing out on.' She gestures towards the street outside. A tattoo parlour that got shot at last month, the glass still visibly shattered. A Korean restaurant they've never seen anyone eat at, so they assume is a drug front of some sort. A twenty-four-hour chemist, where it always feels like it's three in the morning, no matter what time you visit. A pub that Adella was once followed home from. When she began sprinting towards her street, the man finally stopped and started cackling. He couldn't keep up.

'Ah, well,' Jake says, his tone dripping with hyperbolic pity. 'I'm sure she cries into her ski gear while flying down the Swiss Alps.'

She loves Jake in this moment. Neither of them has ever been skiing. This was their shorthand for determining whether someone had money. If they knew how to ski, they were rolling in it. If they owned their own ski gear, well. Their parents must be on Australia's Rich List. Having Jake see it too meant she knew she wasn't mad. She also has no desire to go skiing. Everyone always seems to break their neck. Across from Jake, in Cafe Luxe, is precisely where she belongs.

'What's she studying?'

'She's not. She does something in fashion. I don't really get it, but it seems cool.'

She nods. Girls who went to Blackheath, where she went, didn't go into fashion. Or music. Or the arts more broadly. It's funny, Adella thinks, the choices you must have when there's a soft queen bed, inside a five-bedroom home, waiting to catch you if you fall.

'How's uni going?' he asks. She knows how intensely he does not care, but she appreciates the sentiment.

She considers telling him that the cliché is true – anyone who studies Psychology does so because they secretly think they're mad. They enrol to first diagnose themselves or perhaps someone they love, and then they can move on to diagnosing others. But ultimately it begins as a navel-gazing exercise, where they quiz the lecturers on some very specific symptom of Bipolar II. Then she considers telling him about the letter. There is an award, named after a long-dead professor, she is set to receive next week.

It turns out last semester she placed first in two of her second-year courses. She'd called her mum and then Lottie and then Pa, but found she didn't feel much of anything except, she supposed, a desire to tell people. It's as though she'd called them to try to animate some emotion within herself – to hear their squeals and pauses and gasps and try to absorb some of that excitement within her own body. Her own elation had been too fleeting. Unsatisfying. It made her wonder what any of this was for.

Instead, she tells him about the essay due tomorrow for The Philosophy of Happiness, an extra Arts unit she'd picked up.

'So what's the philosophy, then?' He leans his head back into interlaced fingers.

'I don't know.' She shrugs. 'I keep leaving the lectures early to get a doughnut.'

'I don't need to study a course at university to know the answer is doughnuts.' He looks towards the window display, probably in search of a doughnut. 'I bet the people who chose that subject are really fun and also cool. I'm surprised you still hang out with me.'

'They all smell like . . .' She pauses. 'Ham. Hey, what happened to your hand?' She looks curiously at the space between his thumb and index finger, at a red gash that looks like it is beginning to heal.

'Work. Clipped it with the saw. Could've been so much worse . . .' He trails off.

For two years now he's been doing his carpentry apprenticeship. She doesn't even remember when he made the decision that carpentry would be it. One day it just was. It was strange how since school he had gone on to live one life, with hammers and screwdrivers and circular saws, while she spent much of the week living another. She feels a sharp moment of discomfort, wondering if this is why so many adults don't seem to have any friends. They get pulled away by work first, then perhaps kids or dying parents, and the accidental intimacy of adolescent relationships drips away, making way for something more formal and polite. When she looks at Jake sometimes her mind skips forward ten years and she can see a family barbecue, kids hanging on to bare calves. They are in her backyard, a home she owns with a pool and white French doors that open into a big white kitchen and although she isn't sure, in her imagination, how she earned all of this, she knows she is A Success. Everyone there knows it. She's always thinner in these delusions. That barely warrants mentioning. Sophia is there beside someone lovely and they're laughing about all those men who rejected Adella who must know now about the Success. She has proved something to everyone, but most of all she has learned that life is fair. Good things happen to people who work hard, even when they grow up in the wrong family in the wrong suburb. Jake is always there, though. Saying with a look rather than with his words that he sees it too – how she became something.

'How's your mum, by the way?' He asks the question earnestly, the dimple in his left cheek disappearing.

'Not good,' she says, pushing her empty orange juice glass away from her. 'Mum's not good.'

4

Jake

Kanooble is the type of place that still has phone boxes.

They don't work. In every case someone graffitied the outside, then the inside, then tried to start a bonfire, and then as a last resort took a hammer to the phone itself. Now they work for no one.

There are shelters over bus stops out of sheer necessity. In winter Kanooble is one of the coldest parts of greater Sydney, and in summer one of the warmest. The heat ricochets off the bitumen, onto dilapidated homes and scorched browning front yards. There is no relief.

It is not unusual to see an Australian flag hanging out the front of a rundown fibro home. Some houses wear their Christmas decorations all year round, or maybe have a parked caravan in their driveway, the engine dormant. There are 'For Sale' and 'For Lease' signs peppered throughout every street.

Jake pulls up on the corner of Gallipoli Road and Albert Street and despite himself feels something flutter in his stomach. Two awkward holes sit on the street side of the front fence, left by the 'For Lease' sign.

Sam's car pulls up behind his, with their mum in the passenger seat, the back seat packed up so high the rear-vision mirror is rendered useless. They have a few cardboard boxes, but mostly everything is packed into laundry baskets and garbage bags bursting at the seams. He opens the boot, picks up a basket full of pots and pans, and makes his way into their new family home.

It smells damp and faintly of another family's cooking. The corridor is cold and dark, and the floorboards appear to be made of some sort of hard plastic. He plonks the basket down on the off-white kitchen bench and heads to the little patch of grass out the back, just to double-check. Good. Nothing but a corrugated iron fence, a Hills Hoist and a bush that looks like it's never been watered.

For the rest of the afternoon, they go between Edgar Street, the only house the boys have ever known, and Gallipoli Road, packing, unpacking, putting things in temporary places they mean to fix later but probably never will.

When he arrives after his fourth trip, dust settled under his fingernails, he imagines what this place might look like to Georgette. He notices for the first time how strange it is that there's a single white plastic chair that doesn't belong to them sitting on the verandah. He thinks that this place looks like it belongs to a lonely old lady who lives in the dark, hoarding lolly jars to bribe her grandchildren with. Would Georgette think that? Might she not care? Would she notice that no other residents on this street appear to have mowed their front lawn, their own new yard well manicured only because a real estate agent insisted on it?

While he packs away his toothbrush and razor in a bathroom he'll share with both his brothers, he thinks of Vili on the other side of Sydney, moving in with Adrian and Timi. They're moving closer to the city, which they'd spoken about doing since starting their apprenticeships years ago. He is moving even further away, still with his mum. Imagine, he fantasises, knowing your parents would be okay without you.

'Do we have toilet paper?' Sam shouts from the toilet attached to their mother's room.

'Seriously? We've been here a few hours and you've already christened my toilet?' she yells back.

'Jake's in the other one. Seriously, can someone bring me some toilet paper?'

Annie and Jake begin rifling through baskets and garbage bags, full of items that don't belong together.

'Did you want a wall clock?' Jake calls out.

'How about a kettle? Oh look, it's still got water in it – that's helpful,' Annie quips.

'I've got your birth certificate?'

'There are three copies of Dad's funeral booklet. Genuinely might work?'

Finally they find half a roll of paper towel. The booklets go into the bottom kitchen drawer.

As the light in the house turns from orange to grey to a dull blue, miscellaneous items become scattered across the bench and the living room floor.

'Can we get Maccas?' Sam shouts from under his bed, twisting an allen key he's been working with for hours.

'I feel like you shouldn't be under the bed while you're constructing it,' Jake says, sticking his head in his room.

'I'm really hungry. Can you ask Mum?'

The three boys start chanting for Maccas, just like they did when they were kids, Paul finding a knife and a pair of tongs to bang on the bench for extra effect.

'I don't . . . you can all drive and have your own money, why are you asking me if we can get Maccas? Whoever's going, I'll have a large McChicken meal.' Annie throws her arms in the air and goes back to her bedroom, where clothes are sprawled across her maroon doona cover.

That night, they eat on the lounge room floor, sitting on upside-down washing baskets. The light above them begins to flicker.

'Ah, fuck, do you reckon this house is haunted too?' Sam points to the light above, his mouth full of chips.

'The old house wasn't haunted. We just got Vili to do the electricity and it turns out he's really shit at his job. That's why the ceiling fan would randomly turn on and the lights were fucked,' Jake says. He picks up a Maccas bag, looking to see if there's anything in the bottom.

'Nah, I like the idea that wherever Dad is, he has the energy to turn the lights on and off just to annoy us.'

Paul scrunches up his burger wrapper and says with conviction, 'I think they have, like, an obligation to tell you if a house is haunted.'

'You serious?' Jake looks at Paul and lifts his eyebrows.

'Yeah, like that house where the guy murdered his parents and sister. They had to tell potential buyers because it's the law or something.'

'That's not because it might be haunted,' Jake says, rubbing his tired face. 'That's because there was a triple murder committed there?'

'This house isn't haunted,' Annie says, face blank. 'We've earned ourselves some peace.'

Jake returns to his bedroom, putting away the last of his clothes and moving his small wooden desk into the corner of the room. This house does feel different, the air less thick, the walls and the ceilings telling no stories yet. It is not haunted like Edgar Street. But at least at Edgar Street he knew where his dad was. He could still vividly see his body moving from room to room, his outline walking through the front door, and sitting down at the dinner table.

Growing up, his mum always had extra spaghetti bolognese, which meant Adella was there multiple times a week. Every time his dad sat down at the dinner table and took a mouthful of food, he'd remark, 'This is nice, Annie,' and Annie never seemed to get sick of hearing it. Adella would sit beside Jake, while his two younger brothers, Sam and Paul, sat across from them. Sometimes Angelica and Megan would join them, Jake's two older sisters from his dad's previous marriage, but that was rare.

Jake's dad was a brilliant storyteller. He'd begin, 'You'll never believe what happened at work today,' and then tell an outrageous story about picking up boxes of used catering supplies that hadn't even been rinsed, with maggots finding a home on someone's uneaten potato from three days ago.

'And I said, I said,' Malcolm would say, "'Couldn't even give 'em a rinse? Tell me, what did your last slave die of?'"

Malcolm had worked at a party supply hire company, where he'd drop off hundreds of plates and forks and wine glasses for a fancy party, and then pick them up afterwards. The fact he never left that job made Jake suspect that maybe he hadn't actually said all those one-liners out loud, but he never challenged his dad on it. Looking back, maybe it was his dad's way of reclaiming power around the dinner table, playing out a version of events that couldn't have happened, but he wished they did.

Here, in this house, his dad doesn't exist. He never opened a window or hosed the garden. He never put his arm around his wife or told a story that took too long.

In dragging the desk, the top drawer now sits ajar, full of paper and pens Jake had forgotten about. He rifles through, finding a report he remembers hiding from his mum. He tosses it into a garbage bag. But at the bottom he finds a sketchpad. Inside are designs he had to do for Woodwork, of boxes and a bedside table he never turned in. As he flicks, he finds other sketches that weren't for school. Windows and doors, imagined backyards and a renovated back shed. They're not bad. They're not perfect, he can see that. The proportions are sometimes off and he can tell where he'd got halfway through a drawing and given up. But he remembers how it had felt to lose himself on a page and visualise a reality different from the one he was living in. Was this what he'd once expected from carpentry? Is that why he'd pursued it in the first place?

He leaves the book on his desk with some pencils he finds in the drawer below and makes his way back out into the living room.

He notices that most of the lights are off and his mum is curled over the coffee table, rummaging through her handbag.

'Mum, do you have any toothpaste?' he asks, lowering his voice. 'I don't know where mine is.'

'No toothpaste, but I do have Dad.' She smiles, her voice a whisper. In her hands is the framed photo that had sat atop his coffin, a picture taken on a holiday when they were little, his nose sunburnt and his forehead shiny with sweat. He'd had more hair than Jake could ever remember.

He smiles. Can't remember the last time he saw it. The picture once sat on the table by the front door at Edgar Street, where everyone threw their keys and hats. But Annie kept finding the silver frame face down and quickly realised its placement wasn't an accident. Since then it had lived in her bedroom, the only thing on Malcolm's bedside table.

She places the frame on the coffee table and murmurs goodnight.

Jake finds toothpaste in one of the baskets meant for the kitchen. As he brushes his teeth, he makes his way back into the living room and looks at the photo. He is only now beginning to see the resemblance: the deep brown eyes, the fair skin, the shape of the hairline and how when he is hot, a vein protrudes from his left temple. He holds the frame, heavier than he expects, and places it back down, face first.

By morning the picture has disappeared. He assumes into his mother's room.

5

Adella

Her phone vibrates between the couch cushions.

She's been lying on her back, head against the armrest, legs half hanging over the back cushions for hours. It's raining outside, loudly then quietly, though Adella has barely noticed. Lottie is out somewhere and her mum is at the hospital, finishing up a day shift.

As she fishes for her phone, woken from a trance she was quite enjoying, she realises she's done more of this assignment than she expected and the sun hasn't even set yet. That's unusual for her. The only way she gets anything done is through a blend of guilt, shame and adrenaline. At school, Sophia was always starting her assignments weeks before they were due, and it made Adella irrationally irritated. Do you have nothing better to do? Do you honestly think you're going to write your best essay on a Monday night, two weeks before its due date, at a leisurely pace?

Adella liked to pretend her process was chaos, but in fact it wasn't. She'd wait until the voice in her head yelling at her to get something done became deafening, and then she'd sit down at her laptop, and virtually not stand up until it was finished. The thing that drove Sophia, and everyone else, mad, was that she would inevitably achieve almost perfect results.

Sophia would lean over in class and whisper, 'Bullshit you started at midnight last night,' and as Adella swore she had, she also knew there was something she wasn't sharing.

She had completed her assignment in a state of magic. Something took over. It wasn't her. Words would come from nowhere, and ideas would dawn on her as though she were hearing them from someone else standing in the corner of the room. It would flow with urgency, her fingers unable to keep up with her thoughts, spinning into an essay she didn't have to structure or plan because it simply came out that way.

It was never easy. Instead, it was as though she fell into a puzzle, right on the edge of her capacity, and the feeling of slipping a piece into the right spot was so addictive she couldn't look away.

The only person she'd spoken to who seemed to understand precisely what she was talking about was Pa. For most of his life he'd worked as an English teacher, and he'd said to her once, laughing that he was slightly butchering a very eloquent Gloria Steinem quote, 'Reading and writing are the only two things where when I do them I don't feel like I should be doing anything else.' Even in his late eighties, he still wanted to read the essays she wrote. The problem was that he couldn't remember his email address and so his preference was that she post them to him. That was about three too many steps, and so they'd agreed on a middle ground where when she came to visit – he lived in Port Macquarie, about four hours' drive north – she would bring the essays she'd written that year and have him read them. Mostly he had thoughts or a comment, but never really criticism.

Writing in this way – almost in a trance – had become her sanctuary. In this state, she wasn't Adella anymore. It didn't matter that Leah had whispered to Jessica that Adella's fake tan at the formal had been 'embarrassing'. Or that every time she went out with her boyfriend, Finn, he spent more time speaking to all the girls in Freya's group than her. That was the stuff of real life. Writing, oddly, didn't feel like a performance. The words, tapped out into a document, couldn't be taken away by someone who didn't care about her. There was pride, or maybe something much uglier – a sense of superiority over the people around her. Writing afforded her something they didn't have. Options. Freedom. Possibility. In this space, in this trance, she was special. It was a world that belonged only to her. She had something she was sure – if she was truly honest with herself – that others didn't. Perhaps, she'd consider for a fleeting moment, she was great. Capable of achieving remarkable things. Everyone thought like this, though, didn't they? That life had a plan especially for them. That they were capable of contributing something no one else could, if only the people around them would pay attention. Once she'd even admitted it to Jake after a puff of a joint being passed around in someone's backyard.

'I think I might be destined for something great.'

She searched for recognition in Jake's eyes, a sense that he felt the same, but if it was there she never saw it.

She unlocks her phone.

Nathan 5:14 pm Sunday
How was your weekend x

Why did he message every Sunday as though he was at all interested? She scrolls through their text history spanning the last few weeks.

Nathan 11:59 am, Friday
Hey, what are you up to this weekend?

Adella 1:10 pm, Friday
Hey! Not much yet. I have a family thing on Sunday x

Nathan 1:02 am, Saturday
You out?

Adella 1:06 am, Saturday
Haha, nah I'm at home in bed. What did you get up to tonight?

That's when she vowed to stop texting back. He was making her look stupid and she was better than this. Surely she was better than this.

Nathan 4:55 pm, Thursday

Just found myself thinking about you. Drink tomorrow night?

Adella 6:50 pm, Thursday
Yeah I should be free, what time?

Nathan 6:52 pm, Thursday
Let's do 7 at Rooftop

They had done Rooftop. They'd ended up back at his place. For the first time they actually had sex, and Adella could almost convince herself she enjoyed it. Or maybe she just enjoyed the idea of it.

She spent more hours thinking about him than seeing him, which sometimes made her feel like she was going mad.

Adella 11:03 am, Saturday
It was nice seeing you last night. Any weekend plans?

That message had gone unanswered. And now it was Sunday, more than one week later. Had Nathan not seen her question? Did he not notice the grey bubble above his green one? Or was there – as Adella had long been suspecting – genuinely something wrong with his phone? Her house had notoriously bad reception. She had to step out onto the street to have a phone call without the line dropping out. So perhaps he wasn't receiving her messages at all. Or perhaps she was only receiving one-third of the messages he was sending. That would make more sense than the incoherent conversation she was looking at.

She puts her phone on the armrest where she can't see it. She tries to return to the paragraph she was finishing, but all of a sudden the water she'd been swimming in has turned to ice. The essay has become impenetrable. What if Nathan was messaging her because he wanted to see her tonight? It was still only a quarter past five; they could go to dinner or she could get the train to his house. She imagines herself lying in his lap as they watch a movie, him stroking her hair and realising that she is a person who exists on Sunday nights as well as Saturday nights. Before she can stop herself she replies.

Adella 5:16 pm, Sunday
Pretty quiet. You free tonight?

It makes her look desperate and boring. But anticipation shoots down her stomach, and she likes how it makes her heart race. She throws her phone down near her feet, and huffs into her open laptop screen. She has nothing to lose. Nathan isn't hers to begin with.

She hasn't even reread her last sentence when she feels her phone vibrate with such urgency she knows it is him. Snatching it, she reads the words, 'Yeah. Parents are away for the week. Want to come round?'

She smiles to herself and feels sweat prickle under her arms. This is what she wants. It does not matter if he is her boyfriend or not. All she wants is someone to spend a rainy Sunday night with, watching a British murder mystery set in a dreary small town. She wants someone to ask what she did today, a reason to

45

have an interesting answer. Someone to touch her bare skin. And to look at her like she exists.

*

It is nearly eight when she arrives at Nathan's front door, swallowed by an oversized navy hoodie that has 'HARVARD' printed across the chest. She hopes it makes her look like she's not trying too hard. Lottie gave her a lift, a favour she'll be paying off for weeks.

When he answers the door, Adella thinks this is how she wishes she saw him all the time. In grey tracksuit pants and a white t-shirt, he looks stripped bare. Relaxed. Like he belongs to her.

'You never told me you went to Harvard,' he says with a raised eyebrow, leading her down the dim hallway.

'Yeah, well. There's a lot you don't know about me.'

He does a double take.

'I . . . didn't go to Harvard. This was a gift from my cousin, I think.'

She notices how much homelier this place seems on a Sunday night, when lamps are on and a TV is humming in the back-ground. There are baby photos of Nathan hanging up on the walls of the hallway, along with his brothers, and she thinks how looking at these feels much more intimate than having his penis in her mouth.

'Maybe you'll end up there one day. With a brain like yours. I believe in you.' He is joking but takes both his hands to her shoulders, and gently kisses her on the forehead, like he adores her.

She stops at one of the photographs on the wall. 'Okay, baby photo shoot. Is that you?'

The photos were clearly taken by a professional. He is playing with the lush cream carpet beneath his chubby fingers, a nineties green backdrop behind him. His brown hair is straight, standing up tall, as though he's been slightly electrocuted. It's his almond eyes which are most distinctive, a deep brown, with a smile that reveals four tiny teeth. Beside the photo is a shot of his mum and dad, his mum Filipina, short with long, dark hair, and his father white, tall, with no hair at all.

'Yep, that's me. Every time we went back to the Philippines my aunty would set up a photoshoot . . .' He points to the photo of his parents.

'Men inherit their hair from their mum's side. Just so you know.' His voice even sounds different on a quiet Sunday night. He speaks more slowly, calmly, smiling with his whole face, not just the corners of his mouth.

They watch *Mad Men* on his dark grey corduroy couch and order pizza. She thinks she's hungry, but once the food arrives she can barely stomach a whole piece.

A gas heater sits in the centre of the room, filling the air with cosy warmth, and his dog, Henry, curls up on her lap as though it is the safest place in the world.

'He likes you,' Nathan smiles. 'He doesn't like anyone.'

Adella has always believed dogs are the best judge of character. She had a friend at school, Lexi, whom she always suspected was a psychopath. She'd say things like, 'Oh, are those bumps on your forehead sore?' as though she was genuinely concerned.

Or, 'Are those jeans new?' When Adella would reply, 'Yeah, why?' she'd look shocked and say, 'Oh, no reason.' Then Adella would catch her whispering in the ear of someone else, her gaze fixed on how the jeans flared out at the ankle. Adella would look around at everyone else, and notice for the first time that their jeans became tighter at the ankle.

When Lexi had come over for dinner, Adella's dog, Teddy, had growled and barked, as though he'd detected an evil spirit in his immediate vicinity.

'Stop, Ted! It's fine, it's just Lexi!' she'd say, feigning embarrassment. But secretly she'd loved it, and most of all she'd known he was right. Something in her stomach was growling at Lexi too, but she'd spent years trying to suppress it.

Henry's snores make her feel like maybe she is good – whatever that means.

When Nathan gets up to go to the bathroom, she wonders when – if at all – he is going to kiss her. They've watched an episode and a half and she is barely following any of it, focusing instead on the plot playing out in the reflection of the television screen, the one between her and Nathan.

When he returns, though, he sits closer to her, clearly distracted. After a moment, he whispers, 'Come here,' kissing her gently.

For the first time he doesn't taste like alcohol. He kisses her more slowly, like how boys kiss you in their high school bedroom, as opposed to how men kiss you in dark, loud nightclubs, detached and apathetic. Her heart races, and Henry climbs down off her lap, sensing he ought to make himself scarce.

Everything is different this time. He doesn't lick or bite,

but takes his time undressing her, and then penetrating her as though she is precious. He buries his face into her breasts, like he can't get enough of her, clutching at her hips and thighs. When she'd slept with him a few weeks ago, it had hurt, and she'd worked hard at making her discomfort sound like groans of pleasure. The next day she'd been sore and swollen. This time he doesn't pull her hair or turn her over without so much as a word, he doesn't spit on his fingers, like he did when he was unsatisfied with her lack of lubrication. And when she looks into his eyes, what she sees is different. There's no disgust or irritation or impatience. She wants to ask him, 'Isn't this better for you too?' but she'd so convincingly pretended she enjoyed the other sex, even asking him to choke her when he hadn't come yet. She'd learned that. Say something they don't expect you to, and they'd finally finish. Pretend you're coming, clench muscles, pull faces. Then the fucking – and it was fucking, it certainly wasn't sex – would stop. And then maybe you'd get what you came here for. To lie beside someone in the dark, without inhibitions or distraction, and talk. About anything. To have the conversations you can only have once everyone has their clothes off and the rest of the world has gone to bed. That's what Adella so craved. Sex just seemed like the only way to get there.

This time when Adella pretends to finish, she actually feels close. Her body is warm and relaxed, moving in ways that aren't intentional or contrived. Afterwards, she feels self-conscious.

'Did you want to stay?' he asks, popping his head through his t-shirt.

She never stays. She doesn't stay because she knows she won't sleep and she doesn't have any of her things and he probably won't like what she looks like in the morning.

There's a pause. And then she says yes.

6

Adella

Adella nods as the nurse slides over a white plastic cup, smaller than the length of her thumb, with a pill in it.

She feels an odd sense of pride that while she may be quiet, unengaged and anti-social, she remains obedient. With a gulp of water the pill slides down her throat. In Ward C she has watched grown men refuse, their lips tight like a child who won't accept a spoonful of peas. On her first day, a younger man, maybe in his mid-twenties, had been convinced that whatever was in that cup was poison. He'd begun to scream in terror as a nurse tried to reason with him, shouting that there was nothing wrong with him. He cried that they'd been trying to get him for months and he wasn't ready to back down, and his conviction was such that for a moment she thought maybe she believed him.

To him, that was the truth.

Abigail, the woman who occupies the bed beside her, would tell her later that Jimmy – that was his name – had watched his father kill his mother as a kid. It had been in the papers. She shook her head, as though the sharing of this information was born out of sympathy and not pure titillating gossip.

'If I had my phone I could show you the pictures of the house,' she'd said, her gaze fixed on Jimmy.

Someone lived on his shoulder now, Abigail told her. He was here because that voice had told him to set his girlfriend on fire. It was unclear how Abigail knew all of this, or if her stories were simply a part of her own delusions.

Adella sits at an empty table, covered in sprawling puzzle pieces, hoping she'll be left alone. It's not even 9 am. If it were up to her, she'd go back to bed, but she is dressed now and in an hour she will be meeting with Dr Black about her medication. She stares at the puzzle pieces, deciding she shouldn't interfere. She's watched Abigail snap at other patients who touched whatever she was making with Lego, and all you had to do was look in the direction of Mika and she'd shout, 'What are you fucking looking at, you cunt?', working herself up even when the other person left the room.

But she can see the corner piece. And the one that belongs above that. Whoever started on this puzzle has grouped all the pieces by colour, and it would be so easy to just establish a border. She glances around her. Everyone seems distracted. Abigail is sitting in the courtyard, its grass brown and its garden sad, with a plastic bag full of God knows what. Jimmy is on another table, eyes red with a vacant stare directed at the 'No Smoking' sign on the glass doors leading out to the courtyard. Even Mika looks tired, sitting beside Kirra who is talking about how they can't keep her here between wicked laughs.

Adella lifts her hand and pulls the corner puzzle piece into the right bottom corner. She glances around again. No one says a word. She picks up the connecting piece, and feels the click as it fits above it.

'Adella!' The call is loud, coming from right behind her.

Her whole body reacts, jumping from her seat, gulping in air.

'Didn't mean to scare you, love!' Cathy says as she approaches. 'You just got this lovely bunch of flowers and I wanted to show you before I set them up next to your bed. Look here, hydrangeas, we've got some eucalyptus, oh, smell that, would you? What an interesting mix. Aren't you spoiled!' She beams from behind the bouquet. 'These'd be worth a bloody fortune!'

Adella looks at Cathy blankly, half attempting a smile that never comes, hoping it will fast-track the end of this interaction.

'How about I read you the card?' Cathy asks, not looking at Adella before sitting beside her and reciting the words on the little piece of shiny cardboard.

She reads out the name. Adella recognises it, though a part of her is surprised.

'You got an admirer!' Kirra shouts, doing something suggestive with her eyebrows.

'I'm sure there's a line out the door!' Cathy responds, jumping back out of her seat and heading in the direction of Adella's room.

*

There's something suffocating about Dr Black's office.

The walls are grey with nothing on them. She imagines a framed painting. Would banging it over one's head cause any real damage? Could you try to stab yourself with the corners? Being placed in an environment designed specifically to mitigate any harm a person might do to themselves has made her somewhat obsessed. She notices there are no sharp corners. No long charger cords. Shoelaces were taken from her runners and a drawstring removed from her hoodie. No tweezers or razors. It has made her imaginative. Is this suicidal ideation, she wonders, or simply curiosity? How much thinking about one's own death is 'normal', given it is the only certainty, waiting in all our futures? Isn't it more bizarre how little so many of us think about it? And talk about it? How is it possible that we talk about anything else?

Dr Black clears his throat, and switches his crossed legs. He asks her a broad, meaningless question, the preamble before the inevitable.

'All right, well, let's start where we left off yesterday.' He slides his glasses slightly down his nose and looks her directly in the eye.

'Jake.'

7

Jake

Eight years ago

He slides into the passenger side as Adella throws her bag into the back and adjusts the driver's seat, forward then back.

He rubs his eyes. He'd stayed at Georgette's last night, a decision he'd regretted while driving home early this morning to make it to church, after maybe four hours of sleep. After the service he wanted nothing more than to climb into his unmade bed, but the guilt of not going to the gym ever so slightly outweighed the pain of going, so he messaged Adella and said he'd pick her up in fifteen.

It wasn't just that he was tired, though. Something about Georgette was bothering him. Even though she talked a lot, it was as if they didn't really have all that much to say to each other. Or what they did choose to say to each other wasn't actually true.

He didn't quite know how to explain it. To Georgette everything was so exciting or so funny or so cute, and work was always wonderful and she loved her parents and she had, literally, the best group of friends in the world, and none of it felt real.

Sometimes when he touched her it was like she wasn't even really made of soft pink flesh, but something cold and impenetrable like glass. Even when they fucked, the tone of her voice felt engineered and the shape of her mouth purposeful. Once, a few weeks back, he awoke before her and found himself examining her face. Finally, she wasn't trying so hard. Her eyes weren't fully shut, her lips gently parted. She was beautiful when she didn't know she was being watched.

'If I go to the gym three times a week,' Adella says, still fiddling with mirrors, 'I feel like a lazy piece of shit . . . a slug of a person. But if I go *four* times,' she flicks on the indicator but Jake can tell she's not really concentrating, 'then I feel like this fit . . . strong . . . disciplined success of a person. Actually, I feel like an athlete. I start checking myself out in mirrors because I reckon I can see definition in my arms. It's like the difference between me being good and bad is whether or not I . . .'

'You're just not a good enough driver to be this distracted,' he says, the words falling out of his mouth at precisely the moment he thinks them. She shrugs her shoulders as if to concede.

'We are what we do most days,' he recites from something he probably once came across on the internet. The only time he truly felt like exercising was just after he'd exercised. Adella assumed his relationship with it was uncomplicated because it was something he did almost every day without complaining.

But to not exercise was to deprive himself of the one real opportunity in his day to feel really, really good. And that would leave him feeling ashamed and empty. He wasn't motivated. He was simply self-aware.

'Some real rainy, foggy conditions today,' he says dryly, leaning his head against the headrest.

'Yeah, really good practice. And good to get my night hours up.' The weather is perfectly fine, and it's ten-thirty in the morning. They both just know that she needs to satisfy all the requirements of her log book in order to go for her licence.

'It's like, whenever you have to stop it's a surprise,' he says, finding the grab handle on his left. 'I shouldn't physically hit the glove box every time we approach a red light, just so you know.'

She grins at him with no teeth.

'You sound like Mum.' Adella had stopped driving with her mum months back, complaining that snappish instructions and erratic movements in the passenger seat were not conducive to learning how to drive, but Jake can sort of see where she's coming from.

Like she can read his mind Adella mutters, 'Nowhere does it say you need to be a *good* driver. Just that you need to pass a test. And not lose all your points.'

As Adella pulls up outside the gym, he wonders out loud: 'Do you think we're negative people?'

'We're depressive realists,' she says, without taking a beat. She must notice his expression out of the corner of her eye. 'Okay, so we're pessimists, but more importantly, *we're right*.'

'Are you depressed?' he asks, still confused.

She thinks for a second. 'No, not at the moment. I think I've definitely been depressed and that I'm generally a depressive person . . .'

'Is that bad? Does that make us bad company?'

'No. It makes us funny,' she says defensively. And he must admit, Georgette is not very funny.

'Pa is depressed,' she says matter-of-factly. 'I think he's been depressed his whole life, although some periods are worse than others. He was hospitalised once when I was little, I think.'

'That's your mum's dad, right?' He pulls his swipe out of his gym bag.

'Yeah. And who the fuck knows what's wrong with Mum. Depression. Anxiety. Bipolar. All of it.'

He doesn't know how to respond, so says nothing.

Their hour at the gym goes by blissfully. Jake pulls up the program Adrian sent him – today is chest and triceps – and puts on his headphones. His mind wanders as he starts on a barbell bench press, imagining a future in which his body is harder, his muscles more defined. That's where the fantasy often starts, but when he allows himself to daydream it always goes further. There's a house with a swimming pool that he buys to live in with his mum. She's always talked about how she'd love one of those 'islands', sort of like a benchtop in the middle of the kitchen. He'd have one of those. He'd be wearing one of those fat watches that demand you pay attention to it just long enough to notice the word 'Rolex' or 'Omega'. Parts of Father Josip's sermon from this morning wash over him, where he spoke about how God has plans for each of our lives. So long as we trust in His word and do good, He will find a way to properly care for those who worship Him. While we don't know what that looks like, Father Josip said, there is no place for anxiety or fear because we will never be alone. Jake likes this idea. That no matter how alone he feels or how unsure about the future or how worried he is about his mum, it's never just him. It makes him feel lighter, somehow. Then Father Josip started talking about 'sexual purity' and he tuned out, reflecting on what he was whispering in Georgette's ear only hours before and how he really needed a shower.

He signals to Adella when he's finished, and they walk back towards the car.

'I was thinking,' she says, taking a sip from her water bottle. 'Remember in Year Ten? I was depressed then.'

He nods. Of course he remembers.

It was a warm night over the summer school holidays when she asked Jake to meet her at the swings. It was past eleven, but both knew how to escape out the back door without their parents noticing. Adella had been quiet lately and whenever Jake had asked to meet up she'd said she was tired or busy.

He approached the swings, and could see Adella already sitting on one, her back slouched, her ankles crossed, swinging slowly.

They talked about nothing for a bit. How they couldn't be bothered going back to school.

Adella cleared her throat.

'Do you ever feel like you're stuck in a dream?' She stared at her feet as her fingers clasped the metal chains either side of her.

He thought for a moment.

'Um, I'm not sure. What do you mean?'

'It's sort of like . . . you're here but you're not here. I get this feeling that I'm watching myself from above, like an ant on a footpath, going about its life, but I don't feel anything. I'm hollow.'

Jake was quiet.

He thought about that feeling he got sometimes, where he'd be at school or on the bus or sitting on the lounge at home and suddenly it was like he was outside of himself. Sometimes he could even hear himself speak, like a spectator. On the bus the year before he'd nearly vomited because he'd thought he was going crazy, and he was never going to be able to get out of it. It was the feeling of being trapped – like you're stuck in someone else's life, filled with another person's thoughts, and you don't know how to plug in again.

The voice inside his head said, 'Yes, yes, I know that feeling,' but he couldn't bring himself to say the words out loud.

Adella looked out ahead into the darkness, her fingers busy, playing with the gaps in the chains beside her. 'It's like I've always had these waves. Even when I was in primary school. I would just have periods of six months where the whole world went from colour to black and white. It becomes really hard to get out of bed . . . and everything is suddenly bad. Like everything starts going wrong. And I can't stop it. I've just got to wait for it to end.'

She cleared her throat, then laughed, shaking her head. 'It's like a part of me is dead.'

Out of nowhere, Jake was confronted with a memory he'd never told anyone about. He was eight or nine, and his dad had been laid off from work. He remembered hearing the word 'redundancy' a lot and not knowing what it meant. When he learned his dad would be around more, he'd felt excited. His dad was always saying how much he wanted to be able to take him to his rugby league training, and this meant he could. Jake had thought how cool it would be if school just said you didn't have to come for six months or something. But things shifted, quickly.

His dad barely spoke. It was like he lost his voice. His facial hair grew long and ugly. He smelt like sweat and sleep. He'd always been a big drinker, but now he started earlier, and once when Jake left his breakfast bowl in the sink, his dad picked it up and threw it against the kitchen wall. He watched television constantly, and Jake would often catch him watching the same movie, day after day, as though yesterday had never happened. One night, Jake went into his parents' bedroom to ask his dad if he could have money for the bus, and he found him lying there above the covers, staring at the ceiling. His legs were shaking like he was very cold, but the room was warm, the air suffocating.

'I'm scared, mate. I'm really fucking scared,' he'd said.

Jake had swallowed.

'What are you scared of?'

With a shaking hand, Jake's dad tapped the front of his head. And for the first time in his life, Jake had watched his dad cry. His face contorted into shapes he'd never seen, and it was the most unnatural thing in the world. He howled, and pain filled the whole stinking room, finding its way into Jake's chest.

Standing there with a blank expression, Jake thought that this must be what it feels like for your heart to break. A shattering deep in your chest – a hot pain that rises through your neck and grabs your throat so it becomes harder to breathe. Whatever was happening in his father's body was echoed deep within his own, and he whispered, 'Dad, it's okay. Please stop crying.'

Later he'd overheard a phone call his mum was having with someone. It was a Saturday afternoon and she was sitting on the back step, and he was eating a sandwich at the kitchen bench. She said, 'It's like my husband is dead and I don't know how to get him . . .' Her voice cracked as she said, '. . . *back*.'

Death before death. That's what Adella was talking about. And he'd seen a living person decay as they breathed, a family mourn as they slept, and be buried alive, their arms either side of them, as though they were powerless against it.

8

Adella

Eight years ago

It's a disaster from the moment they arrive.

She should never have chosen this place. Her mum said she had to choose somewhere, but she doesn't really know any restaurants. She'd seen on social media that Georgette, Jake's girlfriend, had a birthday here last month. She'd scrolled through the pictures, nine women, all legs and big white teeth.

That's how they've ended up at an Asian-fusion bar and restaurant called Reggi's in Watsons Bay, more than an hour from home, where all the women are wearing silk camisoles and the men are in boat shoes and chinos that graze their ankles.

The November sun is still high in the sky at six in the evening, with women perched on the outside stools, sunglasses resting on the bridge of their freckled noses. It is as though they have walked onto a movie set: tanned long limbs, soft curls falling from bleached-blonde hair, women who have effortlessly chosen the right shoes and the right bag and they know it.

A remix of some nineties R&B song plays from speakers, and big groups of young people congregate around tables overflowing with wine glasses and cocktails and half-filled beers.

'Everyone here looks famous,' Lottie says tonelessly, looking at a group of tall, bronzed men wearing fedoras. In the western suburbs, men do not wear fedoras.

They shuffle through the outdoor bar, inhaling designer perfume and cologne, before locating the entryway of the restaurant.

'Ah, a table for three . . . under Adella, I think it should be . . .' she says, staring at the reservation book, sure, as she always is, that there will be no such reservation.

The waiter confirms Adella did not imagine making the booking, and declares, 'Follow me, ladies,' throwing together a bunch of menus and parading through the restaurant.

How out of place they must look, Adella thinks. Her in a cotton black t-shirt and blue denim skirt with years-old sandals, and Lottie in jeans – despite it being summer – and a white, flimsy singlet that Adella is sure she's seen her wear to bed. To be in this restaurant, among these people, is embarrassing. More embarrassing is the way she had imagined while lying in bed last night that they might take photos much like Georgette's, with her miraculously wearing an outfit she doesn't own, smiling with a face she doesn't have. In her imagination, Nathan would see it, and be so overcome with desire that he would say everything she so wanted him to.

As they're seated, the waiter recommends 'we' get a round of spicy margaritas to start, as though they don't cost $15 each.

'Holy shit, there's a main for $125,' Lottie says once he leaves, which they've all of course already noticed, processing the information in their own private ways.

'We don't have to be here,' Adella mumbles. She's not even hungry.

'It's your twenty-first birthday. Shut up.' Lottie pulls a face at Adella while their mother studies the menu.

Twenty-one doesn't feel like a big deal to Adella. She's spent all year at twenty-first birthdays of friends from school and university acquaintances, and bought gifts for people she knew in all likelihood she wouldn't be friends with by twenty-five. Fathers said speeches and friends read awkwardly from the Notes app on their phones. More than once she'd been standing there during speeches, listening to a guy who could barely speak roast his best mate, and whispered to the person next to her, 'That's . . . that's a crime, though?' as everyone cheersed to stories of trespassing and potential assault. Once she heard a story about the birthday girl waking up beside a guy she'd never met and a woman getting changed in the corner of the room. The birthday girl had no idea what had happened. A few people awkwardly laughed while the girl's grandmother tutted and waddled inside. Adella knew a twenty-first would be her worst nightmare. If she never organised one, she could at least imagine it would have been overflowing with people. She could fantasise about the speeches Sophia and Jake would make. In her head, her dress would be perfect and she would look like a different person after her spray tan.

The reality could never be quite as perfect as the dream. Best not to test it.

She has thought about what it means, though, turning twenty-one. Adulthood, maybe. A blink in the eye of a universe that serves up each new generation with a unique set of problems.

Adella Ryan had been born at the end of a war she didn't understand. It took place on the other side of the world, defined by ideology rather than territory, driven by an apocalyptic arms race. The first decade of her life was the last decade of the most violent century in history. World wars and holocausts and the nuclear bomb and Agent Orange. Destruction for the sake of destruction. In the nineties most people had a family camera, though – a black one where you had to get the films developed into photos at a shop. So you had to smile. You were always being told to *smile*.

Her grandfathers had fought in wars they never talked about. One dead and one still alive, they told stories about men they killed. Illnesses they contracted. Hell on earth. Acts that would constitute a crime in the town they grew up in were considered an honourable act of patriotism in a country where they didn't belong. They couldn't reconcile that paradox. Of course they couldn't.

She is a member of the last generation that will remember what it was like when no one had mobile phones. She knows, when she looks at the 'phone' symbol, that that's a call back to the home phone. The kind that was stuck on the wall, or sat on a table in the hallway. She remembers what it was like to sit in the corner of the kitchen, with the phone to her ear, keeping her voice low so no one would overhear what she was saying. She also knew the 'click'. The sound that meant someone else had picked up, and was listening from another room. Lottie. Listening in, breathing deeply.

She is old enough to remember the internet dial-up sound. The yelling that happened when her mum needed the phone at the same time Adella needed to be online. Phone books and video shops, toll booths where you threw coins in and supermarkets with no automated checkouts. They were a distant memory now – but they were a memory.

If you'd asked when she was at school if anyone was mentally ill, she'd have said no, and if you'd asked if anyone was gay, she'd have said no. She never thought too much about whether that was true. Just that it was what was understood. No one had blue hair. No one was in a wheelchair. It was easy to imagine that everyone was, largely, the same.

She's old enough to remember when the planes crashed into the Twin Towers. The moment is etched into her memory like the images of Princess Diana's funeral and the Black Saturday bushfires. Events she knew were important, but wouldn't yet know why.

As a teenager, the two worst things you could be, of course, were ugly and fat. That probably hadn't changed much since her mum was at school. There were other things you didn't want to be. A try-hard. A bludger. Desperate. A weakling. Unco. Stingy.

In high school there was a career advisor. It was compulsory to see her in Year Eleven. You filled in a questionnaire and then had a meeting, where she suggested you become an *archaeologist* like it was the most obvious thing in the world. She suggested Sophia be a *fashion designer* as though there was more than one in Australia, and you could simply study a course and then, *boom*.

The school was intent on not putting too much pressure on the students, but hard work meant you had more *choices*. And you wanted *choices*. To *choose* what to study. Where you wanted to go. But even if you made the wrong choice, you could always make a new choice and decide to be a nurse instead of a teacher or an events planner instead of a retail manager or work for Coca-Cola instead of an NGO. *There was always another choice.*

Adella secretly thought, when anyone at university brought up the word 'privilege', that there was no privilege like being able to write. We can lie to ourselves that that is simply a product of hard work, but it isn't. We are born with the brain we are born with, and some allow us access to university, and others mean there are thousands of professions their owners will have no access to. It's not a matter of being 'smart' – Jake, for example, is one of the smartest, most interesting people she knows. But he can't write an essay. And therefore his life will be different.

'How's work?' Adella asks her mum, who is now staring vacantly out the window at a flock of seagulls fighting over a discarded tray of chips.

'Hmmm?'

'Work, Mum. Is that unit manager still being a bitch?' Lottie gulps down the last of her margarita.

'Oh.' She smiles, but it looks painful. 'No, it's okay.'

Adella and Lottie look at each other. Lottie raises her eyebrows.

'That one only has one leg,' her mum mumbles, gesturing towards the seagulls.

When the waiter returns, Lottie announces she is just going to order for the table, and Adella wants to kiss her. As Lottie asks if that sounds like enough food, Adella scans the room, watching couples speak to each other animatedly and a group of girlfriends laugh so hard they shush each other. Then she returns to her mother, pale and stricken, and Lottie checking her phone. There is something sadder about having a sad moment in a happy place. Where all the variables are ripe for joy – the sun tickles the faces of people on the balcony, the music makes this moment feel like an occasion. How wonderful this evening might be if it were spent with the right people – or if *you* were the right kind of person. It is perhaps more of an effort to make tonight miserable. And yet, her family so effortlessly manage.

'I'm messaging Dad . . . he said he'll be down next month and will celebrate your birthday then,' Lottie says, putting her phone face down on the white tablecloth.

'Ah. Yeah, I've always said that's the great thing about birthdays. How flexible they are. In terms of dates.' Adella glances at her mother. She's still watching the seagulls. 'It can all just wait until Dad's here. And I guess this year was a surprise too. It's never fallen on November fifteen before so that would have been really confusing.'

'Good point.' Lottie nods. 'He missed my twenty-first too, remember? But *then*, oh my goodness, I'd forgotten this.' Her eyes widen. 'He just *happened* to be here for my graduation and got upset that I hadn't reserved him a seat. So I had to ask if anyone had a spare ticket. And then he posted a whole album of pictures as though he had any idea I was studying Occupational Therapy before that specific day? Remember that, Mum?' she asks, nudging her with her elbow.

Their mother slowly nods, and breathes out a vague *ha*.

'Yes! And Suzie commented "smart just like her father xx" even though Dad doesn't, like . . . put spaces after full stops. And says "irregardless" every time we're having an argument . . .'

'WHICH ISN'T A WORD,' they both say at the same time.

Their mum pushes her chair back and leaves the table.

'Mum?' Adella asks.

'I'm just going to the bathroom, be back in a tick.'

Lottie puts her face in her hands and pulls down her cheeks. 'I actually can't. Does she even know she's doing it? How fucking hard is it to put a smile on her face and wish you a happy birthday? It's selfish and it's lazy but like, grow up? Sort your shit out. She's too old to lack this much self-awareness . . .'

Adella watches her mother slowly navigate her way towards the bathroom, her shoulders rounded, her neck looking as though it can barely muster the strength to keep her head upright. 'She reminds me of a dementor from *Harry Potter*. Like a mass of darkness . . . and you can see them coming and then they suck happiness from everyone around them. Do you think that's what J. K. Rowling based them on? Depressed people?'

'I never read *Harry Potter*. But I don't think it's just depression. Apparently her doctor said it's anxiety,' Lottie says, shrugging her shoulders.

'Is she taking her meds?' Adella looks towards the bathroom.

'Yeah, pretty sure. They're next to her bed.'

'They need to triple them.'

Adella checks her phone. There are a few birthday messages from aunties, her boss at the pub, and a missed call from Pa. She'll call him back tonight. But what she sees is a gaping absence. She switches to another app. Uni friends standing on a beach in Mexico. Tight tummies. Laughing with snorkels hanging from their hands. Some friends from primary school at a boozy girls' lunch, draped in dresses in various shades of pastel, as though it was coordinated beforehand.

'Oh, look,' Lottie says, pulling Adella from the world that lives inside her phone, to the much more uncomfortable one unfolding before her eyes. 'It's Mum with her new mates.'

Adella looks up and sees her mum standing slightly pigeon-toed, arms folded, staring at the seagulls on the wharf. A couple walk past and do a double take at the middle-aged woman in white three-quarter pants, watching the seagulls as though she's never seen them before.

'Must be better company,' Lottie says slowly, as they watch one shit on an abandoned table.

Entrees arrive before their mother returns to the table, where she picks up her phone, staring intently at it, her eyes peering down past her nose, her mouth slightly open.

'You know,' Lottie begins, 'our generation gets a hard time for being addicted to our phones, which is like, fair enough. I get withdrawals if I leave my phone in another room. But you guys,' she points at her mum, 'are way worse than us. We're at dinner, put down your phone, Mum. What are you even looking at?'

Her expression is blank. Maybe irritation flickers behind her eyes.

'I was just replying to Colleen about something. She says happy birthday, Del.'

'Ah well. At least Colleen wishes me a happy birthday.' She glances at Lottie, and shoves a forkful of eggplant into her mouth. It is difficult to swallow. Her throat has begun to close up and ache.

'I'm not feeling well,' her mum announces, the most enthusiastic she's been all night.

'Oh, what kind of sick?' Lottie asks, her forehead creasing.

'Nauseous. A bit faint. And I'm getting these headaches behind my eyes.' She rubs them slowly. Pauses for a moment. 'I think I'm going to have to go home. Sorry, girls. Not well at the moment . . .' She trails off.

'Are you sure, Mum? The mains haven't come out yet,' Lottie says, confused.

'Yeah, I can't really eat. No appetite,' she says as she stands up, her shaking hands reaching inside her worn black wallet, a fiftieth-birthday gift from her daughters. 'Here, take my card. To pay.'

Adella and Lottie refuse, but she places it firmly on the table and ultimately wins.

'Happy birthday, Del,' she mumbles, kissing the side of Adella's head.

'Yeah. Thanks, Mum.' She stares at the tablecloth.

After their mother leaves, both are silent for a while. Adella's phone vibrates. It's a happy birthday from a number she doesn't recognise. Nothing from Nathan.

Mains are served to a quiet table, and then Lottie mutters, 'I'm sorry.'

'It's not your fault. It's just a birthday.' She doesn't want to say anything more. Her throat hurts and her eyes are prickling. She feels stupid for having wanted today to be anything, for playing out conversations with her mother they'd never been able to have. Whatever today could have been – it wasn't. Nothing is ever quite what she'd hoped.

Lottie moves around the table to sit beside her.

'Hey, hey, we've got each other. Mum has her own stuff going on. And look!' she says, holding up her mother's credit card. 'We've got Mum's card! Shall we buy some drugs? How about heroin, that might help? I reckon Mum's friend can help us out.' Lottie points to the one-legged seagull who also appears to have a droopy eye.

Adella sniggers. 'Fuck Mum,' she says.

'Fuck Mum,' Lottie nods, offering a toast.

'And fuck Dad, for different reasons,' Adella adds, taking a gulp.

They eat what they can, which isn't much, and Lottie asks if she can have the rest to take away.

As they wander towards the ferry, watching people their age head out, in clothes they could never afford, to sit in bars people travel halfway across the world to visit, Adella is reminded of a quote she learned for uni last semester when she was studying the French Revolution. It was from *The Hunchback of Notre Dame*. The quote she'd remembered was something like: 'A one-eyed man is much more incomplete than a blind man, for he knows what it is that's lacking.'

It would be better not to see this part of Sydney, she thinks. Better to not know people live like this, in a suburb where the sun shines differently upon the skin of people destined to live a better sort of life. They would spend their Saturdays eating brunch at outdoor cafes, well-trained dogs at their feet, before they made their way to Pilates. A few Pilates classes would cost more than Adella made in a full Saturday shift. Their cars smell different and their buses don't break down and their schools aren't made up of dozens of demountables and their pubs aren't full of old men, gambling away money they never had to begin with. As a kid, Adella had forever been rearranging her bedroom, putting her Ikea desk under the window, and having her single bed face the door, thinking maybe if her environment looked just right then everything would become easier. But no amount of rearranging her tiny bedroom would grant her access to a life like this.

It was easier when she was blind, she thinks to herself. When she didn't know just how a place like this *felt*. Now she knows what's lacking. And she has to go back to the other world, where everything is a little more dark. And a little more sad.

9

Adella

She knocks on the door and takes a small step backwards. A Christmas beetle has settled on the mat beneath her feet, and she watches it scuttle into the darkness. She shifts the plastic bag full of leftovers from her right wrist, inspecting the mark it's left.

She listens to the thumping of bare feet down the hallway, and watches a light switch on, before she sees Sophia beaming in the doorway. Her place is small but cosy. She used to share a bedroom with her two older sisters, but they've long since moved out. Now it's just Sophia and her mum, and her place mostly smells of clean washing.

Tonight, neither of them says much. Sophia asks how her birthday dinner was and Adella pulls a face. Sophia nods and puts on *The OC*, disappearing into the kitchen to get M&Ms and Diet Coke.

Adella thinks back to this morning, when she'd allowed

herself to fantasise about what today would be like. She wonders if everyone feels this – a sense that they're never doing the right thing at the right moment. Because nothing is quite like how you'd hoped it would be. Not a relationship. Not a novel. Not a day or a meal or a job. The idea is always greater than the sum of its parts. Whereas all anything can be is the sum of its parts.

Sophia's phone lights up on the armrest. A notification from Daniel. Adella doesn't mean to look, but in a glance she absorbs the message by accident.

'If I knew you were going to bail I would have gone out after?'

She feels a pang of guilt. It's a Saturday night and Sophia had probably been planning to see Daniel all week. She is struck by her own neediness. Why does she always end up on Sophia's couch, while her mum recites all the food they have in the pantry in case anyone gets hungry? She looks at the box sitting on the coffee table: a pair of topaz studs, her birthstone. Sophia had even wrapped them up, a fancy bow criss-crossed around the box, and attached a card that reads 'Congratulations on your baby boy'. Adella can't remember when they started buying irrelevant cards for each other, but it had become a tradition.

'Would you like your Diet Coke in a wine glass? Because it's your birthday?' Sophia calls out.

'Yes, please.' She crosses her legs and rests her head back.

They stay up until past one, mumbling, 'Should we watch one more?' every time the end credits run.

'I have to work in the morning,' Sophia eventually says, yawning. 'You take my bed. I'll sleep out here. There's towels and stuff in there if you want a shower.'

'Sophia,' she says, still curled up so she doesn't have to look her in the eye. 'Shut up. Obviously I'm sleeping out here. And thank you.'

'Don't make things weird,' Sophia says, visibly cringing. 'We never go full Mel,' she adds definitively, walking to the linen cupboard.

Mel was a girl at school who used to narrate their friendship. They'd all be hysterically laughing and Mel would stop and say, 'You're honestly the funniest people I've ever met,' and suddenly things would become uncomfortable. If there was a pause in conversation she'd fill it with, 'Do you guys find me annoying?' or 'Are we as close as we used to be?' and they'd audibly groan. Adella and Sophia's friendship was something they did but never examined. To put words around it would make them both feel exposed and vulnerable, like it was some sort of performance rather than a means of survival neither could live without.

Best not to tell the other how much their friendship means, in case it becomes so hyper-examined they discover cracks they didn't know were there.

'I'm sorry, good point,' Adella says, lifting herself off the couch.

As she follows Sophia to the kitchen, both holding glasses and empty packets, all the years concertina together. Birthdays and sleepovers and parties they left early. When that guy Adam had cancelled a date a few years back, after she'd done her make-up, it was Sophia who said 'I'll be there in halfa' and decided they'd both go out even though it was a Tuesday night. Touch footy and netball and getting her period at the swimming carnival. Sophia had a pencil case full of everything she could need, and sat in the cubicle beside her explaining angles and positioning.

If, at twenty-one, she's ended up on Sophia Fraiser's couch, watching *The OC* for the fourth time, then perhaps she's done something right. She has somehow ended up with a best friend who makes everything fun by accident; the type of person she does not deserve.

She will think about that a lot in the years to come. Whether she ever deserved Sophia in the first place.

10

Jake

Gold tinsel hangs from the metal handles at least a dozen people are clutching, their hands clammy from the December heat despite the air-conditioning.

Every time the bus stops and the rear doors open, a wave of thick air pours over everyone inside despite the fact the sun disappeared an hour ago. It's as though someone has opened an industrial oven.

Damp patches have formed under Jake's arms and he sticks his nose under the top of his t-shirt, sniffing.

'You right there?' Adella says too loudly.

She takes another sip from a water bottle filled with straight vodka and leans forward from the back seat, inspecting Jake, who sits in front of her. She sits beside Nathan.

'Yep. You right there?' he asks back, signalling his eyes down to the water bottle that's nearly finished.

She giggles in the way she only does when Nathan is around and he hates it. It's not that he minds when Adella is seeing someone – he couldn't care less – it's just that the pitch of her voice changes and she is entirely oblivious to it. Sometimes she stops listening to him halfway through a sentence to smile at Nathan, as though if she ignores him for three minutes he might just walk away and never come back. He wishes he could grab her by the shoulders and shout, 'You're *less* likeable like this, not more,' but he knows he can't.

'Are you at least going to tell us what happened with Georgette?' she asks, her eyes opening wide. She glances at Sophia, who sits beside Jake.

'Just wasn't feeling it anymore,' he says, looking in the opposite direction.

'You seemed really into her last time I saw you,' says Sophia, taking the water bottle from Adella.

'Yeah, I was. I don't know. It became a bit of a . . .' He pauses to find the word. 'Burden. Kind of like a responsibility to see her all the time. And she'd get weird if I didn't text back for a few days. It was a bit suffocating.'

He catches Adella swallowing.

'Ah. I liked her,' she says, her face suddenly serious, and he knows this is a lie. Introducing them to each other had been like introducing two people who did not speak the same language. Georgette could not believe that Adella had never eaten sushi and Adella had to insist more than twice that it was true, and Adella did not seem to think Georgette's jokes were that funny. In Adella's defence, they weren't. But Georgette had the kind of smile that meant whenever she smiled, everyone smiled with her. And that had given her a false sense of things. The feedback to her particular brand of comedy had been skewed, whereas for ordinary-looking people, no one laughed if what they said wasn't genuinely funny. They had to work harder. The feedback was harsher. And perhaps that was why so many comedians were, you know, strange-looking.

As Jake gets his phone out of his back pocket, Nathan asks if he has the score up. For a moment they talk about the rugby league game on tonight, and Jake thinks maybe he isn't that bad. Even so, he's looking forward to finally getting to The Balcony, where most of his footy team have been for the last few hours. It's a strange dynamic between the four of them, and will be even stranger when Daniel arrives.

Sophia and Adella talk about their trip next month to Thailand and Jake suddenly wishes he'd had more to drink at Sophia's place before they all left. He is far too sober to be on a bus on his way to a club in the city at 9 pm. But it's also Christmas Eve, and he knows he has to be careful on Christmas Eve. He always has to be careful on Christmas Eve.

The line for The Balcony creeps around the corner and Adella has the hiccups. Sophia keeps trying to scare her by shouting 'BOO' in the middle of a sentence, but then they start laughing and Adella just hiccups harder.

A message pops up on his phone. It's from his Aunty Liz.

'Thinking of you today, mate. If you ever need anything I'm right here x'

All day his phone has been going off. It's nice, in a way.

To know people are thinking of you. But he hasn't replied to any of them. He should probably say he's thinking of them too, but the truth is he's not. He's trying not to think at all.

Big groups of men are turned away from the entrance, and Jake can see why his footy team had to get here so early.

'Tell me more about that feminism you're always on about, Adella,' he says, gesturing to a group of six men who are clearly pissed off.

She raises her eyebrows. 'I'd choose being rejected from a club over being physically or sexually assaulted . . .'

'How many times have you been punched in the face?' he asks, half laughing.

'How many times have you been followed home?' she snaps back. Her eyes dart towards Nathan. She wouldn't ordinarily speak like this in front of him, as if she was some bra-burning, hairy-armpitted angry feminist who thought all men were predators. She knows it's ugly. A turn-off. Usually she would drip-feed this part of herself to anyone she was having sex with, a context in which she loved being small and weak and dominated. Female oppression was something she had difficulty explaining to the person with whom she had a distinctly gendered dynamic, where she didn't want to be a brain but a body.

'I reckon I'd rather be followed home than have someone literally break my eye socket . . .' That was two years ago. Technically it was a cracked cheekbone, and it happened at someone's house party where the music was too loud and everything was too dark. There was a girl, long brown hair. Maybe if he'd been paying more attention he would have noticed she was having a fight with her boyfriend. But all he saw was her dancing, then she had her arms around his neck, then she led him towards a bedroom door. But they never made it.

'So would I,' Nathan adds. Adella shoots him a look.

'I'm just saying, for all you go on about how tough women have it, you can literally show up wearing a paper bag and these guys will let you in. Last time I went out to the Cross they didn't let me in because my shirt didn't have a collar. And another time it was like forty degrees and I got turned away because I had shorts on . . .' Jake's smiling but he means it.

'Yeah, I get that,' Adella says, exasperated, 'but you also don't get routinely harassed for what you're wearing. Again, I'm not going to protest in the streets for your right to wear shorts when literally five minutes ago I was whistled at by an old guy who was staring at my chest.'

That had happened five minutes ago. Jake had laughed as the man passed. He noticed that Adella had not.

'Okay, but Adella,' Nathan says with a smile, putting both his hands up defensively. 'I don't know how to say this without you blowing up at me . . .'

'I have never blown up at –' Adella starts.

'That dress is very low-cut. You had to have known when you left the house that men were going to look at you. Isn't that why you wore that? Like,' he gestures to her chest, 'they *are* out.'

Jake thinks Nathan has a point. But there is something about how he delivers it – as though it is embarrassingly obvious. Jake has always challenged Adella on the way she sees the world, even when he doesn't believe it himself, just to see how she responds. Nathan, though, has not earned that right.

'Fuck off,' Sophia scoffs.

Nathan puts his hands up in defeat and says something about 'devil's advocate'. Jake says nothing.

'So, because I wear this dress, I deserve to have every single man I walk past staring at me? And calling me a slut from their car window? It's . . .' Adella searches for the word, caught up in the cruelty of what Nathan has just said. She doesn't want to speak to him like this but she can't help it. 'Victim blaming. I should be able to wear what I want without feeling objectified . . .'

Jake stops himself from rolling his eyes at the word 'objectified'. He hates it when she speaks like she's writing a university essay. And isn't the whole point of wearing a dress like that so people will look at you? That's fine, of course. But it's a bit like yelling in a quiet movie theatre and wondering why everyone keeps staring.

He notices there is redness crawling up her neck towards her cheeks. Sophia is making an awkward point about how men should learn to look away, and Nathan says he'd quite like it if people complimented him on the street, but all Jake can see is how Adella's body language has changed.

'Anyway, I've gotta piss. Be back in a sec,' Nathan says, heading for a backstreet around the corner.

'I don't think he meant it to come out like that,' Sophia says as soon as he's out of earshot, placing her hand gently on Adella's arm.

Adella groans and looks at the heel of her shoe. The line shuffles forward a little.

Something Bad is Going to Happen

'It's just . . .' Jake notices her eyes have become cloudy and her arms are crossed. She looks up at the black sky. 'The reason I'm wearing this stupid dress is so that *he* will look at me. Him. And instead it feels like every creep on the street looks at me before he does . . . And now he's mocking me for it. It's like I'm in this stupid game I never wanted to play and I'm being made fun of by the person who invented it . . .'

Nathan eventually returns and puts his arm around Adella, while Jake texts Vili inside to get him two drinks.

'Have we calmed down?' Nathan whispers, and Adella nods, leaning her head lightly on his chest.

Jake wants everything in his head to go quiet. He has no patience for whatever is going on between Nathan and Adella.

When they finally make it inside, they squeeze through damp bodies towards the bar and order a shot and two drinks each. Jake spots Vili and the others sitting on the couches in the corner, and announces as he greets them that he needs to catch up. He sculls the two drinks Vili bought him, and then two more that Adrian returns with. Daniel arrives and he loses sight of Sophia, Adella and Nathan for a while. Vili tells him it's his round and places a Santa hat on his head, pushing him in the direction of the bar.

He stands in line and the hat is too tight. He feels suddenly claustrophobic. His head is hot and he can't catch his breath and his heart beat is thumping in his ears. Without consciously deciding, his feet lead him to the bathroom, abandoning the hat on the floor on his way. The door of a cubicle with a blocked toilet hangs open and he runs in, locking it behind him. Breathe.

He rests his head against the door, closing his eyes and clenching his fists. His phone vibrates again. His mum.

'Tried to call. When will you be home? Will you make it for midnight mass? It's okay if you can't. I love you more than anything. And so did he. Love Mum.'

He wants to throw his phone at the wall, but instead he turns it off. He closes the toilet seat, trying not to glimpse what's inside the bowl, and sits, rubbing his eyelids with his fingers.

It was late afternoon six years ago when his mum had appeared at the park up the end of their street. She wasn't wearing any shoes and asked if he'd heard from his dad. He didn't like the question. There was something in her tone, a veneer of calmness that was unconvincing.

'No, why?' he asked. He was kicking a footy around with his brother Sam.

'Not to worry,' she said, 'it's just that we can't find him. He left me a strange voicemail, that's all. I'll try him again . . .'

'What was the message?' He picked at the stitching on the ball.

'Oh,' she scoffed. 'I'll speak to you about it later. I'm going to try him again.'

He'd later learn the message had been just ten words, although he never got to hear it.

'I love you, Annie. Tell the kids I love them.'

Jake left the park immediately. Something in the air had changed and he felt like you do right before it rains, when the sky has suddenly turned dark, and ants have begun to scuttle purposefully along the cracks in the pavement.

When he walked in the door, at a pace designed not to panic Sam, his mum was calling uncles and aunties, trying his dad again in between each call.

He'd overheard a conversation at the wake. His mum was in the backyard, sitting on their white plastic chairs with her sister, finishing the last bottle of spirits she could find in the house, an overflowing ashtray on the table beside her. She was speaking louder than she realised, her speech slurred and careless.

'I knew he was in there, you know,' she said. Jake could sense her gesturing. 'I knew as soon as I saw the message.'

There was silence. Jake threw the last of the cardboard plates in the kitchen bin.

'Will I ever stop hating him?'

Her sister whispered, 'Yes.'

Annie had been gesturing towards their corrugated iron shed, which housed the lawn mower and a rake Malcolm rarely used. The corners were covered in cobwebs, and when the boys were little they used to throw each other in there and hold the door shut, laughing as whoever was inside imagined redback spiders climbing into their shirts.

His mother's face had changed that day when she decided to check the back shed. The expression – the way lines framed her mouth and forehead – it all stayed there. Their father had always warned them not to pull funny faces in case the wind changed. That afternoon, the wind had changed.

She walked slowly to the door and pulled it open. Jake can still hear the scream if he shuts his eyes. He was sure it wasn't his mother's voice.

The neighbours heard and ran through the front door. They picked her up as she dry-retched on all fours, having seen the man she loved suspended in the air. Floating. He looked like he was floating.

Jake sometimes thinks he sees inside the shed in his dreams, except it's not really his father's face he can see. More a mouth, gaping open. Hollow eyes. Dark. His face is always so dark.

There's a bang on the door. He doesn't know how long he's been in there but his hands are shaking. Another bang and he unlocks the cubicle, to find a security guard towering over him.

'What have you been doing in there, mate?' the man asks, glancing towards the toilet, clearly trying to find some white powder.

'Nothing. Wasn't feeling well.'

'Had too much to drink?' The man raises his eyebrows.

'No. Something I ate maybe,' Jake says, standing up straighter, running his hand through his hair.

'You watch yourself.' The guard steps back, a scar through his top lip.

By the time Jake returns to the table, he has a tray of ten drinks, not including the two shots he did at the bar. Adrian gets his phone out to show him some footy tackle that was going viral, but Jake realises he can't really see. When he tries to respond, his tongue feels heavy in his mouth and he stumbles over his words. Everyone laughs. He finishes his drink, and another half-drunk one sitting sticky on the table.

Next comes a big black spot, a memory that's never formed. Maybe he danced. He must've found Adella. His bank statement will indicate that he bought another round. Who knows if they even made their way back to the table.

The streetlights are bright as he leaves. Adella tries to flag down a taxi. Her arm up, waving, then back down. Up again. A taxi pulls up, sees him, then drives away.

'We need you to move along.' Jake watches him say it, in slow motion, through his scarred lip.

'We're trying to get a taxi,' Adella says.

'I don't give a fuck what you're trying to do,' the guard says, mocking Adella's tone. 'Or your dropkick mate. Just get the fuck away from the front of the club.'

Adella shakes her head and turns around, starting off down the street. But Jake stands still. He's staring at the security guard, watching him chew a piece of gum with one side of his mouth.

'You got a problem with your hearing?' He sees it, in that moment. An expression he recognises so well he could be looking in the mirror. Fury.

When the man puts his palms on his shoulders, everything, all the rage, comes from somewhere deep inside his chest and his arms do something he can't remember telling them to. His hands ball themselves into fists and punch and punch and for a moment nothing has ever felt this good. He can't see anything, as though pure emotion has leaked into every region of his brain, and shots of electricity infiltrate muscle fibres, telling his body to hit. To hit. To hit.

Then knuckles come towards his face and his jaw cracks.

Finally, the world goes quiet.

11

Adella

Present

Dr Black looks over his glasses at Adella, a finger smudge on the right lens, and asks about her mood today. How she would rate it out of ten.

She looks up at the ceiling, her clammy hands squeezing each other. How do you tell a person whose job is to assess your level of madness that today you do not feel like killing yourself, because it is as though you are already dead?

She swallows. Answers about a three. Maybe. It is clear he is not sure what to do with that.

He asks about her appetite. Her sleep. Emphasises how important eating and sleeping are to getting well. If her body knew how to laugh, she would've. The food in Ward C is inedible. Mashed potato that tastes like powder. Grey meat tougher than cardboard. Egg sandwiches on white bread, the smell making her nausea worse than it already is. Then there's knowing that a few steps down the corridor, Jimmy smeared shit across the toilet door, trying to write a message no one could quite make out. She imagines that the faeces has made its way into her meals, her orange juice, her lukewarm water.

Then there are the sounds of the night. The nurse checks. How Kirra cries for her mother from about two in the morning, moaning the word 'mum' over and over again. She hears Abigail scribbling in her notebook, the scratching of pen on paper, in the bed beside hers. New patients who seem to be withdrawing from something yell profanities at nurses half their size and her heart rate speeds up, waiting for the sound of a fist smacking a jaw, the collapse of an unconscious body onto the floor. She sleeps lightly, if at all, for only an hour or so at a time.

He asks how she feels about being in hospital.

While this room, this ward, is a new kind of hell, a place where you do not necessarily learn to get better but rather how not to die, there is something oddly gratifying about the gravity of it. About it being a place one goes when they are unwell. It is *stabilising*. That is the word she uses to describe it.

Last night, night four, she had her first dream in as long as she can remember. It was so vivid she pinched herself to check if it was real. It stung.

Jake was there. He was a patient beside her in the hospital. She kept trying to catch his face, obscured by shadows, until finally she recognised him. She said his name out loud and after a beat he turned to her. There was guilt in his smile. A look she had seen so many times. He had mouthed the word 'sorry', and then pulled his hoodie over his head, the drawstring tight around his neck. She had tried to wake up. Screamed but no sound came out. She tried to throw herself out of bed. To squeeze her eyes shut, and take her back to the other world where Jake wasn't there anymore. Was she awake or asleep? Awake or asleep?

'I had a nightmare last night. Could that be the medication?' she asks, hoping he doesn't ask her to recount what happened. He does.

'I can't remember exactly, but it felt so real. Like it wasn't a dream. It made me really confused.' She looks at her knees.

'Then when I did wake up, I think, I didn't know if I was still in the dream. This feels sort of like a dream. And the dream felt like real life.'

He nods, rests his pen on his notebook.

'That must be very distressing,' he says, his brow creased. He scribbles something.

'When you go to bed tonight, keep a cup of cool water on the bedside table. If at any point you're confused as to whether you're awake or asleep or whether this is a dream, pick it up, take a sip. If the cup is cool against the palm of your hand, you're awake.'

She commits his advice to memory, surprised that it is somewhat useful. Thinks, *Imagine if every piece of advice you gave people was this practical. Might actually make a difference.*

When she returns to the common area it is late afternoon, but the sky remains a brilliant blue. She stands before a thick-paned window and looks up at the cloudless sky that she knows, intellectually at least, is beautiful. This is a picture that Australians wait all year for – that she used to wait for. A sky full of promise and hope, leaving you with a red nose and freckles in new places. As soon as Lottie had got her licence, she'd drive them to the beach, the windows open and the radio loud. The water always felt cold at first but once they committed, diving under a wave, they'd find it impossible to get out. They'd groan in pleasure and lick their lips, the salt settling on their faces, rattling their head side to side, trying to dislodge the water caught in their ears. Was she happy in those moments? Or only in retrospect? Would she still be able to feel the tingle of the water on her skin? Would she ever know that freedom again, the ocean as far as the eye can see, meeting the sky at some point in the distance, the blues melting into one another?

A movie is playing on the small television. One woman is dumped. Another is a workaholic, conveyed mostly through how much she huffs. Adella sits in an empty lounge chair, unsure of what else to do. John is sitting cross-legged beside her, sunglasses on, a baseball cap covering most of his face. He is afraid of being recognised by fans, despite the fact he has none. Jia is silent, borderline comatose, watching *The Holiday* with her mouth slightly agape.

She has fallen into a light sleep when Cathy taps her on the right shoulder and whispers, 'There's someone here to see you.' It takes her a moment to comprehend where she is.

She stands up too fast, blood rushing from her head. When she turns around, Sophia is standing there, freckles in new places, her cheeks and nose blushed pink.

They stare at each other in stunned silence.

12

Adella

Eight years ago

'You're sunburnt,' Sophia says, pressing the skin on Adella's arm which goes from white to a deep red.

Adella is standing in Nathan's kitchen, Sophia sitting at a stool opposite, waiting for Daniel to shout from the barbecue that the meat is ready. 'A bit.' Adella hates when people tell her she's sunburnt, as though she doesn't know. As though she can do anything about it now. Sophia's skin doesn't burn like hers; it might go a little pink, but becomes golden overnight. Adella, on the other hand, needs to make sacrifices in order to develop any colour, which usually involves layers of peeling.

She glances at her phone. Still no reply from Jake.

'How's Jake going?' Sophia asks, elbows on the bench, chin in her hands, as though she can read her mind.

'I can't believe he punched a bouncer,' Nathan announces from the back door, shaking his head. The smell of barbecue wafts in behind him. 'How dumb do you have to –'

'He's not dumb,' Adella interjects, smiling in an attempt to soften her voice.

Nathan walks into the kitchen, pulls a beer out of the fridge and takes a seat on the stool beside Sophia, resting his elbows on the bench. 'The guy wears a crucifix,' he says, as though speaking only to himself.

'What's wrong with a crucifix?'

He shrugs. 'I think believing in a man who lives in the sky is a sign that maybe you're not very smart.' He speaks slowly, as though to a child. 'And believing that we go to a place called "Heaven" after we die is deluded.'

'I think it would be nice to believe in something,' Sophia says, trailing off.

'Might be nice. It's just not true. We rot in the ground like every person before us.' He sips his beer loudly.

It's probably easy to believe that the skin of human bodies liquefies and blackens, their hearts and livers decaying, like we are no more than a maggot-infested possum who has fallen from a power line, Adella thinks. Easy until that skin belongs to your own father. What a luxury it is to speak about death so callously, a trait that seems most common in those who have never lost anyone they love.

'In my defence, all I know about your friend is that he punches security after a few drinks and wears a crucifix. Sorry if I don't think he's Einstein.' He does that thing with his hands again, as though Adella is attacking him and he is trying to calm her down.

'There's more to it than that. I told you . . .' She tries to gently dismiss his comment. To draw this conversation to an end.

'Yeah, yeah, I know, his dad died. That's obviously fucked, I get that. But you can't go around punching people. Even bouncers who, like, probably sometimes do deserve a punch in the head.' He turns around, heading towards the back door. She can hear the sizzling meat, Daniel with tongs and sausages.

'Of course it isn't, but I don't think any of us can really understand what that day must be like for him.' She speaks quickly. 'And Jake wasn't even punching him that hard.' The screen door closes behind him. She directs the rest of her sentence to Sophia. 'The bouncer didn't need to knock him out.'

'Did he have a concussion in the end?' Sophia asks.

'Yeah.' She crosses her arms over her chest. 'He couldn't remember where he was. I spoke to him on Thursday and he was still feeling pretty shit. A bad headache and stuff.'

She'd called him every day this week. An impulse partly born from worry, but mostly born from guilt. She knew what Christmas Eve meant to him and hadn't wanted to bring it up. They'd made it a ritual to go out and celebrate, to pretend it was just the night before Christmas and nothing else, a likely fruitless attempt to get his mind off it. As a family, Adella knew they marked Malcolm's birthday. But they had never quite worked out what to do with the day he died. So his mum went to church, sometimes with one of his brothers, but more recently the boys have scattered across Sydney, as if by avoiding each other they would also avoid the memory. Usually she would send a text first thing, but this year she'd been distracted, and when they met up she didn't want to acknowledge the anniversary in case he had been managing to think about something else, just for a moment.

Mascara had run down her face in the ambulance, dry and itchy by the time they arrived in Emergency. She was surprised to learn he would only need four stitches. While the doctor explained she'd be administering a local anaesthetic to the wound, Adella had decided to distract Jake with his favourite story, the one about Lottie being on a boat with her new boyfriend and blocking the toilet so severely they had to return to land. She had begged the boyfriend to tell the skipper it was him, but instead he quite literally pointed at Lottie while explaining what had happened. That was when Lottie knew this man was not for her. The skipper then had to make a call that began with 'We have a situation', followed by 'I've just never seen anything like it'.

'Apparently there was a team of four waiting for them on the dock. And they had this industrial-sized pump,' Adella added. Jake laughed, trying desperately to stay still, and even the doctor was suppressing a smile. Adella figured that the only advantage to how much Jake had drunk was that he could no longer feel a thing.

She never asked why he'd punched the bouncer. The answer was obvious; he was angry. Anger isn't rational. It's immediate and all-consuming and directed at the person standing closest to you. She came over on Boxing Day and they didn't talk about it. As they watched television, her eyes darted to the plastic Christmas tree, askew and sad-looking, three or so presents below it, still wrapped. She knew they were for Malcolm. Every year Annie would disappear for days doing the Christmas shopping, and on Christmas morning Malcolm's gifts would appear under the tree, as though he might just come back to open them. Adella thought about Annie wandering alone through Kanooble Plaza, working out what Malcolm would have wanted this year. Smiling at the cashier as they scanned the tie or the shirts or the socks that would forever remain unopened. What did she do with them? Adella wondered. Did she hide them in her bedroom? Throw them in the bin?

Apparently she'd cried when Jake had walked through the door, blood plastered all over his white shirt, in the early hours of Christmas morning. He'd made Adella promise not to tell his mother anything. Now she could see why. Annie kept shouting about 'legal action', as though they'd be able to afford it, and interrogating Adella about the details. Jake had also, of course, conveniently left out the part where he had thrown the first punch.

He did ask that night, on Boxing Day, if 'Sophia and that' knew. She wished she could have said no, but in the ambulance she'd seen a series of missed calls and sent a rushed text.

Daniel finally calls out, 'Meat's ready!' They move to the outdoor table. As they eat, he asks them questions about their trip, where exactly they're going and for how long.

'I went on a family holiday to Thailand when I was like sixteen,' Nathan says, shovelling a sausage wrapped in white bread into his mouth. 'Hated it.'

People who pay for their own holidays rarely hate them, Adella thinks. She feels sorry for Nathan sometimes. It would be an exaggeration to say he had grown up with everything, but his upbringing could probably be summarised as 'comfortable'. She imagined him as a teenager boarding a plane, with no sense of what it cost or what they might be doing at the other end. Adella had fantasised about going to another country since she was a child, and no matter how hard she tried she couldn't imagine what it must be like to look beneath her feet and see land that wasn't Australia. The last few nights she'd been struggling to sleep, overcome with anticipation, her gut whirling with excitement.

'Neither of us have been overseas before,' Sophia says, looking towards Adella. 'With the tour, there are heaps of add-ons you can do, like snorkelling and hiking and visiting temples . . .'

'Of *course* you're doing a Contiki tour,' Daniel says, shaking his head. 'I thought they were just for people on their gap year. Everyone will legitimately be eighteen – you guys will be the oldest ones there.' The boys both laugh. Sophia pushes him playfully.

'No, I'm kidding. It'll be fun. And it's super cheap, right? Like you won't have to have saved that much?'

Adella's body tenses at the question. She's been trying to save for six months but has still only saved a few thousand. When she asked Lottie for a loan, she said no but then told her to go to the bank and apply for a credit card like everyone else. A week later Adella had access to more money than she'd ever seen, and bought herself an expensive Dior perfume to celebrate. Sophia doesn't need to know any of that.

Before either of them can answer Nathan interjects, leaning back in his chair, 'The real question is how much money you're spending on my present.'

'However much you're spending on mine,' she says, offering him a big smile, wondering what kind of gift you'd buy someone in Las Vegas. He kisses her on the side of the head.

It's late when Sophia and Daniel leave. Sophia offers her a lift home but she wants to speak to Nathan, alone.

He pulls himself up onto the bench as she closes the fridge door and asks, 'Are you going to miss me?'

She leans with her back against the stainless-steel fridge, her arms folded.

'I hate to ask this,' she says. 'But what . . . what are we?' She pulls a face, as though she's in pain as she says it.

The smile fades from his eyes but stays on his lips. 'What do you mean?'

She leans back further, staring at the ceiling.

'I mean, are you sleeping with anyone else?'

He groans and puts his head in his hands, running his long fingers through his thick brown hair. Even when he is trying to find the words to tell her how little she means to him, she still finds him sexy.

'No I'm not,' he says, as though it's an unfortunate observation rather than a choice. 'But aren't we having fun?' He raises his eyebrows.

'Can we not be exclusive and still be having fun?' She matches his tone.

'I don't think . . .' He pauses, searching for the words, '. . . I can give you what you want.'

Her stomach falls as a voice inside her head whispers, *But I haven't asked for anything.*

'We're both going away and I just thought we should have the conversation before . . . it's been months, so I think working out what we are would be fair. Would be good.' When did she become so inarticulate?

He stares back at her but doesn't say anything.

'Are you planning to, then? Sleep with anyone else?' No part of her wants to ask this question, which, she realises, means she already knows the answer.

'Do you want me to be honest?'

Has anyone ever said no to that question?

'Yes.'

'I don't know. Maybe? I'm just not looking for anything serious right now, does that make sense? Whatever you're asking for, I can't give it to you.'

'What am I asking for?' She laughs, looking confused.

'Commitment? Me calling you every day? I just don't know if I want this to be a girlfriend–boyfriend thing.' He pauses. 'I'm just trying to be honest with you . . .'

'So you don't think I'm someone you'd like to date.' It comes out like a statement.

'Well, yeah. I don't know if you're the kind of girl I'd date. If that's how you want to put it.'

Why would that be how I want to put it? she thinks.

'Why?'

'Adella,' he groans, like she's being childish. He is already sick of this conversation.

'Why not?' she asks, as though the answer has no bearing on her whatsoever. She hopes her face is not the colour it feels.

'I don't know. It's just how I feel. Something is missing, I guess.'

'So do you know if you'll ever feel like I'm someone you might date? Or have you made up your mind?'

'Don't know,' he says again, without even giving himself a moment to think about it.

'Okay, well, good to know,' she says, standing up straight. 'I didn't want to go away thinking we were exclusive if we're not.'

'Are you going to sleep with people?' he asks, his eyes wide in mock excitement, as though it's a joke.

'Fuck you.'

13

Adella

The bright lights from the street, beaming from billboards and nightclubs, turn the right side of Sophia's face from pink to blue to purple.

They're drinking mango daiquiris at sticky metal tables and even though it's past eight, their foreheads are prickling with sweat.

Phuket, their first stop, is louder than Adella expected. They've been here three days now and she still finds it overwhelming. Music blasts from nightclubs and shops and blends with horns and the revving of motorcycles. The city is covered in low-hanging electricity lines, some of which look like they're only seconds from falling onto the footpath. The smell is all-consuming, but not necessarily in a bad way. Fuel and cooking food, burning and dampness – the smells of life.

'You are beautiful and smart,' Sophia covers her mouth, stifling a burp, 'and Nathan is probably already regretting his decision. The best revenge is to enjoy every second of this holiday.'

Adella had imagined the greater her distance from Nathan, the less space he would take up in her head, but the inverse seems to be true. Her mind keeps slipping back to him, mostly when things are quiet. She imagines his eyes every time she asks Sophia to take a picture of her here or there.

'This isn't a point-and-shoot situation,' Sophia had said earnestly at the hotel pool on the evening of day one. 'When either of us asks for a picture,' she held Adella's gaze intently, her eyes wide, 'we are asking for *the picture*. If it takes fifteen minutes, it takes fifteen minutes. We did not come to Thailand to get a handful of blurry images where I look bloated and you look . . . tired.'

She opened up her camera roll, scrolling through the pictures they'd taken that afternoon. 'See this one here? You've gone from below. We need to be taking it from above. And more candid. So take photos as I'm, like, *preparing* to have my photo taken, you know? You nailed it here,' she said, pointing to one. 'This is what we call growth.'

The two nights already felt like longer. Adella has felt caught between two distinct versions of herself. There was the Adella who believed this would be the best holiday of her life, one she'd dreamed of for years. She was here with Sophia, free of Nathan, a person she knew, logically, was not good for her. She wanted to drink too much and use this time to recover from him – to come back as an entirely different person. And then there was another Adella. This version did not want to be here. She was a parasite, sucking any energy the first Adella had. She knew this holiday was doomed the moment Nathan paused for a beat too long, and the problem wasn't so much Nathan the individual, but what he represented. Rejection. Seeing her for what she was. Lacking something. Empty. He could see, as everyone would eventually, that there was something wrong with her.

An off-key rendition of a Kings of Leon song blasts from one of the bars across the street, and at the same time they visibly cringe at each other. 'I'm sorry if I've been a bit quiet,' Adella says, running both her hands through her hair. 'I think I just had to let myself be sad for a bit. But I'm done.'

She'd been having the peculiar experience of being a spectator to joy, but not being able to touch it. She knew when she stepped off the plane that this was a moment she'd been waiting for, but her body was devoid of sensation. As she ate she was sure the food tasted good, but was unable to experience it. She felt like a floating device desperate to be plugged in, to turn on, to feel everything as wholly as it deserved to be felt. But instead she was numb.

'Oh!' Sophia leans forward. 'Let's write the list. Why haven't we done that yet?'

Adella had forgotten about the list. Every time one of them went through a break-up, they had to write a list of all the things they'd always hated about the other person. The pettier the better. Once Sophia had written eleven dot points about an ex's backpack, from the colour, to how the straps were too narrow, to how it made him look like the kind of person with body odour.

Sophia disappears to the bar and comes back with a pen and a napkin. She is wearing a brown fedora and a white prairie dress.

'Let's start with the fact that he thought he was fucking Calvin Harris . . .' Sophia mumbles as she begins to write, Adella getting flashes of the terrible songs he used to play her off his laptop.

The game helps. It always does. After an hour Sophia looks up at her and says, 'In conclusion, we ran out of napkin.'

They drink and talk about things that don't include Nathan or Daniel. Sophia tells the story of a psychopath she's working with who keeps listing impressive places he's worked at, but after some rudimentary digging it's clear he didn't. After the weekly newsletter, he replied to all, adding in one of his own 'wins' he thought had been overlooked. They diagnose him with at least four disorders. They discuss various ways to avoid getting food poisoning.

Sophia starts telling a story about her friend who dropped five kilos after a week with salmonella, when a sandy-haired, fair-skinned man approaches their table.

He places his hands down flat and says, 'All right. Sorry to bother you, genuinely, but my mates and I have been trying to guess where you're from and now we have a bit of a bet going. Please tell me you're . . . European of some sort? Swedish, perhaps?'

'Oh, yus,' Sophia begins in the most terrible accent. She realises she can't keep it up and mumbles, 'We are from . . . Sweden.'

'Bullshit,' the guy says, smiling.

'Nah, we're Australian,' Adella says, as Sophia hits her from across the table. They introduce themselves and learn that his name is Mike. He is travelling with his cousin Joe and his best friend, Lachy.

'Whereabouts in England are you from?' she asks.

'Manchester. Unfortunately.'

They laugh even though they don't get the joke.

'How long are you here for then?' He looks from Adella to Sophia.

'Got in a few days ago,' Sophia says. 'We're doing a tour, it starts tomorrow. For ten days . . .'

'No way! Contiki thing?'

They nod.

'That's what me and the boys are doing, aren't we, lads?' He gestures back to his table where two others sit – she assumes Joe and Lachy – lifting their beers in acknowledgement. 'Do you know anything about it?' He slides up a chair and takes a seat. 'We haven't really had a look. We're spending two months travelling around South-East Asia . . . weren't prepared for the heat.'

She notices that they are all horrifically sunburnt. The tops of their ears are purple and their noses and cheeks reveal they've been wearing sunglasses without sunscreen.

'How old are you?' Sophia asks.

'Forty-nine,' he replies.

'How old are you really?'

'Twenty-six.'

She smiles, catching his eye.

It's the distraction Adella needs.

14

Jake

'How do you wind up living in a place like this?' Ant asks Tommy as he sips an iced coffee.

Jake listens for an answer.

They're on a re-roofing project in Vaucluse at the moment, one of the most expensive suburbs in Sydney. He'd never heard of it until Tommy picked him up early one morning and said they were about to see how the other half lived.

'He's a developer of some sort so this has got to be his third . . . maybe fourth property. I think he does actually plan to live in this one, though. Seven bedrooms. Eight bathrooms. A gym. The view itself has to be worth ten mil–'

'But how do you become a developer?'

'His dad was a developer. It's family money. You gotta have money to make money, as they say,' Tommy says with a shrug.

Jake is finishing off his sausage roll, sitting in the gutter under a tree, relieved to be out of the sun. 'If I want to be really rich one day,' he says, swallowing the last of his mouthful, 'and own a fuck-off house like this, what do you reckon? What do I have to do?'

Ant says 'inheritance' at the same time Tommy yells 'marry rich'.

'This guy have a daughter?' Jake asks, half-joking. 'Or a son. I could be swayed.'

'Ah.' Tommy waves his hand as though shooing away a fly. 'Money isn't everything, mate.'

That's what people like them say to each other all the time, Jake thinks. His dad used to say it. And when he was a kid, he believed him. He remembers sitting in the passenger seat of their Holden Barina, where the air-con no longer worked and the back window wound down but not back up again, and they stopped at a set of lights beside something loud and low to the ground. He can't remember what type of car it was, only that it was yellow and it looked like a toy car Paul played with a lot, making a really annoying 'vroom' sound as he launched it at someone's ankles.

'People who drive cars like that are trying to prove something,' his dad said, nodding his head towards the neighbouring driver.

Jake looked over too. The man wore sunglasses that even he could tell were expensive.

'Flashy cars . . . it tells you a lot about what someone values,' Malcolm said, sitting back as the yellow car launched at full speed the second the light turned green.

His dad had thought there was something more virtuous,

more morally superior about owning things that were objectively worse. That it said something about your character. But all it said to Jake was that you couldn't afford the better version. Every now and then his dad played golf with a mate from work who was a member at a fancy club. They'd be teamed up with a few other guys. When his dad walked in the door he'd grumble over dinner, 'You shoulda heard these blokes! Talking about bloody private school fees and real estate. Never been so bored in my life.' At the time, Jake thought that did sound boring. But now he wonders if those men had made his father feel bad about himself. If he even knew the unleashing was a twisted defence mechanism; a way of appeasing himself from the guilt of not being able to provide such things for his own family.

Jake takes another bite out of his sandwich. He lets Tommy's words sit. 'Money isn't everything' is a lie people without money tell themselves so they don't think too much about how much better life could be. Or sometimes it's parroted earnestly by people who have enough, themselves ignorant of what life looks like without it. Both types of people are delusional.

Tommy takes a call while Ant heads back into the roof, where it must be nearing fifty degrees. Jake scrolls through his phone for a few minutes, putting off getting back to work.

He watches as three women, around his age, wander in the direction of the beach, towels thrown over their shoulders. They're holding different-coloured smoothies, each as big as their own heads. He checks his watch. Just after eleven. He wonders what their days look like. They move slowly and peacefully. Clearly not at work, even though it's a Tuesday. He thinks about Adella on holiday. You wouldn't have to go on holiday if you lived here. Every day you'd be waking up in paradise.

He gets up and makes his way back to the worksite. One day he'll live here, he decides. But then he finds himself immediately wondering if that will ever happen. He's been trying to save, but whatever begins to accumulate eventually disappears. He helps out his mum with rent and food. Tearing his ACL last year ended up costing him probably thousands just in physio fees. Then he'd had his wisdom teeth out, which he'd put off for as long as he could. That cost him a month's salary.

Money even matters once you're dead, Jake knows. It dictated the casket his family chose. The headstone. The shit cold food selection at the wake. His dad had had no money, and that didn't change once his heart stopped beating.

A few weeks after the funeral, when he'd been looking for something in the bottom drawer, Jake had found an envelope marked with his dad's handwriting. On the front it said 'Gold Coast', with a list on the back of all the expenses he'd need to save for. The petrol for the drive up. Theme parks. Accommodation. Jake found $75 in there. In the end, his mum used it on groceries, and another dream of his dad's went unrealised.

As he pins off the rafter, he remembers the months before his dad died, a period of his life his brain has worked hard to forget. Two of his uncles had spoken at the funeral. They had said how much Malcolm had loved his kids. How he'd never missed a footy match. That wasn't true, though. He'd stopped coming – hadn't been on the sideline at all that season. That was part of Malcolm's story too.

They kept using the word 'happy', telling anecdotes about how he always made everyone laugh and would put people before himself. That wasn't the father Jake knew anymore. That man had been replaced by a monster he hated. He clenched his jaw as he sat in the front pew at that funeral that didn't feel long enough, wanting to shout, 'My dad was his own murderer!' He stared at the crucifix that hung from the wall behind the altar, Jesus's head flung to one side. Flecks of blood marked his hands and feet, and Jake thought about suffering. His father had suffered like that, maybe even worse. He just hadn't bled. If only he had bled.

Instead he'd been awful. Disengaged. Mean. He drank too much and sometimes he would yell at his children who were always making too much noise. He didn't tell stories anymore around the dinner table; he barely ate. As Jake's eyes went from the crucifix to the casket, he was overwhelmed by the complexity of the person they were burying. There was the man from last week, with vacant eyes and nothing to say, always making his mum repeat herself because he wasn't really listening the first time. And then there was the dad of his childhood, carrying Jake on his shoulders and driving a little faster down steep hills so their stomachs would drop. The person who would play with them on the lounge room floor, crawling around on all fours for hours, carrying at least one kid on his back. The dad who took him to the beach for the first time and taught him to dive under waves, always beside him as he re-emerged above water. As the flowers in their house died, and the phone stopped ringing, Jake found that the memory of his father began to take the shape of the man from his youth. He liked that.

Something Bad is Going to Happen

Jake's thoughts turn from his father now and back towards the work in front of him. He falls into a sort of flow as his hands measure and sheath, measure and sheath, breathing in the earthy fresh scent of plywood. His feet ache inside his heavy mustard boots. He imagines the place he will buy his mum and his brothers one day; so different from the place they're renting now. As he reaches for another sheet of plywood, he sees a Rolex and a Black BMW 1 Series and a fridge with an ice machine. All of it.

For him, this is just the beginning.

15

Adella

Adella wakes to the sound of a running tap. Moans. Rolls over, pulling the doona up over her face, trying to block the stinging sunlight. The next time she wakes is to the sound of a zip, then the *clunk clunk* of suitcase wheels being pulled down the stairs right outside the door. Her head is pounding and her throat dry.

'What time is it?' she asks as Sophia re-enters the room, eyes slowly opening despite a strong desire to keep them closed.

'We're leaving in,' Sophia checks her phone, 'six minutes.'

'Fuck.'

She stands up too quickly and can taste the tequila from last night.

'I packed your bag,' Sophia says without looking at her.

Adella hurries into the bathroom to brush her teeth, an uncomfortable sinking feeling in her gut.

'You didn't have to do that,' she calls out from one side of her mouth.

'I did because otherwise you'd be left behind.'

She hears Sophia now rolling Adella's suitcase to the door, then doing a final sweep of the room.

'I don't know why my alarm didn't . . .'

'It did but you turned it off,' Sophia replies abruptly.

She wants to shut the bathroom door and disappear. Redness creeps up her neck and she is struck by the distinct sensation that she is too conspicuous. Too visible. There's that expression about wanting to climb into a hole, but to do so would be to still exist. She wants to evaporate, if only for a moment, to experience some respite from herself. She can't remember Sophia ever being this short with her. Two mornings ago, when Adella had slept in, Sophia quietly packed her bags and gently woke her up right before they were due to leave. They'd officially been on the tour for three days, so far only exploring Phuket, and it had already become a running joke that Sophia could drink herself into oblivion and would still wake up the next morning at seven, eyes bright, full of energy. For Adella, the hangover would linger for most of the day, and she'd find herself unable to speak until at least lunchtime, breathing slowly in through her nose, out through her mouth.

'Sorry. I mean it.' She spits the last of the toothpaste into the sink. 'I won't do it again. I just feel like shit. I need a can of . . .'

At this, Sophia smiles and opens their mini fridge. Inside is a can of Coke.

'Remember we bought one before we went out last night?'

Sophia hands it to her. 'I'm not packing your stuff again. I don't feel great this morning either but I don't want to get yelled at by Liz if we're late.' Finally, she has said what she is thinking.

'Thank you, you're a lifesaver. I owe you.' Adella pauses, deciding whether to ask. 'Did you sleep here last night? I woke up in the night and I swear your bed was empty.' The acidic taste of Coke mixes with the freshness of toothpaste.

Sophia leans on one of the suitcases. 'I slept in Mike's bed for a bit.' She rubs her eyes.

'What? What happened? Weren't the others in the room too?'

'Shh, they're next door,' Sophia begins to whisper. 'Nothing happened, I swear. We cuddled. It was nice.'

Adella opens her mouth to ask about Daniel, but Sophia has already opened the door, wheeling her luggage out. They've barely spoken about him since they arrived. She figures that's because Sophia, endlessly empathetic, is trying not to acknowledge the elephant in the room. That being, of course, that what Sophia has with Daniel is fundamentally different from whatever Adella had with Nathan. He adores her and looks at her in a way that Nathan never did Adella. He did not dump her because they would be apart for a few weeks. Things like that didn't happen to Sophia.

Adella puts on sunglasses that cover the purple circles under her eyes and walks down the external stairs. As she approaches the road, she offers half a smile to Mike.

'Lachy's chucking,' he says tonelessly.

'I'm in trouble because I couldn't get out of bed,' she says, glancing at Sophia who is speaking to the tour leader.

'I feel you.' They stand in comfortable silence.

The past three days, visiting the Big Buddha and snorkel-ling at Kata Noi Beach and bar-hopping down Bangla Road and wandering through the Naka night market had felt pulled from someone else's life, full of a lightness she found unfamil-iar. Yesterday afternoon, sitting on Freedom Beach with Sophia, Mike, Lachy and Joe, watching the afternoon sky change colour, the sun eventually setting, her mind thought of nothing but the moment she was presently in. She had thought less about Nathan, except for the odd moment she managed to connect to WiFi, where her fingers instinctively opened a bright-coloured app and tapped on his social profile before she'd even made a conscious decision to do so. He'd mostly been tagged in videos, out in clubs and by pools during the day. There was one girl, she'd noticed. Half an arm in a photo of him with a cocktail. One where he was wearing her hat, and her account was tagged. But Adella's impulse to follow her profile and learn everything she could with just the tips of her thumbs was always interrupted by something more stimulating. Her pad Thai would arrive, or Mike would be yelling 'Ten!', which he always did when some-thing was perfect, or Joe would be declaring 'whoopsie', which they always did when, for example, they ordered two full meals and a beer bigger than their head. She felt like a different person from the one who arrived, barely able to speak to Sophia as they wandered through a temple she couldn't remember the name of.

Mike, Lachy and Joe are the type of men Adella and Sophia would swipe past on dating apps. Their haircuts, all short on the sides, longer on the top, do not make sense, and they wear thongs that look like they've been purchased for two dollars from a local chemist. Their clothes are sometimes an obvious joke, matching party shirts purchased from a Thai market, and other times the joke is more unclear – singlets with three-quarter cargo shorts. Green board shorts printed with the word 'Italia'. Collared short-sleeved Ralph Lauren shirts in royal blue, or black t-shirts emblazoned with Jack Daniels logos. There is something endearing about how little they care.

She learned three things about Mike in quick succession. The first was that he had broken up with his girlfriend of seven years a few weeks before booking this trip, and without looking at the itinerary or how far Thailand was from Manchester, he'd purchased the tour online. The second was that to be in his company was to have your cheeks ache and your eyes water. He could make anybody laugh, even a Thai waitress who spoke only a few words of English. The third was that he was taken by Sophia. That much was clear immediately. He looked in her direction whenever he told a story, and asked her questions he didn't bother to ask anyone else. They disappeared sometimes, just the two of them, and would return, Mike piggybacking Sophia, she whispering in his ear.

Joe and Lachy listen more than Mike does and are always offering to carry bags that aren't theirs. Adella has grown close to them, mostly bonding over how irritating they all find the two Canadian girls on the tour.

Ashley and Kayla, the Canadians, love nothing like they love Canada. Over dinner, they'd announce that the food was good, but nothing like what they had in Yukon.

'Have you ever tasted bison? Yukon is literally world-famous for our bison,' Ashley had remarked, while Kayla refused to finish her fried rice.

Eventually Lachy interrupted. 'Have you ever tasted Nandos? The chicken dinner with chips with peri peri salt? Manchester is world-famous for our Nandos.' The girls looked disgusted.

Today, after meeting outside the hotel, the tour group walk the five minutes to the ferry port where they travel to Phi Phi Island. The five of them sit on the upper deck, legs outstretched, comfortable in silence. At one stage Sophia lays her head on Mike's lap. They're sharing a set of earphones. Adella drifts into a half-sleep, warmed by the sun tickling her skin, the slight breeze cooling her face. Soon the hum of the ferry gets louder, a buzz spreading around them, and she sits up, arms hugging her knees to her chest. She sees glistening turquoise water lapping onto white sand, dotted with long-tail boats. Rugged green mountains surround the horseshoe coastline as though it were expertly designed that way. It is unlike anything she's ever seen.

'Ten,' Mike says, standing up to get a better look.

There is silence for a moment, broken by the sound of Kayla's voice, speaking to no one in particular. 'Mmmmm. You should see Yukon in summer.'

Lachy chokes into the water bottle at his lips.

After dropping their bags at their small resort, Adella, Sophia, Lachy, Joe and Mike spend the afternoon swimming and snorkelling, the water a temperature so perfect they cannot bear to get out. The five of them take turns shouting, 'YES, BUT HAVE

YOU BEEN TO YUKON?' Once shadows fall they wander back to their rooms to shower and change, before walking to the Cliff Bar for a drink. Mike slides in next to Sophia, placing his phone in the bag hanging from her shoulder. When Lachy gets up to order a round of drinks Adella asks for a straw, so he comes back with a cocktail full of dozens. Every time someone orders another, they return with a dozen straws in their hand asking, 'Hey, sorry, did you need a straw?', slipping them into Adella's hair and pockets and down the back of her singlet. She leaves them there, laughing when she goes to the bathroom, scooping countless straws from her clothing.

Once the sun has disappeared behind the mountains and the sea turns as black as the sky, they make their way to a strip of beach bars, passing on the way a stall selling sand buckets of cocktail mixers.

'Should we share one?' Sophia asks, glancing at the size of the Smirnoff bottle in the nearest blue bucket.

'Don't share one! They'll last the rest of the night . . .' Joe insists.

'But how many standard drinks are going to be in one of these?' She picks up the bottle of Smirnoff, trying to do the maths.

'Maybe twenty-eight? Thirty-five?' Adella says, shrugging. 'Around that. They're like five dollars, we might as well get one each and we don't necessarily need to finish them.'

Sophia groans and throws her head back.

'We're in Phi Phi Island,' Mike says, holding her by the shoulders. 'If we can't have thirty-five standard drinks here, by the Indian Ocean, with this fine gentleman over here,' he gestures to a monkey on a lead wearing a nappy they've passed twice today, 'then when *can* we have thirty-five standard drinks?'

'No Indian Ocean,' the man holding the monkey says, his face serious. 'The Andaman Sea.' He points in the direction of the beach clubs.

'Should she get a cocktail bucket?' Mike asks the animal, which is sitting on the man's left shoulder. The monkey nods, clapping his hands.

'You can't disrespect a monkey. Not in Thailand,' Mike says, saluting the monkey.

With their shoes in their hands, they amble down to a beach club and one of the boys orders a shisha. Adella likes how it warms up her lungs, and how it smells, or tastes, a little like strawberry.

By the time she looks down at her bucket again, it's half empty. Mike's is nearly finished.

'I need to dance,' he says, standing up clumsily, signalling towards a dance floor elevated slightly from the beach.

'Same,' she says, edging out of her seat. The bucket hangs from her wrist, and she hears the others follow.

They all dance for what feels like hours. At one point Joe starts vomiting just off the dance floor into white sand. Adella thinks, *This is the best night of my life.*

There's suddenly a giant fire skipping-rope, and she watches it, transfixed, wondering how it doesn't set the ground alight. People jump, their minds slow and their legs awkward, and when she next looks up Lachy is skipping as though in a trance. Then the rope smacks his ankle and the hair on his legs is singed. She thinks she would never do that – it's too dangerous – but then she is jumping and the fire is hotter than she expected. It hits her leg and so the rope stops circling, but by the time she realises the bottom of her left foot has landed on the burning rope. She laughs. It stings. The sole of her foot looks black and red. She limps towards the lounge chairs, imagining how much this will hurt tomorrow.

'You need to sit.' Mike leads her to a spot on the sand, leaving her for a moment while he finds a cup of cold water. Her breathing constricts, the way it does when you're about to be alone with someone for the first time, and you're not sure exactly how it will feel.

'You wanted a straw, right?' he asks as he plonks down next to her, slightly out of breath. He extends his hand and she looks down and sees a single straw lolling in the cup.

She stares out at the black sky while he pours the water on the burn, and everything spins. The lights from the bar strobe across the ocean, and her stomach begins to rock as though she's on a boat. She rests her head on his shoulder and for a moment she thinks she might fall asleep.

'So who was the guy you were seeing before you left?' he asks.

'How did you know about that?' She tries to focus her eyes on his.

'Sophia mentioned it.' He looks out to the ocean. 'Said you were pretty cut up about it for the first few days.'

She clenches her jaw. 'Yeah, it just ended badly. He was going away at the same time and I think he wanted to be single. Probably for the best.'

'Ah, his loss.' He smiles and turns to her.

'Do you like Sophia?' she asks.

'Why do you ask?'

'Just seems like you do.' She smiles and plays with the rim of the plastic cup. She reminds herself to speak to Sophia in the morning, and repeat everything she's about to hear.

'Yeah, she's cool.' They listen to the waves come in and roll back out again. There's a shriek. In the distance she thinks she can see two people, water up to their waists, either having sex or preparing to. 'I like you too, though.'

That hadn't been what she was asking. Her head turns to look up at him. She feels a jolt of electricity in her chest – partly shock, partly excitement.

'You're very . . .' He looks upwards, trying to find the word. 'Sexy? Is that a weird thing to say?'

The jolt of electricity courses through her stomach, stirring something she didn't know was there. She likes how he is looking at her. How he is saying things people do not ordinarily say to each other.

'Is that right?' She smiles.

'Today on the beach I couldn't stop looking at you.' He shakes his head. 'I just wanted . . . I wanted it to just be us.'

She thinks back to the beach. He had mostly been with Sophia. Joe had even taken a photo of her on his shoulders, Adella on Lachy's. There had been a moment, maybe, where she caught him looking towards her. She'd smiled. Readjusted her bikini. She'd felt exposed.

She looks up at him. He leans in and strokes the inside of her thigh as he starts kissing her.

'I've been wanting to do that for a while,' he says, pulling away only a few centimetres.

She lies back and he rolls on top of her, his hands reaching up inside her singlet.

She watches herself from above, unable to catch up with the events unfolding in front of her. Her life feels exciting. Thrilling. The more she kisses him, the closer their bodies become, the more she can taste and feel and become the person he envisions. She hungers not so much for him but for *that*. To become that.

The part of her, perhaps a single brain cell, that is still sober sends a message to her hands to claw at the sides of her underpants that he has begun to pull down.

'Not here,' she says. 'Let's go back.' She sits upright, watching the world shift on its axis, stars just out of focus.

'Okay,' he whispers, kissing her neck, and there is something about it she does not like. It is as though he is pretending to be someone else.

They stumble up from the beach, her limping, avoiding the lights of the dance floor where she vaguely makes out the shapes of Sophia, Lachy and Joe. Sophia is laughing, but glancing over her shoulder, as though looking for someone. Adella unlocks her phone and quickly checks for WiFi, so she can let Sophia know she's heading back to the resort. Nothing. She'll message when she gets to the room. It should only take five minutes.

Adella can feel Mike watching her as they navigate the narrow streets, bright with street lamps and full of twenty-somethings with glow sticks and face paint, sand buckets hanging from their hands.

He takes her hand and leads her through the crowds, and she thinks how strange this physical contact would have been even an hour ago.

When they reach her room her fingers find the cool metal key in the bottom of her bag. She feels him watch her struggle to slide it into the door, and wishes he'd either take over or look in the other direction.

'I want this so badly,' he says as she leads him inside the dark, stuffy room, clothes strewn on both beds, make-up scattered by the full-size mirror.

He looks serious now as he locks the door behind him, his mouth straight, eyes focused, and she feels as though this is a different man from the one on the ferry and the beach and the bar this afternoon.

He leads her to the bed and then pulls off her underpants, scaling the length of her body, settling between her legs, as she wriggles down with him. She shakes her head, turning him over onto his back instead, knowing that it's been hours since she had a shower and she could not enjoy an act that would be so unpleasant for the other person.

She instead takes him into her mouth, the sour taste of sweat reaching the back of her throat, and he moans, 'You're so good at that.' The comment thrills her.

It's dark and as he moves her this way and that, she loses sense of which way is up, what side of the bed she's on, if he is behind her or in front. She makes noises he seems to like, and grabs at a body she feels indifferent to. She wants him to stop when he whispers in her ear, something about her 'pussy' and her 'tits', and his breath has begun to smell acidic. Her limbs are tired, her eyes heavy, her head unable to comprehend where she is or who she's with. He keeps going and she moans, confused as to why even as she does it.

Her eyes jolt open and she can see a snake of light making its way in from beneath the curtain. The air outside sounds early. She can feel last night's eye make-up hardened into the corner of her eyes, and spit has dried on the left side of her mouth. Then she is hit by various realisations at the same time. Mike is beside her, his nose rattling each time he breathes in, his mouth hanging open in an ugly way. Sophia's bed is empty. Adella reaches for her phone, wondering if she had the foresight to plug it into its charger. No. Her stomach sinks. Her stomach. It is coated in something sticky, dry. She doesn't remember that. Was she conscious when he finished? Did he think she was? She feels a moment of gratitude for his pulling out. She shifts silently out of her bed and sees her bag splayed by the door. She tiptoes into the bathroom and sits down on the toilet seat, head in hands, feeling the matted knots at the back of her hair. She wants to have a shower but doesn't want to risk waking Mike up, although if he did wake up he'd at least slink back to his own room.

By the time she returns to bed, his hands are tucked behind his head, his elbows wide, eyes barely open.

He sits up. 'The others are going to have questions,' he says, and laughs, rolling over in search of his pants and t-shirt.

He no longer looks at her like she is special. The air in the room has changed from charged and passionate to dirty and stale. He spots her shorts on the floor and flings them at her, and she intuitively puts them on, even though this is her room and she doesn't need to be dressed. He collects the rest of his things and opens the door, murmuring 'ahhh' as the sunlight floods in.

'Oh, what?' He looks down towards the doorstep.

'What?'

A third voice emerges, tired and gravelly.

She hears the word 'fuck', then a sniff.

Adella pulls the door open wider. Sophia is sitting on the ground, looking up at her, eyes red and wide.

'I'll leave you guys to it,' Mike says, helping Sophia to her feet. He turns towards his room without so much as a wave to Adella.

Adella feels like one does at the moment they see a wave forming on the horizon, bigger than the ones that preceded it, gaining momentum as it surges towards you. She holds her breath. It is coming.

Sophia slams the hotel door, then the bathroom door. Adella hears her sniffling before the flick of the shower tap, and she sits on her bed, shoulders hunched, looking at her bare feet. The sole of her left foot stings and the skin feels tight and sticky.

When Sophia finally opens the door, steam pouring out into the rest of the room, two lines sit between her eyebrows and her lips are in a straight line.

Adella opens her mouth.

'I actually don't want to hear it.' Sophia takes the towel off her head, and dries the hair beneath it.

'It was an accident,' she almost whispers.

'To lock me out? I banged on the door, Adella. For half an

hour. You knew we only had one key. Where the fuck did you think I would be sleeping?' Little bits of spit are thrown from between her teeth and evaporate into the air around her.

'I wasn't thinking about . . . next door? Could you have taken Mike's bed?' Her tone rises.

'Both the boys took girls home. Not that that is even the fucking point. All I wanted was my own bed.'

'I didn't know. I didn't hear you banging.'

'The phone calls? I must have called you fifty times last night.'

'My phone died. I only found it this morning. I was drunk, I was really drunk. I'm sorry,' she pleads, her arms outstretched.

'You weren't too drunk to fuck Mike.' The tension that has been floating in the room is suddenly captured in a single word and thrown at Adella with the force of a slap. *Mike.*

Sophia, it is clear, is making fun of her. Her voice is laced with disgust, her eyes fixed on the clothes she's now throwing into her suitcase.

'What does Mike have to do with it? You should be mad at him, he's the one who locked the door last night.' Adella's fingers are splayed in frustration.

'This has *everything* to do with Mike.' Now Sophia looks at her. 'You knew how I felt. You knew. But the second anyone pays you any attention, even if they don't actually like you, you fall for it.'

Adella's chest is shaking and heat is rising from her neck up into her cheeks.

'Why is it so unbelievable to you that Mike might like me?'

'Because Mike likes *me*, Adella.' She laughs mockingly, looking up at the ceiling. 'He's been telling me since our first night.'

She must clock Adella's expression. 'I didn't want to rub it in your face after what happened with Nathan, but are you really going to pretend you haven't seen it? We slept in the same bed,' she proclaims. 'Why can't you see what is right in front of you?' There are tears forming in her eyes.

'I am sorry about locking you out,' Adella says slowly. 'But you don't get to just collect men and giggle as they follow you around because they boost your self-esteem.'

'At least I *giggle*,' Sophia says, exasperated, leaning forward. 'Do you know what your face looks like most of the time? How hard it is to counteract your energy in every room we walk into? I just want to scream *cheer up*. Cheer the fuck up.'

'I thought . . .' She swallows. 'I thought I'd been good this trip.'

'Good?' Sophia's eyebrows rise halfway up her forehead. 'Like when you barely spoke for the first three days because you were heartbroken? Or when you were incapable of getting out of bed and packing a bag like everyone else on this trip is able to do?'

The muscles in Adella's jaw tense and release. Tense and release. She doesn't know how to respond. So she changes the subject.

'You literally have a boyfriend at home and yet you're leading Mike on as if you don't.' She stares at Sophia, her mouth a straight line. 'I'm sorry if I was confused,' she says, making it clear she is not sorry that she was confused.

'Daniel and I are on a break, not that I owe you an explanation.' Sophia folds her arms in front of her chest, her pyjama shirt damp from her hair.

'Well, how was I meant to know that?'

'I didn't tell you,' Sophia says, staring at the ceiling again, 'because I knew you'd get upset.'

'Why would I get upset?' She shakes her head. This is madness.

'We had a fight. About you.' Sophia's jaw shifts beneath closed lips. She sighs, as though telling Adella something that will hurt her is a burden she wishes she didn't have to carry.

'I hated how they spoke about you when you weren't there. Sometimes Nathan would literally say, "Hey, watch this," and text you for the first time in God knows how long and you'd reply straight away. I went to Daniel's place one night and Nathan was there with someone else, arm around her, hardly speaking to anyone else . . .'

Adella's stomach turns. 'Why the fuck wouldn't you tell me?'

'Because, Adella,' she sits on the bed opposite her, 'remember Alistair? I told you that I saw him on Tinder? And then you slept with him that next weekend and lied to me about it?'

That had happened. She'd been so angry. She'd tried to break it off with Alistair as soon as Sophia had told her, mostly because she was embarrassed. They'd been seeing each other for months; had even spent a weekend up at his parents' farm. She hadn't wanted to be hysterical, so simply messaged, 'Hey, can you give me a call when you get a chance?' to which he replied, 'Uh-oh, what's this about?' He never called, so she called him.

He'd been so relaxed when she brought it up. He explained he just hadn't deactivated his account, but couldn't remember the last time he'd used it. He made her feel silly for making such a big deal of it, and made her promise to always *ask* if there was something she was worried about.

That Saturday night she had left drinks with work friends to meet him in the city. They went to a pub until it closed, and then stumbled back to his place. After they slept together, Adella went to the bathroom, and found his phone sitting on the counter. She picked it up before she'd even decided what she was going to do with it. There was no passcode. There was a message from Krystal that read 'wait, tonight? Lol I'm already in bed soz x' and another from Maddy that read 'can't do tonight but am I still seeing you Monday?'.

She tapped on the Tinder icon. Of course she did. There were active conversations with several women who he'd matched with in the last week. She found his bio. It said that he was taking applications for a 'winter girlfriend' to snuggle up to and watch Netflix. It also said that one of his hobbies was 'the gym', which she knew was a lie. She screenshot everything she found, sent it to herself, and then messaged it back to him, which she now thinks was probably an unusual thing to do but it made sense at the time. She picked up her things and slipped out the front door, waiting to see what his explanation would be. Alistair, in the end, never replied.

Of course she never told Sophia. She did tell Jake, though. And so, months later, at Sophia's birthday dinner, when Sophia made a joke about Adella's bad luck with men, Jake had piped up and suggested that it wasn't really bad luck when you ignore all warnings and end up discovering what you already knew. Like Tinder Guy, he said while Adella stared back at him blankly.

'Remember? The guy who Sophia found on Tinder and then

you ended up having sex with him again, only to discover he was – would you believe – on Tinder?'

Sophia had barely spoken to her for the rest of the night. They had eventually made up, though, when Adella turned up at her house the next day, with chips from KFC in hand. 'Extra chicken salt,' she'd said, presenting them like a bunch of flowers and then throwing her arms around one of her favourite people in the world.

'I was embarrassed about Alistair,' she says now, trying to push back the memory. 'I explained that to you.'

Sophia's voice is raised, her face still red from the shower. 'But you never take my advice. I just have to watch on as men treat you like shit, and then listen when you complain about it. At some point you have to take some responsibility. I ended things with Daniel because I didn't like how he talked about you. I was sick of Nathan making you look stupid. But then *this* happens. You're a . . .' She shakes her head.

'I'm a what?'

'You're a laughing stock,' she says, like it's the truest thing in the world.

16

Adella

Krabi is the most beautiful place she's ever been, and she hates every moment of it.

White sandy beaches meet turquoise sea, flat and still, the water so clear you can always see the bottom. Long-tail boats cast a shadow on the seabed below as they take you out to caves and coral reefs, revealing a world just as lively beneath the water's surface. Jungle meets rivers meets limestone mountains and it looks like all an artist had to work with were blues and greens, painting not a place but a fantasy.

As Adella snorkels, she thinks about Sophia, swimming on the other side of the boat, Mike trailing behind.

As she wanders towards the emerald pool, her face expressionless when she finally encounters it, she thinks about Nathan, and what she would say if she ran into him back home.

As she kayaks with Lachy, she can hear his voice but cannot

follow the meaning of his words. She is trapped in that night with Mike, the things he said, the way he touched her, the fact she was no longer, really, in the bed with him when he came on her stomach. She does not know how she feels about that. The whole experience is a knot she cannot untie. It cannot yet be packaged into a neat, funny anecdote for her friends, and even if it could, she no longer has Sophia to tell it to.

For the remainder of the tour, five long days, Adella and Sophia do not speak to each other. The first two nights, they continue to share a room, staring only at the floor when they find themselves inside at the same time. A few times, Adella finds straws in unusual places. One drops from her bag onto the floor. Neither of them acknowledge it. For the final three nights, Sophia sleeps in Mike's room, coming back only to shower and change. Adella wonders how Sophia thinks things unfolded with Mike; if perhaps he has led her to believe that Adella was the initiator and he simply went along with it. Either way, Sophia's sense of betrayal is clear. Mike bears none of the blame.

Adella spends the days with Lachy. She'd forgotten the gratefulness that comes with having someone still speak to you after you've done something terrible. It would happen at school. One day you'd turn up and everyone would look the other way, and then you'd find yourself beside wide-eyed Olivia who had no reason to treat you with such kindness but she would, and would speak to you as though you were anyone else. Lachy behaves like he doesn't know what happened when, of course, he does.

On the final night she will kiss him out of obligation, and feel violated even though she initiated it. She won't know how else to say thank you.

At night, she pretends she feels unwell, which perhaps isn't so much of a lie, and messages Jake or calls Lottie. She flicks through photos from the first half of their trip, zooming in on Sophia, wondering if she hated her that day. Or that day. She zooms in on her own face, photos she'd thought she liked. Now she can only see the emptiness of her eyes, the slumping of her shoulders. She had been living in a delusion.

No photos are taken of her for the rest of the trip. Lachy offers a few times but she shakes her head and says, 'No, it's fine.'

Mike doesn't look her in the eye, though every now and then he says something half-friendly, and includes her and Lachy in whatever conversation the others are having. But mostly he laughs with Sophia, a raucous howl he seems to only ever have with her. Sometimes when they laugh, sitting at the other end of the table, Adella wonders if they are talking about her. The details of what happened in her bed. How mortifying it was that she'd believed he found her attractive. How disgusted he must have been in the morning, as though she were a discarded tissue he'd come in from the night before, and then forgotten to throw in the bin.

She and Sophia are meant to do a trek in North Thailand after the Contiki tour finishes. Deposits have been paid, accommodation and flights booked. But late one night, Adella curls up under her blanket with her phone and, while music from a nearby street permeates the thin hotel walls, she moves her flight home forward by a week. It costs double what she expects it to, and she feels sick as she enters her credit card details, calculating how many hours of work it will take to pay it off.

She messages Sophia to let her know she's leaving the night the tour ends, and in response she receives paragraphs of texts followed by three loaded dots. Still typing. Sophia calls her selfish and says she can't go alone, it would be too dangerous. Then there is the money. Sophia can't get a refund on the accommodation, so is she to pay for both of them? Could we not have discussed this before you booked your flight home, Sophia asks, and Adella says no we couldn't, because we're not speaking.

In the end Adella just sends the words: 'Let me know how much I owe you and I'll transfer.' Then she buries her head into her pillow and cries.

The guilt of spending money is compounded by the guilt of not even enjoying it. Her body stiffens when she pays for a lunch she only picks at, or climbs onto a boat she wishes she wasn't on. She feels sick every minute she spends in a fucking hotel she can't afford and even walking around a market, her wallet closed inside her bag, but knowing the cost of even being here, her feet on this ground. The hours it took to save any money – late nights and shifts where she played games with herself trying not to check the clock – and now all of it, all her savings and more, are just dripping through her fingers.

When she arrives at Sydney airport, a week or so after that night with Mike, there is no one to pick her up. Lottie is working late. Jake's car is in for a service. Her mum would panic and end up getting lost in a car park, then she'd see the cost of parking there and her face would fall and turn white. Adella didn't even bother asking her.

She walks past the people waiting at arrivals, many of them holding balloons and signs, and feels stupid and embarrassed for wishing someone was here for her. She turns her phone back on and feels it vibrate as she puts it back in her front pocket. By the time she gets to the train station, her face is prickling with sweat, and her shoulders hurt from the weight of her backpack. She takes it off and puts it on the floor, sits on it, then pulls her phone from her pocket.

There are twenty-four messages. Nine are from Nathan.

17

Jake

Eight years ago

Music pours out of Jake's house onto the black, still street and a group of four boys, all with their hoods over their heads, turn into the front yard.

'Names?' Jake asks, looking down at the printed-out list Paul gave him a few hours before.

They murmur four names, their voices quiet and cracking, at odds with the size of their Nike TNs that look ready to brutally kick a passer-by at a moment's notice.

'It's like they want the police to stop them and ask them what they're doing,' he says to Adella, leaning the weight of his body against the fibro exterior of the house.

'Yeah,' she says, as though she didn't quite hear him.

'I'm worried that if any randoms actually do show up you're

going to be kind of useless. Like, are you prepared to say "Your name's not on the list, move on"?' he says, trying to lighten the mood.

'Nah. I'd probably just let them in. Don't really like causing a fuss.' She smiles, looking down at her folded arms. 'Can't believe Paul is eighteen.'

'I still can't believe Mum let him have an eighteenth. I had to have that shit lunch at the RSL.'

They stand in silence, Jake looking up at the starless sky, enveloped by a layer of invisible cloud. *That's what life down here feels like sometimes*, he thinks. The stars are there. He knows they're there. Every night they take up their same positions, glowing just as brightly, as true yesterday as they are today and will be tomorrow. He just has trouble seeing them. He hears people describe them sometimes. He even sees them reflected in other people's eyes – like the way Paul beamed this morning opening his presents, and how he nervously tended to the house this afternoon, cleaning the back table and dragging in plastic buckets from Bunnings for everyone to deposit their drinks on arrival. He sees them in Vili's eyes when they win a game on a Saturday. In his mother's voice when he finished his carpentry apprenticeship last week and she kept repeating, 'You've done it! Four years! You must feel so happy and relieved,' and in that moment he felt broken because, no, he did not feel either of those things. Adrian bought him a beer last night to celebrate. His boss had even decided to keep him on and offer him a full-time position, meaning he is on a decent salary – beyond what he's ever earned. And yet, nothing. The stars are there and still he can't see them.

Or rather he can't feel them. They don't penetrate his skin and sink into his insides like they seem to for everyone else. He is beginning to wonder if it doesn't actually matter so much what he achieves or earns in his lifetime, given he has an inability to feel it.

'Have you spoken to Sophia?' he asks, forcing himself out of his own head.

'No. She unfollowed me on everything, though. So did the guy,' Adella huffs and shakes her head.

She had told him about what happened with Mike. Waking up covered in him. She'd tried to pass it off as a funny story – she'd woken up naked, because of course she had. She'd probably fallen asleep, and 'honestly the man deserves credit for pulling out, it was quite courteous'.

'You know that guy,' he says now, two lines forming between his eyebrows, 'that's actually pretty fucked. Like, you were unconscious. I'm pretty sure that's rape.' He tries to introduce the last word lightly, with the same emphasis as any other word, as though it carries no additional weight.

She shakes her head, then leans it back, taking a deep breath. 'I was talking to a few girls from work the other night during closing and one of them used the phrase "almost rape".' She runs her fingers through her hair. 'Like, most women have had a brush with an almost rape. You did something stupid that you regret, things got a bit fucked up, and then you get to decide where you file it.' Her fingers scratch at her scalp. 'Nothing I can do about it now and no point in dwelling on it. But then *he* fucking unfollows *me?*'

'Yeah, good point. You would've had such an enriching, meaningful relationship if he still looked at the shit you post.'

'I'm glad you get it,' she says with a half-grin, glancing towards the two girls walking across the front lawn, their arms interlocked. That probably raises the girl tally to six out of the fifty or so people out the back, which should make Paul happy. Jake doesn't ask their names. Just ushers them in.

One laughs hysterically at the other as they walk into the hallway, then the other laughs.

'That is as good as their night is going to get,' Adella says, nodding in their direction. 'They'll spend the next four hours trying to match the anticipation of getting ready where they probably had four vodka Cruisers and burnt the shit out of each other's hair. And now every conversation will be a let-down by comparison and they'll wonder why every night out just tends to . . . fizzle out. But that's because,' she gestures with her head again, 'that's the good bit.'

He knows she's talking about Sophia. He also knows she's just figuring all this out as the words pass her lips.

Jake thinks for a second about telling Adella to just call Sophia. To apologise. But he stops himself. There's no point; Adella's in more of a talking mood than a listening-to-advice mood. Instead, he says nothing.

18

Adella

Present

Sophia nods as Kirra speaks. Sophia sits on the arm of Adella's stiff, navy chair, while Kirra stands above her, slightly too close. Kirra's black tracksuit, frayed at the ankles, with small holes scattered on each leg, is in contrast to Sophia's sky-blue shift dress. Sophia smells like coconut and something sweet, while Kirra's breath is noticeably stale. Adella is struck by the discomfort of her worlds colliding. Here are two people in her life who were never meant to meet each other.

If you were to overhear Kirra's voice, enough to discern her tone and cadence, but not enough to hear the specific words falling out of her mouth, you would assume she was making sense. She speaks quickly but clearly, about her friend's baby who got sick and the Royal Flying Doctor Service had to come and then the bloke at work who didn't know what was coming to him but he deserved it. Her shoulders are back and her head high, dark hair tied into a loose, low bun. Her words become increasingly nonsensical. Sentences are full of ideas that do not belong together. An oven followed by a husband, a cackle, a mouse, three blind mice, the band, mould growing in the sewage, dancing on the roof in ballet slippers for children, her toddler, burned with a knife, see right here, my broken wrist.

According to Cathy, she is well known to the staff at St John's. Nurses who have worked in the unit for twenty years speak affectionately of her, a woman whose mother they knew too. Sometimes she shows up to Emergency, lucid enough to know she needs help. Other times, she has been sectioned, brought in by an aunty who worries she is a threat to herself.

'A cycle,' Cathy tutted to Adella during her first afternoon there, while they both watched Kirra pace the courtyard, speaking to someone who wasn't there. 'And you know whose fault it is? Bloody ours.'

Kirra belongs to the Gadigal people, and although Abigail is not entirely reliable, she says that Kirra lives with severe post-traumatic stress disorder and an alcohol use disorder, and experiences some sort of psychosis.

'I don't know all the fancy words, but her mum drank when she was pregnant with her, that's what one of the nurses told me last time I was here. And why did she drink? Part of the Stolen Generations. You read about them? You wouldn't believe it if I told you.' Abigail has the ability to speak for forty or so minutes seemingly without taking a breath. She explained the

Stolen Generations, which Adella already knew a fair bit about, and other than a few incorrect dates, she found that Abigail's monologue was relatively accurate.

'Okay Kirra, why don't we let these two chat in private,' Cathy says cheerily, ignoring the stern look on Kirra's face.

Adella leads Sophia into the room she shares with Abigail, and the two sit side by side on the edge of her bed.

'I'm so sorry,' Sophia says in a whisper. 'I didn't know things had got this bad.'

Adella shakes her head, looking down at her odd socks. 'Don't know why you'd think things were bad.' She looks up and meets Sophia's eyes with a crooked smile. It's her first attempt at a joke in as long as she can remember.

Sophia asks her questions about the people, about Kirra and Abigail. She remarks that Cathy seems nice and asks about the puzzles. Eventually the inevitable will come: the question about how she ended up here.

Instead Sophia takes Adella's hand in a way that doesn't feel entirely natural and says without looking in her direction, 'Jake would know the right thing to say.'

All these years later, and she still knows he would.

19

Adella

Four years ago

Adella often wonders what she would say if she were to pass Sophia on the street. It's been years since the Contiki tour, but she catches herself thinking about Sophia frequently.

Sometimes she convinces herself she sees her; a mane of glossy ash-blonde hair or the contours of a profile seem familiar. She freezes and stares, waiting for this stranger to become someone, a laugh or a tone of voice as confirmation. But they never do. They turn around and they are just some nobody, a plain face, wearing years-old sneakers Adella knows would never belong to Sophia.

But she imagines how the next five minutes would unfold. How Sophia would ask her how she's been, and how her own mouth would search for the words. How does anyone summarise four years?

Well. It would depend on her mood.

On a good day, she would say she's doing her PhD in Clinical Psychology. Her work is on the relationship between the locus of control and chronic depression in women of reproductive age. Sophia would say 'that's specific', and she would respond that PhD theses always were, that was kind of the point. She wouldn't bring up the university awards, although she would want to. Awards tend to mean more when you've stopped winning them, a detail she would choose not to share. She'd mention that she tutors now at Sydney University, running tutorials and marking essays. This fact makes her feel proud. There's a thrill she gets right before she walks into the room, knowing she'll think slightly differently by the time she leaves. She becomes someone else, not flesh-and-blood Adella but just a person with ideas, some decent, some not. The students seem to like her and she hopes she's a better tutor than most of the ones she had. She gets paid decently for that, and the university even pays her to study. She'd say she's living in Meadowbank with two housemates who have, she supposes, become her friends. Lottie is living in Parramatta and her mum is working and walking and taking new medication. Life, she would say, is good.

On a bad day, she would say she's twenty-five and still studying while everyone else has a full-time job and is earning an income and reaching the milestones that constitute adulthood. I feel like I'm falling behind, she'd say, forcing a laugh. The tutoring isn't enough – it's only two classes – and the uni money is being used to pay off credit cards she never should have been given, so she picks up shifts at the pub up the road in order to cover rent. She'd say she's living in Meadowbank, which is too far from Jake and her mum and she doesn't have a car and she doesn't like catching the train after dark ever since she found herself in a carriage with one man who kept staring at her, and then stood up right before her stop and was touching himself, like one of those viral videos of a gorilla at the zoo. She'd say her life is too quiet and maybe if she really thinks about it, she's just writing a thesis on what, exactly, is wrong with her mother. And she can't get off her fucking phone. Can you? she'd ask Sophia. Is this just how we live now? Days of our lives swallowed by a rectangle that hypnotises us, a poker machine except without prizes?

And dating. A part-time job she dreads, swiping she fits in while she sits on the toilet or while she tries to fade into anonymity on the train, eyes fixed on a glass screen, digging, digging, for someone who doesn't send her a message like, 'Hey, here's a question. Pineapple on pizza or no pineapple on pizza? :)' as though that question isn't a fucking cliché that people use to try to feign a personality, when ultimately the answer makes no difference to anyone's lives and reveals less than nothing about a person. Oh. And her mum is doing terribly, although she can deny that reality if she ignores her phone calls for a few days, distracting herself with swiping and scrolling and listening to various podcasts about murdered women. She'd smile at that.

'Listening to podcasts about murders calms me down,' she'd say. 'You know it's fucked when that's light entertainment compared to what's going on in my head.'

Sophia would laugh politely, but she wouldn't entirely understand, because she would never listen to a true crime podcast, or watch an eight-part documentary about a serial killer. Just because they no longer speak, or follow each other on social media, doesn't mean Sophia is a total stranger to Adella. She still knows what Sophia would think about this or that, and whenever she meets someone, she imagines what Sophia would make of them. She is a ghost who haunts her, lurking around corners, and visiting her when she can't sleep in the middle of the night.

She wonders if Sophia saw her relationship with Theo play out online. She'd had her profile on public for that reason. They'd met at work – the pub she still worked at on the odd Saturday night. He worked behind the bar too and was always quiet and uncomfortable – everything he said sounded like it had been run over and over in his head until it was memorised. But one night a bunch of them had stayed back for drinks and for the first time she noticed him, how his brown eyes were kind and gentle, how his laugh made everyone else laugh. They began texting. She began obsessively checking who she'd be working with, washing her hair and wearing perfume if she knew it would be him. He kissed her in the car park at one in the morning and from there things were easy. Easy in a way she didn't know relationships could be. Falling in love, she realised, should be an absence of anxiety. Not a feeling of falling at all, but the sensation of being caught. Safety. Home. Quiet. She never worried about when he might message, because he already had. For that reason the butterflies subsided as quickly as they came. When she climbed into bed there was nothing to ruminate on – no unresolved sense of something not quite right. They spent weekends lounging around his family home, taking his geriatric dog on slow walks around the block, and she never once doubted how he felt about her.

That's why she ignored the voice that started whispering, about a year in, *Get out*.

You need to get out of this.

She read blogs about attachment styles and repeating toxic relationship patterns because they felt familiar and she'd nod and catch the train to Theo's house and wonder why the feeling still lingered. She would look at him at parties, how objectively attractive he was, and how clearly he didn't know it, and wonder how, even though all the parts were so perfect, it added up to a person she couldn't love. What was missing?

The voice was always loudest after sex. She would lie flat on her back, looking up at the ceiling, wondering why her gut was churning, telling her something was wrong.

Wasn't this what she wanted above all? For someone to love her? Every year when she wrote out her New Year's resolutions, finding her soulmate sat at the top of her list. The qualities she wanted – funny, kind, emotionally intelligent, driven, gentle – were all embodied by Theo. And yet . . .

Eventually the voice became so loud she couldn't ignore it. She didn't sleep for two nights, and then he came over to her place in Meadowbank, knowing something was wrong. She told him she didn't want to be in a relationship, when what she meant was that she didn't want to be in this relationship. She told him she wanted to be alone, when she knew she didn't, she would just prefer being alone to being with him. She told him she loved him, which she didn't mean, and said sorry, which she did mean. He cried quietly, and kissed her on the forehead. The moment might have broken her heart if she wasn't so full of relief.

After eighteen months with Theo, she has just found herself back on the apps, which are filled with awful men holding up fish, or partying without a shirt on in various exotic-looking clubs. She knows less about what she's looking for. The kindness of Theo left her almost repulsed, and yet she couldn't withstand the cruelty of Nathan.

Without someone in bed beside her, she is left with her own loud thoughts, and the sense that an elephant is sitting on her chest, making it difficult to breathe. This isn't how her life was meant to look – single, in a rundown apartment with mould growing in her dark wardrobe, without any real idea of what a 'career' outside of studying would look like. As the years go on, she finds herself with fewer friends, not more. The world gets quieter. Smaller.

For years she's played out the vision of running into Sophia, how their history would make it impossible to ignore each other. The conversation would span hours and then days and then it would never stop, making up for lost time.

But if she were to run into Sophia today, of all days, she probably wouldn't bring up her mum or her house, Theo or Tinder.

The strangest thing is happening, she'd want to tell Sophia.

That PhD she is in the middle of. The thesis she has been madly writing, that earned her a teaching role and a position, a livelihood, for the time being. A ticket, she's always hoped, to a different kind of life.

She would sigh and look up at the sky, trying to underplay the crisis.

And then she would say, 'I have stopped being able to write.'

20

Adella

Four years ago

When Jake turns up to dinner that night with a petite blonde in one of his baggy jumpers, Adella fantasises about saying something.

She waves as they approach the small table, clearly set for two. Jake picks up a chair from the table beside them, a 'Reserved' sign sitting in clear view. Adella and the nameless woman smile at each other while Jake is reproached by a wide-eyed waiter who has no patience for chaos, huffing as he moves chairs and lays out an additional place setting.

'You'd think this was some fancy restaurant and not Meadowbank's local Thai joint,' Jake says with a smirk.

The dinner is awkward and stiff, the blonde clearly trying to ingratiate herself with Adella to prove something to Jake. She must already know he won't be calling her back.

That isn't because there is anything wrong with her, Adella can plainly see. It is because Jake rarely calls anyone back. He had met this girl, woman, whatever, out last night, and she had stayed with him until morning, when he said, as he often does, that he doesn't want them to leave. They watched movies for most of the day, until Adella suggested dinner, an invite that was clearly just for Jake but he opened it up because he knew Adella would never make a scene. So this woman came, in last night's skirt and a jumper, and is now behaving as though she were the one closer to Jake, laughing particularly hard at his jokes, and stroking him on the thigh.

The whole thing makes Adella furious. Not at the blonde, but at Jake. She feels as though she's been forced into a date that is boring and strange, like she's interviewing a woman five years younger about a life that is completely irrelevant to her. Whenever Jake brings up something the blonde doesn't understand, they have to bring her in, explaining context and backstories that she surely doesn't care about. It is a relief when her phone rings, and she steps away for a moment, clearly being scolded by a parent wondering why their daughter hasn't come home. She is short as she comes back and says her goodbyes, whispering 'message me' into Jake's ear as she kisses him on the cheek from behind and pushes some notes of cash into his hand, which he pockets.

'Why didn't you tell me she was coming?' Adella carefully tilts her head to appear more inquisitive than pissed off.

'I didn't think it mattered. It's not like we had a booking . . . she was still at my house. What was I meant to do?' The waiter drops off the bill. Jake throws his card on top of Adella's, and they wait for the waiter to return with an EFTPOS machine. Adella makes a note to clarify she'll be paying for one-third.

'Tell her you had a dinner with a friend and she would have taken the hint,' she says, looking around as though there is a crowd nodding in furious agreement.

'She was all right, wasn't she?'

'That's not the point. She was fine but I wanted to have dinner because there's shit I actually want to talk about that I can't discuss with a stranger at the table.'

'Oh. Oh yeah, I get that.' He nods, looking at his lap. 'So what did you want to . . .'

'Doesn't matter now.'

The waiter comes over to finish taking the payment and they sit in silence for a moment, until Jake suggests they get dessert at the chocolate place around the corner. She nods.

'You know that feels like shit for her, right?' Adella asks as they push out their chairs and make their way outside.

He doesn't say anything.

'She will spend tonight and tomorrow and the rest of the week wondering why you haven't messaged, and because she's not an idiot, logic will tell her she has some kind of flaw that makes her impossible to care about . . .'

'Okay, this is ridiculous,' Jake says with a smile, still looking ahead. 'We had sex once and she initiated it . . . she got just as much out of it as I did. Isn't it quite "sexist" or whatever to assume she wants to marry me?' He says the last two words like they are unspeakably absurd.

'I don't know how to explain this to you,' she says, stopping and rubbing her forehead. 'Last night, she went back to *your* house because of course she did. I assume *you* came because otherwise you'd both still be having sex. It only finishes when you finish . . .'

He tries to interrupt.

'I need you to understand,' she says, smiling, 'she absolutely did not finish. I know you think she did, but she didn't. This "casual sex" thing is an unfair exchange. It's not equal. You wanted the sex and you got the sex. You know what she probably wanted? Someone to play with her hair. Ask her where she sees herself in ten years. Someone to tell her that she's special and not like all the other girls, because all the other girls are stuck on some sort of carousel being served the same shit men on dating apps who fuck them once and then never text them again.'

'It's a Sunday night. Why am I suddenly in one of your feminism lectures –'

'I just don't know how you do it to people!' She's not smiling anymore. 'Don't you get lonely too? Don't you want someone to call when your boss is being a dickhead and someone to, like, really talk to? About real shit? What is so unappealing to you about building a life with someone who is funny and interesting and smart and *kind*? I don't fucking get what any of you want!'

'I feel like this isn't about,' he pauses, 'her.' He directs his head towards the restaurant they just left. 'Is it about that date you went on the other night? Where is all this coming from?'

She had been on a date with someone she met on a stupid dating app, but it had been mutually disappointing. But that wasn't where this was coming from. 'You're just . . . you're one of the good ones,' she says. 'But you're also one of the shit ones.'

He laughs. They walk into the chocolate cafe and line up to order.

'I know how it looks. When people get too close, sometimes I feel suffocated. Like they need things from me I can't give them. The more they lean into it the more I just want to run.'

'You don't like to rely on people, I think,' she says, as gently as she can. She knows why that would be.

'Maybe.'

They order hot chocolates and sit down at a table near the window. Jake asks, again, what it was she wanted to talk about.

'I exaggerated that a bit to make you feel bad about bringing her,' she smirks. 'I'm just having a weird time. I can't write.'

'What do you mean you can't write? Isn't that what you do? At uni?' He looks genuinely perplexed.

'It's what I'm *meant* to be able to do. Or I could until, like, a few weeks ago. Today, I sat in front of my laptop for almost four hours and I couldn't do anything. I stare at the page and it's honestly like I can't breathe. I'm meant to be presenting at a conference in Queensland in three weeks.' She can feel her heart pounding in her chest. Sydney University has invested in sending her to this conference. She has worked for years to earn an opportunity like this, to stand in front of her peers, lecturers, researchers and clinical psychologists, and present some of her findings. Without conferences on her resume, she could complete her PhD and still be utterly unemployable. In order for a PhD to mean anything, she must present and she must publish. But she sits in front of her laptop, a tool she's worked with for years, and her fingers do not know which keys to type. The letters may as well be in a foreign script. She swallows. 'I'm ignoring the follow-up emails from my supervisor because I'm just waiting for the words to come back. It's like I don't have them anymore.' She's speaking quickly.

'What happens if you force yourself to?'

The question annoys her. It seems akin to asking someone who doesn't know how to play the piano to just bang the keys harder. 'It's almost gibberish. What comes out doesn't make sense.' It's difficult to even find the words to explain. 'Words come out in the wrong order and then I try to fix it and fix it until it's blank again. And I keep trying to email my supervisor to explain the situation. But . . . but I can't even write an email.'

Jake laughs at that, and after a moment, so does Adella.

'Maybe you've had one of those "silent strokes" my grand-mother had. Your face is looking a little . . .' He makes an 'uh-oh' face.

'It's actually not funny, though,' she says, still smiling. She holds up her forehead with the heels of her hands. 'Not presenting at this conference isn't an option. And it has to be brilliant. This could be career-defining . . . and writing is the one thing I'm meant to be able to do. And now it's like the tap has just been turned off and I don't know how I ever turned it on in the first place.'

She tells him she is booked in to see someone at the university psychology clinic, which is staffed with postgraduate trainees, meaning it's only a fraction of the price. She doesn't tell him about the other stuff that's been going on. The sleeplessness.

The hours spent lying under her bed. Why she's been having so much trouble leaving the house. It is too difficult to explain.

'Anyway, I'm just going to go to the GP. See if there's something I can take.'

'Seriously?' He leans back in his seat.

'Yeah. Maybe I just need to stop the physical symptoms and that's what medication would do.' She shrugs.

'But isn't the bigger question why it's happening in the first place? Like, medication doesn't actually solve anything. It just masks symptoms. It sounds as if your head is trying to tell you something.' He takes a sip of his hot chocolate. 'If I were you, I'd listen to it.'

'I don't have time,' she says impatiently.

'They tried to prescribe me something maybe a year after Dad died.' He avoids her eyes for a moment. 'Remember that?'

Adella nods. They hadn't seen each other much during that time, but they'd talked about it since. He'd become stuck. It had happened before; he'd get fixated on a thought or a fear or a concept. After his dad, the thought had been about death – and he'd be unable to talk to anyone. He'd once said to her that he couldn't quite voice the fear, it was something about the endlessness of the universe and how even when you were dead you were stuck in this infiniteness. If he said it out loud, he'd explained, then he would pass the thought on to someone else and then they'd get stuck too. It was better other people didn't know.

'I remember being like . . . I'm trying to figure something out. This is real, human stuff. Why are we trying to numb it?'

'Because you couldn't speak,' Adella says matter-of-factly.

'I get that. But I wasn't "sick". I was in pain. They are two differ-ent things. I was seeing things really clearly. And that – those thoughts, those feelings, they're all a part of who I am. To take those away would be to turn me into someone else. They medi-cated Mum, I remember.' He folds his arms. 'And her dreams stopped. Every night she would dream of Dad. Some were night-mares and some weren't. But the antidepressants meant she couldn't see him anymore. They made him disappear.'

'I didn't know that.' Adella looks down into her drink, then decides to meet his gaze. 'But didn't they make her pain more bearable?'

He shakes his head. 'She stopped taking them pretty quickly. She didn't want to erase Dad from the only place where she could still see him.'

They're silent for a moment. 'I had this conversation with my physio after my shoulder reconstruction. Pain is always trying to tell you something, right? When you take all the painkillers and numb yourself, that's not how you actually get better. Eventually, you've got to feel the pain and use it as a guide.'

'You sound like a life coach.' Adella wouldn't say it out loud, but in the past she has wondered if Jake ever thought about what might have happened if his dad had been medicated. Perhaps the outcome would have been different.

They move on after that. Talk about his work and this weird documentary she found online. There is one other thing Jake says, though, that will stick with her.

He drives her home afterwards. As he pulls into her street, she asks what he's doing tomorrow.

'You've got church?' she says, remembering tomorrow is Sunday, unbuckling her seatbelt.

'Nah,' he says, looking down at her buckle. 'I don't go anymore.'

21

Jake

Four years ago

It is the night he meets Imogen, or more accurately the morning after, that the ground beneath him shifts.

He is meant to be staying at Vili's place that night. That's where he arrives as dusk falls over Surry Hills, birds making sounds as though they are in pain. He has an overnight bag slung over one shoulder and a sixpack looped around the fingers of his right hand. He can hear the boys before he sees them, deep laughs and knee-slapping, electro music playing from a wireless speaker.

The footy season wrapped up a few weeks ago, but no one can remember the night that followed so they've sorted Saturday beers to celebrate. Reg is on the barbecue and Vili has set up beer pong. It has been the first properly hot day in months, and the warmth lingers into the evening. That smell is in the air – the one that signals a summer not so far away.

The more Jake drinks the better his beer pong becomes, which makes him feel lucky when he sees Reg, hands on thighs, curled over a pot plant in the corner.

'He's going to kill my palm . . .' Vili tuts, shaking his head, and for the rest of the night the boys repeat it whenever silence falls.

'*He's going to kill my palm!*' Jake exclaims, strutting flamboyantly towards the pub on the corner, clicking his fingers above his head, eleven men trailing behind him, laughter spreading like fire.

Vili can barely speak when he pulls out his phone a few hours later, and starts trying to message girls he's matched with on a dating app. He tries four before finally one replies that she's at a bar up the road with friends, and will be there in twenty. By the time she arrives, everyone has forgotten she was coming, including Jake, and it takes Vili a moment to work out who she is. Her friend, short with long, brown hair, stands behind her, scowling.

Vili buys his date, Gen is maybe her name, something to drink but spills most of it before he makes it to the table. Jake can't work out why this girl – these girls – don't leave. Surely they have somewhere better to be. He means to be more polite but he can barely see. It is the best he ever feels, when regions of his brain have shut down and he is all instinct and no inhibition. He vaguely remembers promising himself early this morning that he wouldn't do this. He'd woken up with the sensation of a spider weaving a web inside his chest at record speed, his mind working hard to keep up, remembering all the stupid things he'd slurred at Ant and Tommy the night before. They'd meant to have a beer at the pub after work, but he'd hounded them to stay, buying them another round then another, until the sun went down and he changed their order to spirits. He imagines he'd barely been able to sit upright, his eyes half closed, and spit being thrown from the corners of his mouth. After Tommy had left, he'd noticed he hadn't sipped his bourbon and Coke, fiddling with his phone as though looking for an out. The shame lasted until he arrived at Vili's – or more accurately – until he opened his third or fourth beer, and finally, the spider stopped weaving and his mind left him alone.

He doesn't remember opening a conversation with Gen's friend but he must have. Her name is Imogen, and once they start talking her face softens and she unfolds her arms from across her chest. She tells him she's a paralegal. Something about family law. He finds himself hesitating before telling her he's a chippy, and although she is polite and asks questions, he wishes he had a different answer to give her. As she speaks about late nights in the office, nightmare clients and days without lunch breaks, he feels a sense of envy. How great that must feel, he thinks. Being needed. Being in demand. Putting your head down and the next time you look up the sun has disappeared beneath the horizon. Imagine watching your salary pile up in your bank account, and not having the time to spend it. Imagine knowing the potential that lies in your future. He doesn't want to hear about it anymore so starts telling her about the night a few weeks ago when the whole team got so drunk Adrian ended up sleeping on a stranger's verandah and Vili pissed his pants in an Uber without even noticing. The story keeps stopping and starting and he can't remember why he was telling her about any of this in the first place.

She orders the Uber, motioning for him to get in, and he doesn't mind this bit because at least he knows what to do. It's silent for a while as they travel to her place – both perhaps wondering if it's worth it. He does the maths. He's been drinking for more than nine hours. He can't imagine the sex is going to be very good, and that's if it's even possible.

'Anywhere here is good,' she says as the car slows to a halt. He follows her towards a wide gate on the corner.

'What suburb are we in again?' he asks, his palm cupping the back of his neck. Maybe he's been here for work.

'Darling Point.' She smiles as she punches in a code.

As they walk down a paved driveway he can see a car park; three cars nestled underneath a home shaped like nothing he has ever seen.

A Ferrari 458. A Jaguar E-Type. A Range Rover Sport.

He opens his mouth to ask if that's a Ferrari 458, but closes it again, realising it's a stupid question. He can see. That is a fucking Ferrari 458.

She opens a side gate that takes them through to the backyard, an automatic light illuminating palm trees and a pool almost hidden among shrubbery as though it were an oversized pond. He turns to face the house and realises he is not so much taken by the scale – although he can't ignore that – but by the design. The soft edges. The curved glazing blurring the distinction between inside and outside. The intricate detail on the white columns, like every inch of this home is art. A timber canopy extends over an enter-taining area, curved edges making it seem like a part of the ocean rather than a monstrosity settled above it.

There's a pool house she leads him into, which he learns is her bedroom.

'This place is sick,' he says, half-laughing, gesturing at the high, white-panelled ceiling.

'Dad's an architect,' she says, kicking off her shoes.

'Are your parents home?'

'Yeah. But they're upstairs. Everything is, like, soundproof.'

'How loud are you planning on being?' he says, grinning.

The sex is awkward and stiff. She barely makes a noise, except at one point to ask him if he is still hard. He isn't. Eventually, though, some primal part of him takes over, and after too long he finally comes. A relief to them both. As he rolls over, her a little too close behind him, he does not think about her or the under-whelming sex he just had. Instead, he closes his eyes and thinks about the house he has found himself inside.

He wakes to soft sunlight tumbling through panes of glass and it takes his mind a moment to work out where he is. His stomach sinks and his heart races at the memory of last night. The things he said. How as they were leaving he'd stumbled over the words, 'He's going to kill my palm!' and everyone had stopped laughing at the same stupid joke by then. Imogen had asked what it meant and he'd just shaken his head. Flashes of the sex come back to him and he puts his hands over his eyes, wishing it all away.

Imogen emerges from the bathroom in a towel.

'My parents are out this morning if you want me to make

you breakfast or something,' she says, collecting clothes from her wardrobe. He notices there is no warmth in her face when she speaks.

That's when he sees the rest of the house, or at least down-stairs. The floor-to-ceiling windows. The Caesarstone kitchen with a walk-in pantry. The parquet floorboards. The skylights and the timber panelling.

'This is like something out of a movie,' he says. She smiles without feeling.

It is Adella who picks him up an hour later, driving her house-mate's car, a favour she owes him from three favours ago.

As they cross the Bridge, Adella still in tracksuit pants, she turns down the radio.

'If I'm going to drive halfway across Sydney to pick you up, the least you can do is actually talk to me.'

He's been distracted, scrolling and tapping, grunting when she asks him a question.

'Sorry, I'm just finding her . . .'

'Ohhh, so you like her?' She drums at the steering wheel.

He smiles. And then he explains. He does not like her. She was shockingly boring, they had nothing to talk about and the sex was among the worst he's ever had. It's her surname he wants. So he can look up her dad.

'I reckon,' he says, as they drive down the main road, past Thai massage shopfronts and pubs with flashing lights, boxy apartment blocks and homes where the windows shake every time a truck roars past their front door, 'I reckon I want to be an architect.'

22

Adella

She spits whatever bile is left in her mouth into the toilet bowl.

The wave comes again and she retches, as quietly as possible so as not to wake anyone, sure there can't be anything left to purge. Her shoulders hunch and her eyes water, fixated on the bowl below coated with the yellow of her insides. Light is beginning to spill in through the small window in her bathroom and she wonders how long she's been in here.

She groans and wipes her bottom lip with the back of her hand. Carefully, she shifts onto the white tiles and lies on her side, finding relief in the coolness against her cheek. In the quiet she puts together the last twenty-four hours.

Yesterday morning she'd seen a doctor – an older man with a runny nose who bulk-billed. She'd waited for more than an hour before taking a seat in his bare office, where he'd coughed into a handkerchief and asked what he could help her with today.

She stared at the sharps waste box fastened to the white wall and delivered the lines she'd been rehearsing in the waiting room.

'I'm having trouble writing.'

'I'm in the middle of a PhD and I can't meet deadlines.'

'I'm anxious and I'm not really sleeping.'

She squeezed her hands in her lap and did not share any details that did not feel directly relevant. Even as she told the truth, she felt as though she was lying.

He asked about her appetite and she said she doesn't really feel hungry. Some days she might have a sandwich, or pick at some chicken for dinner, but if it weren't for the loudness of meal-times – the way everyone else at the university seems to stop for lunch – she might otherwise forget. Food makes her feel heavy and sick.

They made eye contact and she felt exposed, like he could see beneath her clothes. She looked back down at her hands, her fingers unable to stay still, aware of the deep crevices under her eyes, and her pale, unclear skin. Her hair was pulled into a bun that felt too tight. She had not washed it in almost a week, only partly out of a desire to look exactly how she felt.

She didn't tell him about what has started happening when she tries to leave the house. How she only made it to the front gate yesterday before the panic began, as though the world was full of a danger she had only just recognised. She'd found herself unable to breathe, her heart pounding, painfully, in her chest, her mind not generating coherent thoughts but instead firing feelings she knew didn't make sense.

When he asked if she had any thoughts of hurting herself, she softly mumbled 'no'. She didn't tell him that when she feels like disappearing, she instead turns off her bedroom lights and climbs under her bed frame. For a while, it feels like nothing else exists.

She knows, of course, that how she feels is largely a product of her own laziness. If she exercised and ate properly and journalled and was more grateful and joined a social netball team she wouldn't be here. She felt like a patient presenting with a self-inflicted wound. She was grateful that he seemed to be waiting until she left to appropriately roll his eyes.

He prescribed her an antidepressant and explained it might make her a little sleepy, which he indicated with a fake yawn as though she couldn't understand what the word 'sleepy' meant. She forced a smile. That might be nice, she thought. To be able to sleep. She asked about other side effects. What she could expect. He said that should be about it, and blew his nose into his handkerchief. You'll be a little sleepy.

He told her to start with half a pill, which is exactly what she did. By mid-morning she had set herself up on the lounge with a blanket and watched an old episode of *Sex and the City*, waiting for it to kick in. She could justify the rest, because tomorrow she would sit down at her desk, her laptop open, and put one word in front of the other. She had the research. It was just a matter of putting some structure around it, and communicating it to an audience. She knew she could do it. She always did. The day drew on. She ate a piece of toast. Watched the light outside turn a deeper blue, then grey, then black. When her housemates returned home from work, feeling a little dizzy, she climbed into bed, imagining everything might be better in the morning.

Something Bad is Going to Happen

It must have been past midnight when the electric shocks started, as though her brain were being zapped by currents of lightning. She lay there, eyes wide open, hands in fists beneath her chin, for hours. Her mind presented her with thoughts that did not belong to her. At one point she thought she had a son. At another, she began to scramble out of bed to feed a cat she didn't have.

Eventually, she fell into something approximating sleep, and dreamt of a wave – a tsunami – gathering speed as she sat on the shoreline, frozen.

When she gasped into consciousness, she could not move, and could not tell if she was awake or asleep. She glanced at the clock beside her bed. It was five twenty-two. Her pillow was wet with sweat, and her throat rattled as she tried to breathe air into her lungs. When she mustered the energy to stand, the floor began to move, and for a moment she thought she was standing on the ceiling. It was only when she regained a sense of who she was, and where she was, that she realised how desperately she needed to vomit.

The cool tiles on her cheek are soothing now, but the symptoms persist. For the next few hours, Adella goes from lying on the bathroom floor, to retching into the toilet bowl. By eight, she stumbles back to her bedroom, swallowing down the acidic taste left on her tongue. She doesn't move until lunchtime, when she calls her mum, and explains that she's sick and scared. For the rest of the afternoon she feels like she's on that ride at the Easter Show that spins and spins until you stick to the walls.

The next few days are a blur. She tells her housemates she's sick with some sort of gastro, and stays in her old bedroom at home.

Her mum takes her back to the doctor with the handkerchief. The man sits back in his chair and says it seems that Adella has come down with a stomach bug or a fever, a coincidence rather than a side effect of the medication. She knows this is not the case. It had taken her a simple online search to discover that her reaction was not an anomaly, and that the dosage he had prescribed her was likely too high to begin with.

'Are you feeling a bit sleepy?' he asks and Adella nods and swallows, knowing if she speaks she might scream. She is sleepy because her ears won't stop ringing and her mind is no longer her own and the switch that allows one to fall into unconsciousness is broken. In the end he suggests she lower the dosage and drink lots of fluids.

'I would never have thought drinking lots of fluids would help someone who's vomiting,' her mum says tonelessly as they walk through the door at home and she fills Adella's glass with another Hydralyte. She cooks her meals she doesn't feel like but forces down anyway. They watch Graham Norton and some British police procedural, and she overhears her mother calling the hospital to let them know she won't be in for a few days.

'Am I meant to feel more depressed?' Adella asks on the fourth day. She squints her eyes in response to the glare from outside. The brightness of the sun feels like some kind of assault.

'Give it two weeks. I know that sounds like a long time, but just try,' her mother says as she unstacks the dishwasher. Adella knows she doesn't have two weeks. She'll miss the conference. The emails from her supervisor are piling up.

'I felt awful for a while there,' her mum says, shaking her head, separating knives from spoons. 'But most of the side effects clear up. I promise.'

'Do you feel better now?' There's desperation in Adella's voice.

Her mum focuses her eyes as though she's concentrating and purses her lips.

'A little,' she says, and then she disappears into the laundry.

Adella sits on the navy corduroy couch and pulls her laptop onto her thighs, still unable to sit up straight. She reads the following words: 'Locus of Control is considered an important feature of one's personality. To have an external Locus of Control is to believe that one's situations and experiences are guided by fate, luck, God or external circumstances. An internal Locus of Control is to believe that situations and experiences are guided by personal decisions and efforts. Simply, an internal Locus of Control is to believe we have agency over our own lives, and is generally considered more psychologically healthy.'

Her eyelids drop and so she sits up straighter. Women. She has to establish the parameters of her research. Women who are young. But not adolescent. What do you call them? Adults who are young women. Their Locus of Control is informed by their chronic depression. Or rather chronic depression has resulted in an external Locus of Control. Correlation. Causation. Yes, that's what the presentation is about. But she's getting ahead of herself. She writes.

'Women who are adult, young, and their Locus of Control,

either external or internal, usually external if chronic depression has . . .'

She stops. Doesn't know where she was going. She reads the words back. They do not make sense. *Young adult.* That's the term she's looking for. But why did that phrase take several minutes to find? What is wrong with her brain? How is she to write a paper worthy of being presented at a conference if she struggles this much with the first sentence? Her breathing becomes shallower, her mouth dry. She is furious. Her eyebrows make the shape they do right before she cries, but her eyes won't moisten. She grunts, trying to force it. *Cry. Just cry.* But she can't.

After a week with her mum, she moves back in with her housemates. She tries to go through the motions, greeting them when they walk in the door, but it feels like she is reciting lines, listening to them self-consciously as they come out of her mouth. Mele tells her a story about work, something about crying after receiving some feedback from the year coordinator, but Adella's not listening. It's like Mele exists on the other side of a thick pane of glass, and she can't hear her properly or read her facial expressions. Guilt swirls in Adella's stomach. Mele left a block of chocolate outside her bedroom door when she returned as a gesture of empathy. Kinder still, Mele hasn't said anything about the water glasses left in the sink or the heap of clothes piling up in the bathroom.

The conference is in three days, and she has replied to none of the emails marked 'Urgent' from her supervisor, Polina. She's ignored dozens of phone calls from a mobile she doesn't recognise. Her mother had sent a text message to a course convenor, probably ten days ago now, that explained she wouldn't be able to run her tutorials due to illness, but she's made no contact since then. She tries. She tries to open the emails, but it is as though she is frozen, a rabbit still as a lamppost, hearing ominous footsteps in the distance.

She goes to bed on her second night back in the apartment. Not to sleep, but for another place to be. As soon as she lies flat, it is as though a boulder is placed on her chest. She tries to control her breathing, to trick her way into sleep perhaps, but instead her breath becomes laboured and forced. She thinks, surely, a brain can only focus on one thing at a time: the breathing. But that's not how it works. Her brain also manages to evoke every bad thing she's ever done. Humiliating things. The time she called the course convenor by the wrong name and that other time she ran into a glass door at Vili's twenty-first. All she does is embarrass herself, she thinks. There's a tickle. Then a knot in her chest. A feeling of certainty that something bad is going to happen.

The words are on rotation. She does not know what it is exactly, but she is certain something bad is going to happen. With her head or with her heart or perhaps with her body, but something is off-kilter, like in a movie right before something scary happens. It feels as though her subconscious is picking up something her conscious mind cannot yet.

She lies there and lies there and the switch doesn't flick. She imagines it, at the top of her spine, and visualises her fingers switching it off. Please. Darkness. Black. Nothingness. But just as she begins to fall, her brain whispers *yes I'm falling asleep* and jolts her right back awake again.

Sleep is really important, her brain reminds her. If she does not get enough of it, she won't be able to function tomorrow. Maybe that is why she can't write, she thinks. Her brain isn't doing what it needs to do overnight. Her memory will suffer. And long term . . . well, madness. You can go mad. So really, she needs to go to sleep. And dementia. Every second she is not sleeping is shortening her lifespan. She needs to go to sleep. Why do other people find this so easy? They just shut their eyes and drift off to this other place that is so accessible to them and so inaccessible to her. She tries to drift, but like a block of lead in water, she just sinks. Sinks into a racing mind.

And the waste of time of it all. She could have spent these hours writing, or at least trying to. Up until very recently, her minutes were tracked during the day. Exercise was forgone because there just wasn't enough time. Is there a greater waste of time than lying in bed for six hours before finally drifting off?

And so she lies there, in the quiet. Wind blows. A dog barks. A streetlight flickers. Her eyes feel heavy, her mind as awake as it might be at 11 am even though it's just past three.

The next morning, a Tuesday, she calls Polina, whose tone is clipped and terse. Polina asks that they meet today in her office to discuss her options.

'We're very disappointed about the conference,' she says, before Adella even tells her she cannot present.

She pulls on jeans and a grey jumper and throws her handbag over her shoulder. Perhaps if she could just explain in person. She just needs a little bit more time to sort out whatever is going on and then she will do better. The sunlight stings her eyes as she walks, eyes squinted, towards the station. The whole world looks the wrong colour. She no longer feels tired. She feels almost drunk, like there's a three-second delay between her and the outside world. As she stands on the corner of Elizabeth Road, a bus comes rumbling past, and she watches herself step in front of it. She steps back as the vision dissolves and feels for a moment like her mind is something distinct from her soul, herself, and which of the two is instructing her feet? She returns home after that, distrustful of the soft tissue sitting between her ears.

What she does manage to do is open her laptop. It takes her more than an hour, but she writes the email she has been unable to.

'I can't,' it begins.

She explains she is unwell, but doesn't specify with what, mostly because she does not know. She apologises for missing the conference as sincerely as she can. And then she says she would like to withdraw from her PhD, asking for guidance on the next steps. The email is not written eloquently. She is not proud of it. But her intentions are clear.

She spends the afternoon in a state of numbness, and wonders if this, perhaps, is what relief feels like.

23

Jake

Two-and-a-half years ago

All he can hear is the hum of the fridge and the ticking of the kitchen clock. The house is dark, everyone asleep, and he is hunched over his laptop, a small crack in the top right-hand corner of the screen. Ready.

He leans back, interlacing his fingers behind his head. Sighs. Leans forward again, hands cradling his forehead, his face illuminated by the glow of the laptop screen. There are dozens of tabs open, the computer seemingly groaning from the weight of it all. But now, this is the only window that matters. His cursor hovers over the word 'submit', written in big, bold capitals. His finger twitches over the mouse button, but he doesn't press down. The deadline closes in nine hours.

It has taken him more than twelve months to get to this

point. In three weeks, he will turn twenty-seven.

Applying to a Bachelor of Architectural Design, he realised months ago, was to subject the dream to potential failure. Without filling out the forms, the fantasy would persist, and there would be a future in which he succeeded and became something greater than he ever could have imagined.

But one Thursday, as he sheathed, in the same way and with the same plywood as he had done hundreds of times before, he felt like he might go mad if he had to get out of bed and do this all over again.

He had grown accustomed to spending most of his days playing mind games trying not to look at the time. Waiting for the smoko. Waiting for lunchtime. Then the afternoon would arrive and he'd wait for the clock to crawl closer to three. He would feel a sense of elation when he was free to go, but by the time he got home he would feel so tired. So depleted. He'd scroll through his phone or watch stupid videos that were sometimes funny but mostly not really. Then darkness would fall and he would go to bed, putting off sleep for as long as he could because sleep was a fast track to morning, and morning was work.

Another panel. Repetition. The same thing. Again. His supervisor was always watching, seeing him not as Jake but as a set of unidentifiable hands.

He would never be able to articulate how this felt to another person. Another panel. Without innovation. Or creativity. Or risk. Another panel. The labour suppressed everything about him that was human. Or different. Everything he did was on another man's watch. Every day he arrived feeling less himself than he did the day before.

He knew he could not do this for another forty years. It was not a choice so much as an imperative. A survival instinct.

It was a portfolio, he discovered, he'd have to submit. He didn't get the marks at school to even get close to being accepted into university. Ten pages of 'visual evidence of creative ability'. Even if accepted, he'd be facing at least five years of full-time study, sacrificing income for ambition.

The work began in earnest when he started going to the library on Saturday mornings. He began by looking at images – from ancient megastructures to contemporary San Franciscan homes. He borrowed books about the principles of architecture and the chronology of structural innovation. He downloaded audiobooks and podcasts about Frank Lloyd Wright and brutalism and the future of sustainability. Sometimes in the evenings he would muster up the energy to run, his breath looking like puffs of smoke and his earphones buried tightly in his ears, allowing his mind to marinate in building anatomies and Australian modernism and the future of virtual reality for architectural design. He was obsessed in a way he had never been obsessed with anything.

On a grey Monday evening he rifled through the kitchen drawers in search of a pencil and sat himself down at the desk in his bedroom, which he'd only ever used as a dumping ground for dirty clothes, and began to draw. Doodles. Squares and circles. Straight lines. Sometimes his hand would do something seemingly of its own volition, coming up with a sketch he did not recognise. His hand took him someplace else. Sometimes hours would pass with just him and a pencil. It reminded him of a feeling he thought he'd left in childhood. He wouldn't tell anyone this, but if he's honest with himself he thinks he fell in love with architecture in early high school, when a friend burned him a copy of *The Sims*. The rest of the world would go blurry and silent as he designed mansions on his desktop computer, with both indoor and outdoor pools, gyms, a back shed, a land-scaped garden, arched windows that flooded both storeys with light, seven bedrooms and just as many bathrooms. When Adella came over to play she would rush the house, impatient to get the woman a job and then a husband and then a 'woohoo' session in the spa that would result in a baby. Jake found that part boring. He wanted to knock down and rebuild.

With books open he tried mechanical drafting and architec-tural CAD drafting and it didn't even really feel like learning but, he supposed, that's what he was doing.

He created because he wanted to. Because he felt like himself for the first time since he could remember. That's how he found himself with a book full of sketches. But it wasn't until he sat down next to his mum on the couch, with a Magnum he found in the freezer, that he actually considered submitting them.

It wasn't anything she said. No one in the world, other than Adella, even knew he was considering applying. But his mum happened to be watching *Legally Blonde*, which was on TV that night. Jake had never seen it. As he bit off the chocolate layering, he watched as the main character applied for a degree she was in no way qualified for. The whole movie was about falling upwards, he realised, as he licked the remaining vanilla ice cream. By the end she won a court case, even though she wasn't even officially a lawyer yet, which Jake didn't totally understand, and there was some detail about hair dye that he had to ask his mum about. The point was, she took a risk. And it paid off. Without saying a word, he went into his room, and looked up university admission dates.

And so, it is a sweltering night in December eighteen months later. His bedroom window is open and a slight breeze makes its way into the room. Uploaded are his ten pages, with brief descriptions of his sketches and designs. He is most proud of his sketch of an imagined university library, a fantasy compared to where he's been spending his Saturday mornings. It felt silly at first – that anything so futuristic might exist near where he lived. But his pencil found the shape of a light bulb lying on its side, a light-filled four-storey atrium, the roof a glass dome that prevents heat from permeating the building. He saw a narrow entryway that opened up to the bulb, curved bookshelves coiling through various levels. It belongs in a world that doesn't exist yet. But that is the point, isn't it?

Now, in the quiet dark hours, his mouse still hovering over the submit button, he is sure it is silly. He feels like it is the work of a child who has drawn something make-believe, like Santa or the Tooth Fairy. He imagines the reviewers opening his file and laughing, calling each other over to have a look at what this guy in his late twenties from Kanooble has drawn.

It feels like buying a lottery ticket. A pathetic bid for a different life. You know you won't win, but you check the drawn numbers anyway, a feeling rising in your chest as you do. *Maybe.* Then you laugh at yourself when the numbers don't resemble yours at all, and put your ticket in the bin. Served you right for hoping.

For every success story – the kid who had nothing and became something greater than he could have imagined – are countless stories with a very different ending. Men and women who aspire and work hard and take risks and the world punishes them for it. His uncle Evan is a failed musician. Most of us end up where we started, don't we? The problem with trying is that we learn that it is not by choice but by force.

He looks at the time. Twelve-thirty. Four-and-a-half hours until he has to be up for work. He'll have to blast the air-con in the car so he doesn't fall asleep behind the wheel. The deadline will pass while he sculls his second coffee.

He doesn't click 'submit'. Instead, he slams the laptop shut.

As he crawls into his bed, he hears the voice of his grand-mother, his mother's mother, who moved in with them for a few years after their dad died. For someone who rarely moved, her presence filled the house, and he preferred her company to just about anyone's. She kept the very best biscuits, which she always snuck to them when their mum wasn't looking. If they were leaving the house to meet friends, after a thirty-minute fight with their mum about how much money they actually needed, she'd slip an extra twenty dollars into their hand. But she believed the worst thing someone could be was proud. Whenever one of the boys would come home from school or sport with a trophy in their fist or a medal around their neck, she'd smile and then say, 'Watch out or your head won't fit through the door.' Once when Sam was admiring himself in the mirror, flexing his muscles this way and that, she'd thwacked him with her walking stick and asked him through gritted teeth, 'Who do you think you are?' Jake remembers him and Paul laughing so hard they cried. He can't quite remember the Bible verse, but she'd always recite a passage about not thinking of yourself more highly than you ought.

In the dark of his bedroom, with the buzzing of his laptop, he realises that is exactly what he's doing. Thinking of himself more highly than he ought. 'When pride comes,' he remembers her saying, 'then comes disgrace. But with humility comes wisdom.' The Book of Proverbs. He hasn't been to church in months, but that doesn't mean the faith of his family, the faith of his ancestors, does not still run through his blood.

Do not believe you are more than you are, he thinks to himself.

To do so would be stupid.

*

His alarm fills the room, waking him from a dreamless sleep.

He fumbles for his phone. His eyelids feel heavy as they adjust to the blueness of the morning.

Before he finds a conscious thought, he is standing over his timber desk. He opens his laptop. The window is still open.

Submit.

He hits submit.

24

Adella

Two years and four months ago

It's strange how when something terrible happens – shocking – the worst thing that can happen in a life, there is no voice that whispers in her ear. No intrusive thought that warns her. There is no bolt of lightning or strange apparition.

Instead, Adella is sitting on the deck of their cabin in Port Macquarie, Lottie and her mother inside. It's late February and they're here to see Pa, their mum's dad. Adella looks out over the river, her legs stretched over the outdoor table as she watches the surrounding families huddled under camping gazebos, eating ridiculously early and shouting at their children to sit for a minute and finish their sausages. As kids they camped here a few times, back when their parents were still together and their dad could make it until sunset without a drink. Lottie would braid her hair on day one and for a week she wouldn't wash it, swimming every day, and feeling it go stiff with salt water. They hadn't been back in years. This time, Adella's mum had booked them a cabin and they feel like royalty. Since they arrived they've been looking at the families covered in sand and mud, and saying a silent thank you as they ascend their three stairs and wipe their feet on a straw mat.

But as Adella sits quietly, she is struck by the paradox that she can't stop worrying she might be a narcissist.

It crosses her mind, as it so often does, as she scrolls through her own social media profile imagining she were someone else viewing her account for the first time.

Her last picture is from this summer holiday. Her in a black bikini, the white of breaking waves behind her, as she looks out and slightly to the left as though unaware the photo is being taken. In reality, she was looking at the lopsided bin near the carpark, and she'd demanded Lottie take it while she sucked in her stomach. Her hair looks long and curly with sea salt, as though she's the kind of girl who dives beneath the waves without thinking twice. She actually took a few steps in, decided it was too cold, and scrunched the water into the ends of her hair before running back out again. The picture before is from November, her twenty-seventh birthday, taken by Mele at their small dining table. A smattering of candles illuminates her smiling face. She looks happy, she thinks. The length of her hair, just grazing her shoulders, suits her.

She worries that all she does is think about herself, which is another thought about herself. *How do I come across? Do people talk about me once I leave a room? Is there something 'special' about me, like I suspected when I was a kid? Am I brilliant and special or decidedly average? Am I considered ugly or beautiful or somewhere in between?*

'Can we get fish and chips for dinner?' she hears Lottie yell from the bathroom where she's been drying her hair. Her voice competes with the sound of light rain falling onto the tin roof. Adella checks the time and realises it's past eight. Still, she can't really be bothered to get up.

'Sure,' her mum calls back from the couch, as she marks the page and closes the book she's been reading all afternoon. If it's possible, she says even less on holidays. It's funny, Adella thinks, how people's personalities become intensified when they're away from home.

The cabin itself is more a stationary caravan, with two small bedrooms and running water. It sits in a holiday park, just up the road from where their grandfather lives in Port Macquarie. Adella's mum lives in a state of perpetual guilt about how rarely she sees her own dad. Mostly she visits after a health scare – a fall, or more recently a stroke. But this year they've decided to design a holiday around him in late February, and have been spending long afternoons playing cards in his back room.

Adella realised as they pulled up five days ago that she has begun to share some of her mum's guilt about not seeing Pa as often as they should. When he first came to the door Adella didn't know what to say. Whereas once he had been maybe six foot, agile and strong, he was now barely her height. His jeans sat low on his hips, fastened with a belt to keep them up. His forearms were skin and bone, coloured purple and red from sun damage and bruises and blood tests. He shuffled around his home, his gaze focused squarely on his feet, the beads of his spine poking out from beneath his buttoned-up shirt. It was as though he couldn't bend his legs properly, so he was always unsteady, full of concentration. His face had lost colour and she finally had to concede that at ninety-three he looked like a very old man.

His home is full of books, most of which he's read at least once – half-read books on the coffee table and a stack beside his bed, and dusty bookcases overflowing with encyclopaedias and travel guides and histories of countries she's never even heard of. He'd been an English teacher for more than fifty years. The first night she'd borrowed one, a war novel she didn't expect to find interesting, and by the next day she couldn't put it down.

'That's the one about the bloke who flees Paris with his daughter, isn't it?' he'd asked at dinner, and Adella soon learned that he could just about recite the entire plot. They talked for hours that night, first about the book and then what he could remember from the Korean War. He told stories Adella's mum, his own daughter, had never heard. It was funny how her mother couldn't see how like him she was. How she, too, reserved the best parts of herself for visitors or strangers, never for her own children. One night, Adella's mum told a story about how busy work had been, and how a month or so ago, just as she was about to leave for the day, they'd had three young men arrive who had been in a catastrophic car accident. She had stayed four hours after her shift was due to end, speaking to their parents and trying to calm their siblings down. She saw them most days in the weeks that followed. All three had survived. And when one of the men was discharged, he asked that all his flowers be given to that nice nurse, the one with the short dark hair, as a thank you for her kindness. It was the kind of story she would never dare tell anyone else, but it reminded Adella that perhaps her mum was more transparent than she gave her credit for. All Adella's mum wanted from her father was his attention. And perhaps for him to tell her he was proud. That she'd done a good job of whatever the hell she'd set out to do. That she was a good person who did good things. It was ironic that these were the very things she couldn't give her own children. Perhaps she'd never heard how the words might sound, or come across sentences that she would be able to recite. As Adella watched her mother scrutinise her own father, as though if she looked a little harder she might just really know him, she thought how funny families were. How gaps emerge, wide and gaping, and yet no one ever addresses them. No one at this table really knew each other, and it took Adella to ask a basic question about the end of the Second World War for them to learn something new.

She is being hard on her mother, of course. She has been making an effort. Yesterday they'd gone for a walk along Town Beach, her mother always pacing either two steps ahead or two steps behind.

'You still on that medication? That the doctor prescribed in October or whenever it was?' her mum had asked from behind, the wind taking the majority of her voice.

Adella stopped for a moment, waiting until they were side by side.

'I'm still on it. I don't know how much it's worked but maybe it's taken the edge off a bit.' She considered elaborating but couldn't find the energy. Then she asked, 'You know when you're a kid and it's Christmas Eve or something, or the last day of term, and your stomach is full of butterflies and excitement? I remember some nights when I was maybe six or seven, and I couldn't sleep because I was just so excited about the next day. Do you get that anymore? I suppose it's anticipation or something.'

There was silence and her mum dropped her pace again. Adella looked over to her, noticing that her gaze was straight ahead. She looked resigned as she shook her head. No. She didn't know that feeling anymore.

'That feeling has gradually come back, I think,' Adella said, watching her feet sink into the sand. 'Like life is happening to me, not around me, and I can reach out and touch it.' She got the sense her mum didn't really know what she meant.

They didn't speak for the rest of the walk.

Adella had never spoken, in person, to her supervisor or course convenor again. After she'd sent the email withdrawing, she'd received a brusque response with details about how to formally pull out of her PhD. She completed the paperwork, and then attempted to erase all traces of it from her memory.

Before she'd officially withdrawn, she had one appointment with a psychologist. The young woman with cropped brown hair, slim in a European way with flawless olive skin, asked about family history and childhood and trauma and whether she had thoughts of self-harm, and none of it was relevant. Eventually Adella simply announced that she couldn't write and something was seriously wrong with her brain, at which point the psychologist paused, scribbled something down, and then asked a total of two follow-up questions.

'Unrelenting standards' was the phrase she'd used. The psychologist went on to explain that while panic and adrenaline can often stimulate the fight or flight response, Adella was experiencing the third response, freeze.

'It seems to me that every time you sit down to write,' she said evenly, 'you believe that your entire worth as a human being hinges on your ability to formulate the perfect sentence. That's too much pressure for anyone.' Adella had never thought of it like that.

There had been a vague reference to a deer in the headlights, and 'performance anxiety'. As though Adella were an Olympic swimmer who choked the moment she was about to dive in. The woman pushed her fringe out of her eyes, and explained that we all have a sweet spot that allows us to perform at our best. Then there was a drawing of a wave and something about riding it and eventually the panic would pass. Adella wanted to explain that it doesn't, though. She wasn't an idiot, she'd tried that. But the woman had started to talk about their next session and it was clear this one had ended, the receptionist just outside ready to sort payment.

The following semester, beginning at the end of July, Adella still had three tutorials, which was at least a source of income. She never ate at the university or visited the library, terrified she'd see all the people she'd let down. As the semester drew to a close it was clear they were not going to offer her any classes in the second half of the year. She was no longer studying, so it wouldn't have really made sense.

It had been a relief to discover that no one in her life really cared that she'd dropped out of her PhD. Perhaps what happened in her life was of no consequence to them – a reality which was either depressing or liberating. She went straight from tutoring to working at a cafe up by Meadowbank station, where people bought a coffee before commuting into their real jobs. In the afternoons she would browse job ads – research positions, anything in admin, government roles and coordinator positions at a number of charities, sure that she was getting close to having applied for every full-time job in the state. The only jobs she didn't apply for were ones that required her to write. Six months later and she had received two responses for a second round, both of which were unsuccessful. Finally, her housemate Mele had mentioned one night that the school she worked at was looking for a learning support teacher, and she was pretty sure you didn't need any special qualifications. Within a week Adella had been offered a full-time role at the school, teaching a program to a small cohort of students who spoke languages other than English at home. She starts next Monday.

The panic attacks had stopped once the medication had properly kicked in, and one night she had fallen asleep without thinking about it too much, and there began a habit. Jake started trying to drag her to the gym again, as he did every so often, which she only resists half the time. He is convinced that all positive feelings exist on the other side of exercise, which Adella thinks sounds a little like addiction, but she'd never tell him that.

Something Bad is Going to Happen

'All right, girls, we'll have to leave in a minute,' her mum says as she stretches and yawns, standing by the open front sliding doors looking out over the river. Fatter raindrops have begun to fall and no one is really outside anymore. Darkness has just about descended.

'Oi Adella, your phone keeps ringing,' Lottie calls out from the bedroom they're sharing, her phone hanging from a charger.

Adella wanders in, passing her mum in the doorway, thinking about what clean clothes she still has left and if she needs a quick shower. She's thinking about brushing her teeth as she taps on her phone, and sees six missed calls from a number she doesn't recognise.

She calls back as she unhooks her bikini top from underneath her singlet. The voice on the other end she recognises.

The tone she doesn't.

25

Raheem

Raheem is thinking about scorecards. If he packed them. Shit. Will they have spare ones? No, he's sure he threw them in his sports bag, which is sitting on his leather back seat. Or was that last week? Maybe they're still in there from last . . . No, did he take them out? His thoughts keep cutting themselves off, trying to solve a problem that feels significant in this moment, but will not in the next.

The radio is playing a song by the Red Hot Chili Peppers. It annoys him, but not enough to change the station.

There are drops of rain pattering on the windscreen which appear to have come out of nowhere. He nearly opens his window a fraction to smell it – that smell of cool rain on a hot road that wasn't expecting it. But he's on a freeway and it will be too loud, the wind too intense.

He's making good time. His maps app says he should be

at Easttown Football Park just before six, which is perfect for a six-thirty match. He runs through the process. He'll have to change into his uniform. Check the field. A few droplets of rain won't have affected the grounds much. Check the nets and the corner flags. Warm up. Talk to Scott about the bloke he red-carded last week for calling him the 'n' word. Everyone keeps checking if he's okay and he just wants to stop talking about it. It's embarrassing. Would Scott have spare scorecards? he wonders. If they're not in his –?

For a moment he thinks it's a bird.

It's the movement that attracts his attention, some fumbling on the overpass that crosses the freeway.

He sees a figure in a black hoodie and dark tracksuit pants. What the fuck is someone doing on an overpass above a freeway in the rain? Raheem wonders, leaning forward in the driver's seat and peering upwards.

Something tells him to move his right foot to the brake. He knows something isn't right. Some part of him has registered that this person in the black hoodie is shaking. That his movements are frantic. That he is the only person he's ever seen who is not crossing an overpass, but has stopped midway across it. These are not conscious thoughts. Raheem may never know what he saw in what must have been less than a five-second window before everything changed. But his right foot rests on the brake, because he knows. He knows before it happens.

At first he thinks the man must have stumbled.

His body tumbles over the ledge. White trainers in the air. In an instant, the laws of the universe have been broken and it is as though Raheem has been thrust into someone else's bad dream. His brain cannot accept this is a thing that is happening, while the world unfolding before him insists that it is.

With the strength of his body he slams on the brake, not checking to see if anyone is behind him, scrunching his eyes closed as he braces for impact.

He hears the thud. He'll hear the thud for the rest of his life. The weight of it. The way in which the highway did not make space for him, a blank slate of force meeting his force. He screams 'Fuck!' and it comes from the back of his throat, a place he does not recognise.

Horns beep and cars stop but somehow no one collides with him. The front of his Holden Commodore is barely two metres from the body, which lies still, face down on the road, blood pooling from the front of his head.

He looks away before the image fully takes shape, his brain imprinting details he will wish he'd never seen. As he steps out of his car, he unlocks his phone and dials triple-zero with a shaking thumb.

He massages the front of his forehead, his phone to his ear, and tries not to vomit. Other drivers emerge, asking if he is all right, as though that's what anyone ought to be worried about. Some barely disguise their anger at the man who might have claimed other lives in his attempt to end his own.

'How dare . . .' one middle-aged man says, lines around his tired eyes, his arms stained brown from outdoor labour. 'If you've got to do it,' he shakes his head, 'just don't take other people along with you.'

Raheem's eyes are wide. He nods.

'The bloke might have gone through your windscreen. I was a few cars behind you, mate. It was like he was timing it.' The man rubs his eyes. 'You just don't forget shit like that.'

The police arrive first. They fall into a process that looks horribly familiar to them. An older female officer mutters something about the scaffolding above – how it had been damaged in a storm last week. Raheem notices that caging usually prevents anyone from falling. Or jumping. Except from where he saw the man. A panel is missing. The man must've noticed it. He can't comprehend that this man made such a decision based on a logical observation. Just as Raheem had been trying to problem-solve his missing scorecards, this man had been trying to problem-solve achieving his own death.

The police politely tell the onlookers to leave. They thank Raheem for calling. Say something about someone he can call, but he's no longer listening. When he climbs back into his car, he sees that only ten minutes has passed. He doesn't know what to do, so he finds himself driving to soccer as though nothing were different, as though he did not just witness a man end his own life.

He decides that evening that he did not see a man die. He saw a man *almost* die, which is a very different thing.

As days and nights pass, Raheem feels further from what he saw that evening. Sometimes, years down the track, when he's drifting off to sleep, he will see a flash so vivid he swears it is happening all over again. But then he will remember he is safe, in his own bed, and that was not a man he knew, but a stranger in some sort of crisis he could never understand.

He will be all right.

The stranger – and the lives that he touched – will not.

26

Jake

27

Adella

Two years and four months ago

Jake was pronounced dead in the same hospital he was born in, on that damp Tuesday evening in February.

She sits in the second row at the funeral, between Lottie and her mother, fixated on the framed photograph resting on the coffin. One of his teammates must have taken it, a big grin on his face after their grand final win a few years ago. You could almost have believed he was happy.

St Michael's church is overflowing. It smells of incense and beeswax and polish. She is wearing a borrowed black dress from Lottie that is at least one size too big. When she turns her head she can see silhouettes standing in the doorway, young men in too-big suits holding funeral booklets in hands hanging below their waist. She can see cars still pulling up, people spilling out over to the other side of the street. They won't be able to see or hear anything, but they will stand in silence.

The priest knew Jake – as well as a priest ever knows anyone. He emphasises his dedication to God, and how much he was loved by his family, friends and parish. Adella has seen him once before, at Jake's father's funeral. At points throughout, his voice shakes in a way she's never heard from a priest before. He does not look in the direction of Jake's mother.

He says Jake has returned home to God, the Father, and his voice catches on 'Father'.

It is Jake's uncle who delivers the eulogy. He refers to his death as an 'accident', a tragedy that never should have happened.

'He was a young man with so much to look forward to,' he says, flatly, 'and if he was here right now, we'd give him a scolding for being so stupid.' There is a huff of acknowledgement from the congregation.

Adella knows that Jake's family believe what happened was a fall. That's what his brother Sam told her on the phone the night he died.

'He fell,' he said. 'Mum says he fell and he hit his head. He's dead. Mum says he's dead.'

The sound she made was one she didn't recognise. The next thing she knew she was on the floor and she could not stand up, Lottie now on the phone asking what happened, and her mother holding her shoulders and repeating 'it's okay'.

In the days between that phone call and today, the funeral, she visited Jake's home, bringing flowers and food. She didn't know what you're meant to do but Jake's living room was where she found herself.

'Why was he up there?' Annie, Jake's mum, kept repeating. Her sisters sat either side of her shaking their heads, while uncles stood silently.

The second time she visited, photo albums were scattered throughout the house. Annie looked ten years older, dark circles stretching down her cheeks, her face pale and expressionless. When Adella walked in, she looked up with big dark eyes, pointing to a photograph.

'Look, look, Adella,' she said. She was pointing to a picture of Jake in preschool, at about four years old. He was wearing a Superman costume, a wonky fringe hanging down past his eyebrows. 'He always wanted to fly.'

Adella held Annie as she sobbed with her whole body, her shoulders and her knees, her chest and her jaw. Seeing her distress made Adella feel sick.

During that visit, conversations turned to the funeral and finances. Adella moved into the kitchen and tried to do something moderately helpful. She was rinsing out Tupperware when Sam came up beside her and said, 'No note.' Adella paused and turned to look at him.

'There wasn't a note.'

They watched the suds in the sink and said nothing to each other.

On one of her earlier visits, she went into his room, to see if there were any clues. His bed was made. She didn't know if he'd made it, or Annie had. She didn't know which would be sadder. She turned her phone on and off again to see if there was a message she had missed, or a desperate phone call she hadn't seen. Still nothing.

On her way to the church she had been in a state of shock that the world seemed to be moving on. How could cafes still be open? People seemed to be going to work. She was receiving text messages about exclusive sales and the woman in the car beside her appeared to be singing along to the radio. How?

Now, in the church, Adella watches as the captain of his football team drapes a blue and yellow striped jersey over the coffin. Vili stands broad-shouldered, tall, a stance that always takes up space, his eyes the only indication that he's crying. Sniffs echo through the pews, tissues retrieved from handbags and pockets.

We're not meant to die yet, she keeps thinking.

Sam approaches the casket and places Jake's crucifix beside the jersey. He offers a sign of the cross.

A projector lights up the white screen at the back of the altar, and photos of Jake as a baby come into focus. The first chords of 'Hallelujah' by Jeff Buckley play from the speakers, and a series of small chokes reverberate around the congregation. Adella swallows, not knowing how she is going to get through this. Lottie squeezes her hand tightly and somehow that makes it worse.

Jake at twelve flashes up on the screen, on what must have been his first day of Year Seven. She remembers that Jake, skinny with buckteeth and flat mousy-brown hair. Her chest begins to burn and she grits her teeth, hot tears running down her cheeks, all the way to her neck and her collarbone. The photos she sent Sam pop up, pictures at parties and each other's formal and schoolies. As he gets older she squints to see if anything in his eyes changed. The congregation lets out an accidental laugh as a picture of them both sitting in her car appears, Jake's smile missing a front tooth he'd lost playing footy the day before. He'd had to wait a full week before they could replace it, and Jake had lived his life as normal, going to someone's costume party and showing up at work. *Why aren't you more embarrassed?* she remembers thinking at the time. She is reminded of the last time she heard him laugh. He'd come over to hers maybe three weeks ago, and they'd started watching *The Office* together. The American one. They'd already seen the UK one. When he was leaving she made him promise that he'd wait until she was back from holidays to watch the next episode.

'I'll see how I go,' he'd said, shrugging his shoulders. 'If I get bored one night . . .'

She'd thought after he'd left how their friendship was always best when neither of them was seeing anyone, and so essentially had nowhere better to be. Had he seemed different? How careless had she been to not see him – really see him. When she had been struggling with medication he'd dropped in with a card that said 'Bitch don't kill my vibe' and a block of chocolate. He'd even gone to her wardrobe to find activewear for her to put on so they could go for a walk together. It had made her laugh. And yet where had she been for him? Why hadn't he *said* anything? She was sorry but she was also angry. Furious. How could he do this to her? And more than that, how dare he do this to his mother?

She knows her face will be covered in black smudges but she realises she doesn't care. She looks down at her feet as Jake's two uncles and two brothers take a corner each of the casket, and carry it out of the same church he'd been baptised in. His mother cannot stand up to leave.

Outside is a sea of black suits and sunglasses. Slumped shoulders. Silence.

Every other funeral Adella had been to, for her paternal grandfather, both her grandmothers, her aunty Mary, people had tried to tell jokes. Every interaction was punctuated with a joke, as though people were trying to break the tension, and pretend they weren't there because death happened and it is coming for all of us. The jokes were never very funny – but they happened anyway. Outside, though, there are not any jokes. People look at each other in shock. The corners of people's lips do not curl as they recognise each other. Sometimes they put their arms around each other, saying sorry to people they know, as though this is a mistake someone made and not something much, much bigger.

Young men she has only ever seen drunk at the pub, or on some substance or another at Jake's, look out of place in a context this serious. None of them belong here. One friend of Jake's from school puts his arms around her and says, 'We haven't even had our ten-year reunion.' She nods. They silently turn towards the hearse, where Jake's two brothers stare at the casket. No tears. Just shock. She catches Sam's eye and walks over to him, hugging him and recognising the smell. He smells just like Jake.

As she whispers, 'I'm sorry,' she wants to say she's not just sorry he's dead. She's sorry she didn't look after him. It's friends who are meant to notice when things aren't right. Why didn't she call him that afternoon? Interrupt him?

Something Bad is Going to Happen

The family climbs into the hearse and she steps back, not wanting the car to ever start. At least in this moment there is something – a visual representation that Jake was once here – a casket that means he's not gone yet. He's just over there, three, four steps away. Everyone is here and they're talking about Jake and they know this is madness. They didn't go to work and they're not checking their phones and they ironed their shirts because nothing else matters. There has been a fracture in the universe, a mistake. It is as though no one wants to leave because then they will have accepted it – going on with their mundane lives as though it's fair or understandable that they are breathing and coughing and thinking while Jake is doing none of those things. For more than half her life she has known, roughly, where Jake is. At school or at work or at home or on the other end of a phone call. She cannot understand, in this moment, where he is. He's just over there but he's also not. Where will he be tomorrow? And the next day? How can someone so familiar be so far away?

'Adella?' says a quiet voice behind her.

She turns around and feels arms around her sides, a chin on her shoulder.

'I'm just so, so sorry.' Sophia's eyes are wet. It is the first time she has seen Sophia in more than five years. Her hair is slightly darker and longer, but her face is exactly the same.

'I didn't know,' the words fall out of her mouth. 'He seemed fine.'

Sophia puts her arms around her again and repeats, 'I know, I know . . . there is nothing you could've done.' This makes Adella feel better for a moment, even though she knows it isn't true. 'You were his favourite person,' Sophia says with a smile.

She is crying more than she wants to now, redness crawling up her neck, unable to catch her breath. She covers her eyes and blows through her mouth.

Sophia does not leave her side. Not outside the church or at the wake, held at a bowling club around the corner. They do not ask each other questions or attempt to fill the gaps that now exist between them. Mostly, they sit at a high table in silence.

Even though there are distinctly two chairs, others stop to speak to them as though this is a social get-together. Sophia does most of the talking, and Adella notices that most of Jake's friends appear to speak exclusively in resume – trying to shoehorn in every achievement they've had since school.

One of Jake's friends, Dave, approaches and embarks on a monologue about what he's been up to lately, taking Adella and Sophia's silence as encouragement to continue.

'Good news actually,' he says, sipping a fresh beer. 'This week I was accepted into a Masters of Business, which will be pretty full-on, but . . .'

Adella stops listening and the room starts to spin. She is struck with a realisation, her body feeling it before her mind catches up.

Jake's university application. He wasn't accepted. He must've received the rejection letter – had his family even seen it? Without saying anything she stands up and hurries to the bathroom, not breathing until she is inside a cubicle, head between her legs. She can feel it – how despairing he must've been that day. In all the years she'd known him, he'd always been hesitant to admit he *wanted* anything. The eulogy had described him as good and honest and kind, a young man who understood the importance of family more than most. That nothing else matters. But that week, something else had mattered. He had dared to want more. To take stock of his lot in life and say, 'This is not enough.' He'd felt stupid even applying – he'd told her enough times. Through silent tears she mouths, 'I'm sorry I'm sorry I'm sorry.'

How bleak it must've been. Jake hated work, she knew that. He hated that he still lived at home, most of his salary going to supporting his mum and brothers. He hated that he still lived essentially as a child, except school had been replaced with a job site, and his car rego was always due. He hated the present, and now he knew that tomorrow and the day after would look exactly the same.

That must have been it.

28

Adella

She slides on her shoes, hearing Jack rustle in the corner of the living room.

For a moment she sidles up next to his bed which they call the Russian hat, given it looks exactly like a Russian hat. She sniffs the top of his head and scratches him behind the ears, watching him let out a big yawn and paw the sleep out of his left eye. Jack, a one-year-old Jack Russell, belongs to Mele, but Adella jokes that she is the other woman, always taking him for special walks and giving him extra treats.

Tonight, or more technically, at quarter past three in the morning, she shuffles silently to the door. She hasn't slept. It probably doesn't help that she now needs a lamp on all night, unable to lie in bed in the dark. The blackness scares her. It makes her wonder where he is. If he's scared. If he's alone. If he's trapped in a new place, an eternity of nothingness.

When she was little she used to get stuck in the sticky web of contemplating death. It would happen at night, once the lights and television were off, and she didn't have the luxury of distraction. Everything she did, she realised, everything every-one did – petty arguments and yearning for a new pair of shoes and scrubbing the shower and grocery shopping and playing handball and excursions and the Olympics – were just ways to distract ourselves from life's one inevitability, the most terrifying reality any of us will ever face. The blackness of her bedroom would make her think of being buried underground, screaming to get out or worse, not screaming because she had no idea she was there. *Where do my wants go?* she'd wonder. *What about all the thoughts I had that I never told anyone? The voice inside my head that has a sound I can't describe? Where does it go?* When her chest would start to shake, her palms clammy and her mouth dry, she'd whisper to Lottie who she knew was probably already asleep, 'Lottie. I can't stop thinking about it.'

Lottie knew what she meant.

She'd huff and then she'd always say exactly the same thing.

'Just think about what you're having for lunch tomorrow.'

Adella would, and within minutes she'd be asleep, think-ing about three chicken nuggets inside a white bread roll with mayonnaise.

To be an adult, though, is to be alone. She no longer shares a bedroom with Lottie, and so her mind goes to places it shouldn't. Often, as she's drifting off, she feels as though she is falling, and for a moment she is Jake, the smack of the road waking her with a start. The sound rings in her ears, and anticipatory pain spreads throughout her whole body, bracing for impact. She cannot catch her breath.

She thinks now about the questions people asked at the wake, mostly Vili and Adrian.

'Did you know he was depressed? Did he say anything to you?'

She'd moved her head slowly, left to right.

'I knew he'd struggled before, in the past,' she'd managed to say. 'But he's –' she always had to correct her tense, 'he was doing well, I thought.'

How could that be true? she wondered. Isn't suicide the end point of terminal mental illness? Hadn't that been the case with Jake's own father, who had been finding life increasingly unliveable for months, perhaps years? But Jake. Jake could still laugh, couldn't he? Could something like a rejection letter undo a man who was otherwise well? She had looked at the last picture he had posted. It was from eight months ago; he very rarely put anything up. Seven men sitting in Vili's backyard, empty and half-drunk Corona bottles scattered across a green plastic table. Jake was looking towards the camera, beer up as though cheersing whoever was taking the photo. He had a smile that creased his eyes, and he was wearing a ridiculous pink 'party shirt' with too many buttons loose. She zoomed and she stared and she animated the image in her own mind, seeing him throw his head back in laughter and listen more than he talked. There was so much life in a single frame.

She slips her phone into her pocket and is comforted to hear the sound of Jack's pitter-patter on the kitchen tiles behind her. He stretches as she quietly retrieves his leash, directing him to sit before she opens the door.

The night air is cool and fresh, the streets silent apart from Jack's sniffing. She does what she does every night she can't sleep and picks up her phone, tapping on their message history. When she reads his texts she hears his voice.

Jake 5:12pm Thursday
Hey at the gym call you back after

Jake 6:33pm Thursday
Missed call

Next, she had sent a photo of an echidna crossing the road in front of her car on the way to Port Macquarie.

Jake 10:05am Saturday
Someone needs to tell that echidna that those spikes won't protect them from predators such as a truck going one hundred kilometres an hour

Adella 10:09am Saturday
I passed on the message. What you up to today?

Jake 10:10am Saturday
Just got back from a run. I'm doing this weird af online meditation course lol I'll fill you in when you're back. When are you back again?

Adella 10:12am Saturday
Next Thursday! Couldn't think of anything worse. You free
Thursday night?

He hadn't replied. Perhaps he already knew he wouldn't be
here, or maybe he had simply forgotten.

She taps on his various profiles, and sees comments from
people saying things like 'miss you mate' and 'too soon'. She feels
her heart race.

He can't see your fucking message, she wants to shout. *Wherever
he is, the WiFi is probably patchy and you look like a performative
dickhead showcasing your grief for everyone to see and how dare you
make Jake's death about you.*

Her anger is compounded by how badly she wants to send him
a message, just so their conversations can continue. She knows
she's being ridiculous but their conversations aren't finished yet.
There is so much more to say. She wants to tell him about the last
few weeks and ask him what she is meant to do and sit with him
in silence while she grieves.

Instead, she slides her phone back into her pocket and
walks around the block, watching Jack look up at her every
few strides, his face full of appreciation. There is no part of her
that feels tired when she returns to the apartment and climbs
back into bed. Tomorrow will be a long day. It is best she tries
to sleep.

*

Something Bad is Going to Happen

She wears the same button-up shirt and black jeans she wore to work two days ago and hopes no one notices. The pants are a little loose.

None of the kids at the school know why she started two weeks later than she was originally meant to. She loves that about teenagers – no world really exists beyond their own. That's true for all of us though, she supposes.

Some of the teachers must know although none of them have said anything. She assumes Mele has mentioned it, and a few sympathetic looks appear to confirm that's the case. Mele has been kind, the type of kind that makes you feel uncomfortable and indebted. The more generosity she displays, cooking, leaving books by her door, buying flowers which she puts in a water jug, the more Adella knows the friendship is doomed; there is no way she can repay any of it. She finds herself avoiding Mele, suffocated by her endless empathy. Strangely, she feels more comfortable in the company of Helen, who when she found out, simply said, 'I'm surprised this is the first person you've lost to suicide,' and then went to bed. Mele was quick to apologise on Helen's behalf.

The 8.45 am bell sounds and she dawdles on the way to her tiny room, which is really more like a cupboard, beside the library. Already it's too stuffy, the dated navy carpet seemingly absorbing heat, the fibro walls trapping it. She opens the small window which offers virtually no relief. Today she has to do testing. There's a spreadsheet she doesn't entirely understand with a tab for comments, and in a few months these scores will be compared to new scores. Something about a graph. She thinks she also heard the word 'funding'. She waits for her first student.

Pauli is not yet five foot, has a perfectly round face, and speaks in a whisper which seems at odds with his broad frame. He is soft even though he looks hard. He doesn't want to be here, but Adella can tell that after about ten minutes he forgets that. They race through the flashcards, which this week are words like 'cough', 'tough' and 'fought', and she doesn't know how to explain why they all sound slightly different.

'They just do and it's stupid,' she says with a shrug, and he smiles despite himself.

If they get through the test, trying to read out loud a series of fifty words, she tells Pauli they can play Scrabble, which he finds far more exciting than she expects him to. He races through the words he doesn't care about, getting almost all of them wrong, to then try to put 'JIZIQ' on the Scrabble board while looking at her guiltily. He knows, deep down, that it isn't a word.

Her morning goes by quickly, sounding out the same words with Philip, then Ameen, then Shardae. Shardae especially hates reading, so asks Adella if she has a boyfriend. If she likes Mrs Birmingham or if she's mean in the staffroom too. If she's noticed that Mr Stewart smells like garlic. They end up talking about the school dance coming up on Friday, and what she plans on wearing. Shardae shows her photos on the phone she's not meant to have on her. Adella quickly flashes the cards at her again at the end of their session. She pronounces 'cough' like 'koo'. Next time.

When she's with the students, she thinks about nothing else. They make her laugh. They imbue her with energy and often as she leaves for the day, walking towards the train station, she feels something she's rarely felt; that maybe she is a Good Person. This work feels less selfish and indulgent than writing a thesis that might be read by three people and bestow upon her a meaningless title like 'Doctor'. Yesterday she received her first paycheque, and was barely able to comprehend that this much money would be deposited into her account every two weeks. She spent some of it at Officeworks last night, stocking up on pens and flashcards, the smell of the store filling her with a sense of potential.

At lunchtime she sits in the staffroom, eating a sandwich she bought from the station on her way into work. The white bread sticks to the roof of her mouth. Mr Stewart sits beside her and she smiles to herself. He does smell bad. Like a man who does not floss his teeth.

'Does anyone else teach Pauli?' the man across from her asks the table. He is younger than the rest, probably her age, and she knows him only as Mr Pappas.

'Yeah. He's defiant,' Mrs Birmingham says, full of irritability. 'I've got him for English and he refuses to even open his book and follow along when we're taking turns reading out loud. I've been meaning to talk to the Year Coordinator.' While Adella has only been at the school a few weeks, she finds it interesting that she has never heard this woman – Michelle is her first name – say a positive word about a student. Some teachers, she's come to realise, really don't seem to like kids.

'I think he probably just can't read.' The words fall out of her mouth before she can stop them. Her tone is ruder, more abrupt than she intended, but she stands by her point.

She covers her mouth as she chews what's left in her mouth. 'Sorry. I just mean, I've got him in this literacy program. We've only had a few sessions but he's one of the weakest. Maybe he refuses to open the book because he can't follow along.'

Michelle raises her eyebrows.

'I just keep thinking how boring school would be if you're in Year Seven and can't read.' She tries to deliver the statement as a suggestion.

Mr Pappas shoots her a look. He is trying to hide a smile. 'Yeah, I just asked because I was speaking to the principal of his primary school today, just about some of the additional needs kids, and he said Pauli's mum went back to Tonga when he was in kindergarten. Never came back. He lives with his dad's parents and they're doing their best, but they're in their early eighties . . .'

'Gretel's mum died when she was five and she was one of our best students last year,' Michelle snaps. 'Most of the kids have had a rough start but they don't all behave like Pauli.' She closes the lid on her Tupperware to signal that the conversation is over.

'Yeah, Gretel Smith,' Mr Pappas responds, his emphasis on 'Smith'. 'Whose father is an English teacher, whose house is overflowing with books, and who watches television shows in English.' He pushes out his chair from the staffroom table. 'Gretel is great. But I don't think Pauli's bookshelves at home are lined with Jane Austen. The kid just needs a little more support.' He tilts his head in the direction of Adella.

Everyone disperses after that, collecting things from their desks, waiting for the bell to ring. As Adella walks out the staffroom door, Mr Pappas comes up behind her.

'Elias, by the way.'

'I'm Adella,' she smiles.

'I like Pauli,' he says, pulling on the lanyard around his neck. 'He helps me with the tipping comp.'

'It's really nice that you're using a fourteen-year-old to assist with your footy tips. Never too young to get into gambling.' As she speaks she wonders if he'll understand she's joking.

'Pauli is *thirteen*,' he says. 'And the money is going to charity so myself and Pauli are actually doing God's work.'

'I'm very impressed,' she concedes.

'Good luck with the program,' he shouts over his shoulder, heading in the opposite direction. 'I know there's a lot of admin but welcome to helping children by ignoring them and filling out your spreadsheet.'

She laughs at that, and makes her way up to her glorified cupboard where a spreadsheet awaits her.

29

Adella

One year ago

It happens slowly then suddenly, the losing of her mind.

How do you tell the story of what happens not to a person but within a person? There is no lightning strike. No tumour that grows, no lump she discovers, no explanation for a host of symptoms.

It is so mundane it almost feels like a story not worth telling.

Since she began at St Francis, her alarm rings at seven, its sound becoming increasingly aggressive. It wakes her from dreams where she cannot run. Or a city is falling in on her. Or a wave is gathering momentum, hundreds of metres high, tumbling towards her with force.

In the winter months the sky is still grey, as though to signal *There is nothing for you out here. Go back to bed. This day promises you nothing.* She wakes with nausea and a headache, the shock of the morning never quite dissipating, even as the day drags on. She becomes convinced she is unwell. Glandular fever. Chronic fatigue. A flu stuck to her insides, sending aches and pains to her legs and lower back. The tiredness. There are no words for the tiredness.

Where can energy be found if the body is no longer creating it? Doesn't energy beget energy? And no energy rids you of all future energy. Is it a finite resource the body can spontaneously run out of? She is experiencing an energy crisis. Can anything of meaning – anything exciting or transformative or new – happen if one can barely place one heavy foot in front of the other?

When she first started at St Francis, she'd felt energised. She'd had a sense of purpose. The students made her laugh and she believed, truly believed, she could make a difference. It wasn't just that they were becoming familiar with new words but that their minds were learning new rules, instinctively knowing how to sound out a word they had never seen before. Between activities they told her stories. One young girl about fleeing Sudan. How her father had been shot in the hand, the same hand that was moving to protect his wife, pushing her beneath the dining room table so a bullet would not fly in her direction. Pauli started calling her 'palangi', which meant white person, but she could tell he meant it affectionately. Shardae gave her television show recommendations which she watched while preparing new activities, finding interesting passages online that she knew were related to each student's interests.

The students often talked about Mr Pappas, their sports

teacher who didn't care if they had their shirts tucked in or not. Mostly he spent lunchtime in the yard, setting up and supervising touch footy or basketball games. His theory was that most of the naughty kids just needed a run-around – 'to burn off some energy' – and then they wouldn't explode in class. Adella thought he was probably right, but she also liked the days when it was raining or too hot, and so he was around the staffroom table, usually sitting beside her. He was the type of person whose presence could change the energy of a room. It was always a better day when she spoke to him.

But soon her enthusiasm for the job disappeared. Some afternoons between sessions she would find herself quite literally looking for it in cupboards, wondering if Scrabble or a different set of readings might help bring it back. She still presented the flashcards. Asked about their other subjects. Said 'hi' when she passed Elias in the corridor. But it was as though every time she did, she then had to let out a sigh of weariness. How much longer could she keep this act up?

She stops exercising that winter. Not because she doesn't want to but because she is no longer able. Her body is not capable of sitting behind the steering wheel, turning the key, driving the ten minutes, and swiping her pass. It does not know how to perform that series of movements anymore.

She looks back at the life she used to lead and wonders who that was. The person who stayed up until the early hours of the morning, writing essays she believed mattered. How did she once get out of bed, go to work for eight hours, and then meet Lottie for dinner? Where did the conversations come from, those she used to have with Mele and Helen over white wine and take-away dumplings, laughing about something that wasn't even that funny, believing a thought she had or a story she remembered actually mattered? What is the point in saying anything? What difference does it make?

It's not that she doesn't know something is wrong. She does. You see, she is dying. She just does not know what of. She googles symptoms and scrolls through diagnoses. Anaemia. Crohn's disease. Something autoimmune. Perhaps it's her thyroid. Multiple sclerosis. Addison's disease. Ovarian cancer. Endocarditis.

She sees doctors who run blood tests. When the results arrive, she sits in a plastic chair opposite whoever is bulk-billing that day, hands clasped in her lap, awaiting the prognosis. She longs for them to tell her they can see her pain – there it is – in her blood work. She refrains from asking if there is some sort of scan that might reveal a reason for her pain, how it moves but is a constant.

Her results are normal. Iron a little low, but nothing to worry about. She feels her throat tighten, and nods imperceptibly. Might they do the tests again? Could they have missed something?

The pain, she thinks. I feel it and therefore it is true. But is it true? If I cannot point to it? If it cannot be seen? If a doctor cannot identify it, explain it, pathologise it, how can I know it is true?

It is on her third visit to the medical practice that a female doctor, with jet-black hair and thin, stiff lips slowly reads her file and curiously juts her head to the side, like a dog trying to interpret a command.

'Are you still on antidepressants?' she asks, clicking and typing with her two forefingers.

'Yes.'

'You feel like something is wrong. Would that be fair to say?'

Nods.

Then there is a questionnaire. The pen barely works. She slides the A4 page across the desk, and then fixes her eyes on the small step beside the bed. She wonders if she might need a pap smear.

'You're depressed,' the woman announces, typing something, scratching the front of her head.

'I'm going to write you a referral to a psychologist. And I think we need to increase your dosage. It can be a bit of a process getting it right, but it can really make a difference.'

She watches as the woman types, a silver band around her left ring finger. There is so much this woman could never understand. She wants to say, 'I'm not depressed. I just don't want to do anything ever again,' but she suspects the doctor has stopped listening.

She calls a psychology clinic a few days later. It's the third of August. A woman answers, short and impatient. Adella nearly hangs up, but instead she asks for the next available appointment. It's six and a half weeks away.

'So there's not anything sooner?'

The woman on the other end sighs and says she'll put her on the cancellations list. She considers for a moment asking about cost, but stops herself. She doesn't want to know.

She hangs up. And climbs back into bed.

The strangest thing, she finds, is the paradox of feeling as though everything is going very wrong, while at once being convinced that her *perspective* on it all is very right. She has heard depression described as being like a fog, or a dark cloud descending around you. While she relates to that – and the sense she is walking through quicksand, the difficulty of moving invisible to everyone but her – it is also as though a fog has been lifted. For the first time, she thinks, she is seeing clearly, seeing the world for what it truly is. She is unable to believe in the delusions she used to be so invested in. She thinks about death as soon as she wakes up, and in the hours it takes her to fall asleep. Everyone will die, she knows, especially her. There is no inherent meaning. No grand plan or hero's journey. That's all made up by people who know that humans need false hope or else they will never do anything.

Her phone becomes an extension of her hand, her thumb perpetually bent, and a dent in her pinkie finger where it rests. She scrolls and taps and disappears and flicks through photos of girls she went to school with, on their wedding day or holding their newborn or presenting at a conference with hundreds of attendees. Sometimes she looks up, her eyes stinging, and realises she has lost hours of her life. *No one else can be spending this much time on their phone*, she thinks. Through her scrolling, she becomes obsessed with careers. Managers and executives and heads of departments. How did they get there while she sounds out the word 'fatigue' with thirteen-year-olds? How the fuck did any of this happen?

That's the epiphany she has about life. Growing up, she had this fantasy about fairness. Sometimes you're behind, sometimes you're ahead, but it all evens out in the end. It's blatantly not true, though. Some people are dealt a shit hand. She knows her hand is not the worst, but it's far from the best. She is unexceptional. Unlucky. Boring. Weird family. Barely any friends. Not considered beautiful. She has no card to play.

For Mele's thirtieth, she throws herself a house party one Saturday night. Too many people come. Adella spends the first half of the night thinking that the worst type of crying is the kind you do in a room full of people, with a smile on your face, not a tear in sight. That is the crying that hurts the most – like your chest is being eaten from the inside, your brain shouting 'liar' every time you laugh.

And then she meets a friend of Mele's, Luis.

He is half-Filipino like Nathan. For a moment she forgets herself, a relief she only ordinarily achieves through sleep. He asks her questions, and answers hers with the confidence of someone who talks about themselves a lot. He is funny, truly funny, and with every word his face becomes softer and warmer.

'That's cool . . . the stuff you do with the kids,' he says, blowing out a puff of smoke on the balcony.

'Yeah. It's just, it was never the plan. It's not what I was meant to do and I'm very stuck in it.'

She can tell that wasn't the answer he was expecting. Probably wasn't the response he wanted.

'What is the plan, then?' He turns to face her.

'I wanted to be a clinical psychologist. Or a researcher, sort of like an academic. But I couldn't. I dropped out during postgrad.' She wonders if he'll ask her why.

'What would you do if money was no object?' He taps the edge of the cigarette on the railing, ash falling into the black below.

She hates this question. There is no world in which money is no object. It's like when people ask what superpower you wish you had as part of a pathetic get-to-know-you game. The answer reveals nothing interesting about a person, and is an impossible hypothetical. There is no point in giving the answer any meaningful thought.

'Write and paint by the ocean,' she says, her voice dripping with sarcasm.

'Do you write and paint now?' He raises an eyebrow.

'No.'

'There's your problem.' He leans back and looks up at the stars.

An hour later he is choking her in her own bed. She doesn't mind it, if she's honest. It makes her feel something. The sex is rough but passionate, something her life lacks. He whispers dirty things in her ear about where he wants to put it and how she's a dirty little slut and her stomach tumbles in ways it hasn't for more than a year. He doesn't have a condom so she says it's fine, she'll take the morning-after pill. That turns him on. He pulls at her hair and grabs at her face and spanks her as he finishes and she makes noises that are slightly less contrived than usual. They lie in bed and talk until the sun comes up, about their parents and their loneliness, their childhoods and their futures. She tells him about Jake in the pitch black of her room, how he died. How nothing has been the same since.

'One of my mates, sort of, we were in the same year at school, killed himself. It was just after Schoolies. Stepped out in front of a train. Really fucked up the train driver, apparently.'

'I'm sorry,' she whispers.

'I don't think we treated him well enough at school. When people gave him a hard time I didn't stick up for him. Feel sick about it.'

They talk about what happens after you die. What they believe in and what they don't. Then the room falls silent and she hears his breath deepen, his nose start to rattle. She drifts off, feeling the heat of his body beside hers.

He asks for her number before leaving the next morning. Things feel different with the sun flooding in through the window, alcohol now settled in their bellies rather than their bloodstream. He offers her a stiff hug and disappears out the front door.

She never hears from him again.

30

Adella

Two months ago

She was meant to leave her place thirty-two minutes ago if she was going to arrive at Lottie's engagement party on time.

Instead, she's standing under the fluorescent lights in her bathroom, pulling a face wipe across her cheeks with more pressure than she intended. The room is stuffy and somehow even the mirror has make-up on it. Her foundation isn't the right colour, a shade too dark, and it makes her skin look pink and sickly rather than the intended bronzed and glowy. Her jaw clenches as she spots her uneven, imprecise eyeliner, jutted out on one side and not the other, and her hair, flat and thin. She traces her forefinger along the sore, red bumps that sit on her chin, and progress all the way up her cheeks. Is it possible that anyone, living or dead, has ever hated themselves this much?

She is so struck by the ugliness of what she sees that she cannot breathe. The way her face is composed looks mean. As though she is a person impossible to like. As she slumps onto the toilet seat the room begins to spin and the inside of her mouth starts to taste funny. Wherever she is going, she cannot make it stop. She puts her head between her legs, feeling her heart thump against her left thigh, as though trying to punch its way out of her body. Sweat prickles at the back of her neck and she tries not to think of the time.

It's now a quarter past eight, and it isn't just the way she looks that throws her into a state of abject terror. It is what she has – or rather, doesn't have – to say. When people ask her about work it takes all her energy to even fumble through an answer. Yes, she still works at the school. When they remark, 'Well, that must be fulfilling,' (the only thing to say to someone who, one can only assume, has reached their earning potential) she nods politely, while reflecting that, no. It really isn't fulfilling. It's repetitive. The students are disengaged. She can't really blame them, because so is she. The room is layered with different degrees of boredom. What difference does it make if they can sound out the word 'leapt' – a word they'll rarely use? Of course, in some long chain of reading means learning means opportunity means job means money, theoretically it might make a difference, but she does not have the energy to get there. Today, it makes no difference. And she stopped thinking about tomorrow a while ago.

People can see that moment, she's learned. Where you nod that a job is 'fulfilling' while every part of your being screams 'no it isn't'. You reek of the truth. They might follow up with 'weren't you studying psychology?' or 'do you see yourself there long term?' and she opens her mouth, her vocal cords feeling like broken glass. The person she is speaking to does not know what it is to work without ambition. To live without a plan. To be unexceptional and small, someone no one notices.

She was meant to leave forty-five minutes ago and barely anything she owns is clean. She pulls at a pile of clothes sitting in the corner of her bedroom and finds a long-sleeved black dress, which sits low at the back, but as she pulls it on she realises it's wet, having sat under a damp towel for days. She tries jeans but they're too casual for an engagement party, let alone her own sister's engagement party. Finally she finds a navy silk halter-neck dress, crinkled but wearable. As she pulls it on she knows that tonight she will have to go and be more than she is. She cannot stop picturing the greeting of people, all that enthusiasm she is expected to muster. Stories she's already heard will be repeated and laughs manufactured. And then the goodbyes. Who gives a shit that anyone is leaving? There will be pleasantries about 'see you soon' or 'so good to catch up' when really neither has thought about the other in years, and they just can't wait to get back into the car, throw their head back and exhale. She finds the formula of it all exhausting, a script they're all reading from but pretending not to, whispering later about anyone who happened to forget their line.

'Adella managed to not ask me a single question,' she can hear her aunty muttering to her husband. Never mind that's because she was cross-examined – rapid-fire questions thrown at her – her sluggish brain trying to keep up. It's funny how we call people 'cold' or 'rude', when really they are probably just sad.

For months, probably longer, she has been plodding along, one foot in front of the other. If she just did the normal things – went to work, visited her family, saw Sophia, watched the true crime series everyone else was watching on Netflix, ate meals occasionally, washed her hair, bought a new dress when she was invited to something, swiped on dating apps, then maybe she would become normal. In the same way you must pretend to be asleep to fall asleep, maybe if she pretended to be alive she would become alive, the veneer of normality muting all those thoughts and impulses and habits that are decidedly unnormal.

A while ago (months maybe? She had lost sense of time) she had decided it was the pill. The pill was making her feel like this, as though her head was underwater and she couldn't hear properly. She felt sexless and irritable and cloudy and one day, as she deposited the little yellow pill onto her tongue, she decided that was the cause. For a few weeks, she'd relished in feeling her body 'deflate' as she called it, and the texture of her skin change. She was becoming more herself again, and now this dark veil would lift.

It didn't, though. Her skin returned to adolescence, and her hair became wet with oil. Her mood remained unchanged, except now she bled for ten days at a time. Sometimes she would sit at work imagining she was a wounded soldier, bleeding out, but instead of medical attention she just had to keep working – nodding and smiling and repeating the same fucking word that every student inevitably got wrong.

She was meant to leave fifty-seven minutes ago, and slowly makes her way back to the mirror. Her reflection is worse than she remembers. She grits her teeth as she dabs and fixes her smudged eyeliner. It somehow makes it worse imagining how perfect Lottie will look, her make-up professionally done and a dress that cost her three hundred and fifty dollars. How much has changed for Lottie in two years. She met Clinton at work Christmas drinks, and they have barely spent a night apart since. They have moved in together, adopted a cat named Otis and a dog named Sushi, bungee-jumped in New Zealand and got potentially lethal food poisoning in Bali, and on a spontaneous weekend away he had proposed with his dead grandmother's ring.

Now it is late August, and tonight is the engagement party. There will be at least two hundred guests, fewer than ten from her family, and more than one hundred from his. Adella's lateness will be conspicuous. Her mother will be watching the door, and Lottie will be pretending she hasn't noticed that her only sibling is so far a no-show.

She was meant to leave an hour and ten minutes ago when finally she collects her keys. She grabs a pair of earrings and rifles through her wardrobe to try to find two of the same shoe, wondering how the same two years that transformed Lottie's life could have given her so little.

There have been no relationships. She sees Sophia sometimes, for a scheduled dinner or a walk along the river. There is always an end time, and they don't watch *The OC* anymore. They talk as though they are marking off items on a meeting agenda.

'Now, your work. Still a bit bored? Have you applied for anything else?' Sophia will ask. Action required.

'How about Leon and the kids stuff? Do you think he'll change his mind?' Adella will ask.

The answer is always yes. Of course he will. As soon as his friends start having kids, he will see how much he wants this. 'It's not that he's sure he *doesn't* want kids,' Sophia rationalises. 'It's just that he's not sure he *does*. Which is very different.' Adella doesn't think it's that different.

Leon is Sophia's boyfriend of four years. Of all the men she might have ended up with, how it became Leon Adella might never understand. He is not particularly attractive, a few years older than Sophia but looks significantly more. He is quiet. Cynical. Doesn't even appear to like Sophia all that much. Most of all he is unambitious. Well. He is ambitious in what he *says* he's going to do – a business idea or a position he's applying for. But ultimately he spends a lot of his life playing his Xbox, telling Sophia to 'shush' because he's in the middle of a game right now.

Sophia staged an intervention and he said maybe he just needs some more time, but not this year or next. The man is in his early thirties. Adella isn't sure what he's waiting for. But, tick. Agenda item marked off. It's ironic the opinions we have about our friends' boyfriends when we're twenty, what we're bold enough to say out loud, what we feel we owe them – but once they hit their late twenties and meet the person they'll likely marry, have children with, live alongside, nurse into their dying days? Not a word. That, we reason, is their business.

Then there is sleep. She is sleeping a lot, but she is also an insomniac. She doesn't sleep at night, but at about four or five in the morning she drifts off. On weekends, she sleeps right through until the late afternoon, waking up feeling drugged but also relieved that for a while she experienced respite. When she's asleep she feels the least like herself. As though she is floating without an identity or a face. She cannot say anything stupid. When she is unconscious she is leaving everyone alone. On weekdays, she nods off on the train on the way to work, and when she returns home at five, she crawls back into bed, sleeping for a few hours until dinner time. Her sleep schedule has the effect of making her feel perpetually jet-lagged.

She parks around the corner from the Blackford Hotel, and the freezing air bites at her bare legs and sends a shiver down her spine. She wraps her arms around her chest, head down, and tries to find the entrance.

'What's there to be so sad about, love?' a grey-haired man remarks as she passes him.

She looks up, eyes wide, wondering, for a brief moment, if he is really asking. Beside him is a slightly younger man, tall with dark hair, thongs on despite the cold.

'Would it hurt ya to smile?' he laughs, revealing small yellow teeth, crossing his arms over his swollen belly.

She can feel her ears go red, and focuses her eyes back on the ground, hurrying her pace.

'It'd help with the boys!' he cackles, his voice breaking as he does. His friend laughs harder, as though it is a laughing competition, and says loudly, 'No one's gonna approach ya looking like that!' She can sense them both imitating her.

A bouncer asks for her ID at the door.

'Those old dickheads bothering you?' he asks, glancing at her licence.

'No.'

As she climbs the stairs she tries to smile. Really tries. But her face does not make that shape anymore. Since when? she wonders. In the same way she can no longer touch her toes or do a cartwheel, her body has forgotten how to raise the edges of her mouth with the strength of her cheeks. She feels suffocated the closer she gets to the top of the stairs – the demand that this is a Happy Occasion that must be met with only Happy Feelings is being yelled at her from the sound of the music and the chattering of strangers. She wants to be able to feel this so badly. For Lottie. For her. There are people she loves in this room. But even the music sounds like words without a melody, something so fundamental missing. This, her own head, is a thief. Tonight it will steal another moment, another experience, that she won't ever get back.

Her mother spots her as she reaches the top of the stairs, struck by how many people are here. She raises her eyebrows and almost imperceptibly shakes her head, before turning back to Aunty Liz. The room is loud, but Adella can't really hear anything. No conversation seems penetrable. Cousins and friends of Lottie's and people she doesn't recognise but assumes belong to Clinton clutch at wine glasses and shout over the band playing in the corner and call out to the waitstaff that they'll actually have one of those spring rolls. Immediately, she feels tired. As though her brain is in the wrong mode for this environment, and to communicate with anyone would be to betray some kind of essential truth about who she is and how she feels. She is not an actor. She is not in possession of the kind of energy this night requires. Hell, an old man had spotted that before she'd even entered the venue.

She decides to find the bathroom.

'Adella! You've finally surfaced!' she hears, knowing before she turns around that those words belong to her father.

'Did ya have a more exciting offer tonight?' he asks, his arms outstretched, leaving it to her to walk into them.

Beside him is Suzie, his partner of thirteen or so years, whom Adella has only met a handful of times. She wants to hate her – perhaps it would be more interesting that way – but she doesn't. Suzie has a kind smile and doesn't force anything. She nods her head and occasionally asks a follow-up question.

She remembers hating Suzie in the beginning. It was their father's birthday, and Adella, fifteen at the time, and Lottie, who would've been just seventeen, were surprised to receive an invite to his place for dinner. She watched as her dad listened more attentively to Suzie than he ever had to her, laughed with a depth she'd never heard, and touched Suzie's arm and back tenderly as though she were precious. Surrounded by half a dozen friends and Suzie, her dad was a man his daughters didn't recognise. To Adella, he was a man who grew distracted whenever she tried to tell a story. He didn't laugh when she said something funny, and generally looked at her with an air of indifference. In her entire lifetime, she had never been enough to capture her dad's full attention. Awards he remarked upon. Success he could momentarily understand. But who she was on a Saturday night didn't seem to interest him. That night at her father's birthday she'd felt like a monkey performing tricks to court her father's attention.

Tonight she wonders if this is why she's so pathetic, desperate for a man – any man – to love her. And maybe this, the aloofness, the keeping her at arm's length, the dynamic of having to work for recognition, was a feeling that was comfortingly familiar. This would forever be a relationship in which she felt safe. Anything else would be foreign.

She tries to speak. Her speech is slurred and she struggles to find the right words. There are strange pauses and the two people in front of her feel hundreds of metres away, like they're shouting at each other across a desert, competing with the elements.

'Is Pa here?' She cranes her neck, looking towards the lounges in the corner.

'Yes!' Suzie spins around, pointing towards the right. 'Just over there with Clinton's grandparents. I don't think they can hear a word of what the other is saying . . .'

'I should . . .'

She sees relief in Pa's eyes when they spot each other.

'Adella! This is Eponi . . . Eponi, was it? And John, Clinton's grandparents.' She shakes their hands and agrees with Suzie. They can't hear a word.

She settles in beside him and feels, just for a moment, like she's walked offstage.

'You know,' he says, looking straight ahead, 'I think your mother got halfway here and then realised she'd left me behind.'

Adella looks horrified.

'No, it was no problem. I was having a lie-down in your old bedroom, that's where I'm staying, so I think all the lights were out and she forgot I was there. When I heard the front door slam and the car drive off I just felt . . . relieved.' They laugh.

'Did you not want to come?'

'It's not that. I'm just feeling,' he searches for the word. 'Weary.'

'So am I.' She leans back into her chair.

He looks at her for a moment. 'Everyone fusses over youth, as though it's full of "possibility". But you know where I was at your age?'

She shakes her head.

'Hospital. They didn't know what the hell was wrong with me. But I remember lying in bed, and watching this fly torment me. It would land on my pillow then on the blanket then on the bedside table. And I couldn't for the life of me choose whether or not to kill it. I was frozen in indecision. Two simple choices, and I couldn't make one. That bloody fly sent me madder than I already was.'

'I don't feel qualified to make choices about anything,' she says with a smile. She can see her life in five years or ten years, and she knows for certain that she hates it. But she can barely make a decision about what she ought to do tomorrow, or what time to get out of bed or whether or not to eat something for breakfast. When one cannot make the smallest of decisions, how do you begin orchestrating a completely different life?

She glances around at the room, and catches Lottie beside Clinton – perfect Clinton – in a white cocktail dress, Prosecco in hand. Does she want this? Marriage? Perhaps. Does she want children? What a ridiculous decision for any sane person to have to make. And after all, neither of those are decisions that truly belong to her. They must be done with somebody else, who desires the exact same things she does at the exact same time. Marriage and children cannot be manifested out of sheer willpower or grit.

When she'd left school there had been so many choices. She might've done law or medicine or journalism, she might've gone on exchange overseas or interned somewhere impressive. Instead she had chosen this one silly thing she'd failed at, ultimately. How many times do we make the wrong decision and bear the consequences?

And then we wonder why, when presented with a fly, the decision of what to do with it seems insurmountable. How anyone ever makes a decision is the true mystery.

'Your mum says you've been down.' He looks at his hands.

'Yeah. Just not really feeling myself.' She smiles without showing teeth.

'Depression.' He taps the armrest of the couch as he pulls himself up. 'I've heard some bloke describe it as the family secret everyone has. That's about right.' He excuses himself for the bathroom.

She wanders downstairs for some air. For a while she stands around the corner, the other side of the man with the yellow teeth, and leans against the cool, dark brick. She closes her eyes and scrunches her fist, a trick she read about in a book once. Something about 'get back into your body and out of your head'.

She senses someone to her left and through squinted eyes sees the distinctive movements of Lottie. Flailing limbs and fast gestures. Her cocktail dress is bright white, her hair blonde and loosely curled.

'What are you doing?' she hisses.

'Needed a minute. Sorry . . . wasn't feeling well,' Adella says, her voice quiet.

'Why are you standing here completely by yourself? When did you even get here? We've been waiting for you for speeches to start.' Lottie is panting, her cheeks rosy.

'I didn't realise. It's fine, I can come up now.' Adella pushes her body up from the wall behind her.

Lottie turns without saying a word and leads her up the stairs. Clinton is waiting with a microphone, whispering to someone in a suit, and a wine glass clinks in the distance.

He speaks first, funny and eloquent. When she looks at him, she sees the same thing she always does at events like these; birthdays, pregnancy announcements, engagements.

Jake never got this.

He would have liked to get married, she thinks. Clinton talks about how meeting Lottie was like coming home, a place he'd always been looking for without realising it. She wonders if things might have been different for Jake if he'd found someone to love, and designed a future with them.

No one really speaks about Jake anymore. It's not even been a year and a half since he died. Sam, Jake's brother, posts a lot about his new girlfriend. His friends don't post tributes, and Adella doesn't stay in touch with Jake's mum, except for the odd message acknowledging Jake's birthday. There is nothing left to say. There's just a gigantic hole in the world and everyone has manoeuvred their lives around it, pretending it doesn't exist.

'I am so excited about our future together,' Clinton says, taking Lottie's hand. 'I didn't realise life could be this good.' They kiss and people applaud and Adella wonders what that must be like, to be *excited* about the future and not trapped by it. Does Clinton really feel like that? Or is that just something people say?

The room comes back to life after that, and she finds herself cornered by six of Lottie's friends from high school, all squealing over the top of her. They shout questions about boyfriends and other people they remember from her year before it descends into snapshots of stories from fifteen years ago, misremembered and exaggerated. They perform to her – she is an excuse to retell the stories they've clearly told a dozen times before – and she nods and feigns shock and it's all so boring. Their faces are pink, and four of the six are married now with at least one child. They've had too many champagnes. Is that what happens when you follow the course laid out in front of you? You become the kind of person who writes themselves off at engagement parties, cornering a vaguely familiar face, desperate to talk about anything that isn't the texture of baby poo? Do they know they're sad? Or are they animated by some sort of shared psychosis, where they think happiness is imprisonment with a night out once every six months?

She tunes out for a while, and by the time she tunes back in, Annabel is standing too close to her face whispering to her that she ought to wait to have kids.

'Don't rush it like I did,' she slurs, drinking from a champagne glass, the rim covered in lipstick. 'Enjoy being single. Your party years!' she says, raising her arms as though celebrating, a trickle of champagne escaping from her glass. 'Because then you just become "Tim's mum" and you never sleep again and your husband won't fuck you and –'

'Are you and Craig still not having sex?' Jen asks, overhearing something Annabel clearly didn't want her to.

Adella stands there and listens as they dissect each other's sex lives.

'Why did you have one?' She knows you're not meant to ask that question, and she can't look Annabel in the eye as she does. Her speech is slow. But she wants some exchange, some interaction with these women, to be real.

'What?' Annabel can barely keep her eyes open.

'A child. Why did you decide to have kids?' As she asks, she's aware of how unusually she's standing, her feet too close together. She doesn't know what to do with her hands anymore.

For a moment there is silence. The women without children look at their feet.

'It's just what you do,' Annabel says, shrugging her shoulders. 'That's why we got married. Isn't that why we're here? I love Tim, he's the best thing that's . . .'

Adella stops listening after that. Something about Annabel's words feel rehearsed and inauthentic. She realises she came across as cold and unfeeling. She didn't mean to. The women around her disengage, except for Jen, who seems to look more closely.

'How old are you again?' she says, lifting her nose, the other women distracted.

'Twenty-eight,' Adella responds tonelessly.

Jen nods. 'Saturn Return,' she says, with an air of gravity. 'Feel like your life is falling apart?'

Adella says nothing.

'I cried every day during mine,' she continues. 'It was all "Who am I?", "What am I on this earth to do?", "Do I blow up this life I've created?"' Her tone suggests she now thinks these questions are ridiculous. 'You get through it, though. I saw this great woman, you're going to think I sound crazy but hear me out.'

Adella does not hear her out.

The rest of the night unfolds in a blur. Everything around her is in motion but she is frozen still, unable to react or move. She stands beside her mum and her aunties, and while she thinks of things to say, something always stops her before the words come out of her mouth. It's never worth it. She tries to nod and anchor herself in the present but she keeps being pulled somewhere else.

Her dad and Suzie approach her again. She notices he has a red wine stain on his shirt, another glass in his hand. His teeth have turned a funny colour, and Suzie stands further from him than she did only two hours ago. He asks her about work. Turns to Suzie and explains how smart Adella had been at school. Could've been a lawyer, if she'd wanted. They've had this conversation. They always have exactly the same conversation. Cake comes around and he takes a plate, placing his red wine down on the ground beside his feet, shaking his head at Suzie's offer to hold it. It's not even a minute before he knocks it over, red wine covering his pants and their ankles.

She feels suffocated having both her parents in the same room. Her mother is just beside them, looking off into the distance, pretending to listen to one of Clinton's sisters talk about something inconsequential. These are my parents, she thinks, and everyone here can see the parts of me that exist in them. She cannot hide when they are beside her. Cannot pretend to be someone else. Looking from one to the other, her father speaking with his mouth full, it's like she's in a funhouse full of mirrors and all she can see are warped reflections of herself she hates.

Bar staff pick up the pieces of wine glass, while her dad keeps eating his cake, explaining the plot of some show he and Suzie have been watching.

She has spent most of her adult life full of shame and embarrassment about who her parents are, wishing they'd act less like themselves. Is that because she wants to act less like who she is? Do they see her too clearly?

Adella listens to him, deadpan, before remarking, 'You have cake on your nose.'

It is at that point she decides to go home. On her way out she stops by the couch where her grandfather is sitting alone.

'Pa, did you want a lift?'

Without a word he joins her.

They wander towards her car, him holding her right arm for support.

'What did you decide, by the way? About the fly?'

He looks up from the pavement. 'I chose to let it live. And then a nurse came in with a clipboard and killed it. Turns out we have less control than we think we do, I suppose.'

Later that night, lying in bed, clothes strewn across her doona, four half-full water glasses beside her bed, she feels like her ribs are about to crack under some invisible pressure. It is as though every single person's feelings are stuck on her skin. Her dad's embarrassing moment with the wine glass and Annabel's sadness are stuck to her like smoke, the stench overpowering, and when she closes her eyes that's what flashes. Pain. Embarrassment. Deceit. Regret. Shame. That's all there is. And she's being swallowed by it.

*

Today will be different.

She will be more herself. Or less herself. A better self.

Beside her bed is the gift she bought Lottie for her engagement that was too big and awkward to take with her last night. It's a blown-up photo she'd taken of Lottie and Clinton at Christmas last year. Neither of them even knew the photo was being taken. They are in the front yard of Pa's place, arms around each other's waists, looking at each other as though they are sharing an unspoken secret. She'd had the photo printed and framed – if she's honest it's significantly bigger than she anticipated but she didn't really understand the dimensions when she ordered it.

Her alarm goes off early – just after seven. Mele is up the coast somewhere this weekend and asked that she mind Jack. He needs to be taken out first thing in the morning or he'll piss and shit in the living room. The alarm keeps sounding, the sound of irritation and disturbance. She tries to open her eyes, but her eyelids won't allow it. She sees glimpses of herself in the reflection of her built-in wardrobe, full-length mirrors she's hated since she moved in. Her eyes are pink and puffy and her hair is stuck to her face. She's disgusted, and lets her eyes close again. She only fell asleep a few hours ago. Ten more minutes isn't going to upset the dog, he doesn't even seem to be awake yet. She snoozes her alarm and rolls over, and sleeps more deeply than she has in weeks.

At one stage she hears scratching and crying, but before she can feel anything she is pulled back under into a deep sleep. Then there's quiet. Her alarm doesn't ring.

When she wakes again, she does so with a fright. She grabs her phone and reads the time: nearly a quarter to eleven.

She launches out of bed and the moment she opens her bedroom door she knows Jack hasn't been able to hold on. On the cream carpet of the living room, Jack is sitting, trembling slightly, surrounded by everything he would have preferred to do in the garden.

'I'm so sorry, Jack,' she says, patting him on the head, tasting the smell in the back of her throat. He lets out another cry so she finds him a treat, realising as she gives it to him that she's just reinforced very bad behaviour. She opens the cupboard under the sink and searches for paper towel. Nothing. Eventually, buried up the back she finds a roll of newspaper, bound up in plastic, probably from when Mele would layer Jack's crate with it. This will have to do.

She sprays something that says 'pet odour' on the front and dabs it with the paper, feeling the urine come in contact with her hands. She realises this must have been here for hours, settled into the fibres of the carpet. There's no way it's coming out. She collects what she can of the rest, gagging as she does, accepting all this as her punishment.

She watches YouTube videos and looks up 'how to remove wee stains' and eventually the colour lifts, even if the smell doesn't. She leaves paper over patches to absorb anything that's left. Jack watches on, his round brown eyes sorry and ashamed.

In her pyjamas she takes him out to the patch of grass at the back of their building, where he urinates again. She scratches him behind the ears, muttering, 'I'm sorry.' Despite what had happened upstairs, he'd still tried to do the right thing, holding on.

In her bedroom she finds tracksuit pants and a hoodie to throw on. Pulling off her pyjamas, she catches her reflection in the mirror, marked with fingerprints and dust. She sees creases on the side of her face from sleeping in a strange position, and black encrusted below her eyes. Her skin feels sore the moment she sees it, bumps full of dirt and pus and bacteria. There is one pimple buried in the fold of her nose, bright yellow. Her lips are dry and colourless, her hair greasy, stuck to the top of her head. In just her underwear she sees the way her thighs meet and she thinks of that girl at school who remarked at the swimming carnival one day, as another girl prepared to dive into the pool, 'Shoot me if I ever have baseball bat legs.' She didn't know what she'd meant at the time, but her legs today look like baseball bats, perfect triangles of fat at the top, without definition or shape. Her stomach has developed a permanent crease, and a dimple below her belly button, fat sticking to her middle like mud flung at a wall. She can see blue veins in her breasts, her skin so pale she looks sick. How to describe how she feels? Furious. Revolted. Irritated. How has this happened? This isn't the body she had at twenty. Greed and laziness have landed her in this sack of flesh and when she looks at herself like this it's obvious why no person she has loved has loved her back.

She heads to the pantry, where she finds the plastic tub Mele has filled with household necessities. Masking tape. She wants masking tape. Then she collects the rest of the newspaper rolled up on the bench. Her breath rattles as she tapes the pages to her mirror doors, her reflection disappearing with each patch. By the time she is finished, all that remains is the reflection of her feet, and Jack sitting beside them, wondering what is going on.

With her car keys and Lottie's gift hanging from her right hand, she heads out onto the street. It's a Sunday afternoon and she spots a couple in activewear holding hands, crossing the road, their coffees in matching KeepCups. While her morning was spent dabbing dog piss, they probably woke early, enjoying slow, passionate sex before wandering off to brunch or the gym; how can the same day look so different for different people? The girlfriend laughs with big, white, straight teeth, walking with a rhythm that suggests her muscles work more efficiently than everyone else's and Adella hopes no one sees her, as she catches stains from dinner a few nights ago on the front of her pants.

She slides the photo into the back seat and exhales as she pushes the key into the ignition. It revs, then stops. Revs. Then silence. She examines the dashboard. Fuck. She rotates the right lever towards her. Click. She left the headlights on. Again. This will be the third time since she bought this car. Fuck. Fuck. Fuck. She bangs the heels of her hands against the steering wheel, letting out a grunt through gritted teeth.

She'll have to get the bus. With the present, she trudges to the bus stop a few streets away, the wind biting at her face. People take a second glance at this person carting around a gift as long as her legs, and she has to keep stopping to readjust her grip. Her fingers are freezing, stiff from the cold air. When she arrives she checks the board, only to see that the next bus doesn't come for twenty-four minutes. She waits for a little while, and then decides to go in search of something to eat. It's nearly two and her stomach has begun to growl.

She orders a sandwich made with meat that doesn't look like it's come from an animal. The bread is slightly stale and the mayonnaise overpowering. She munches slowly, getting through half before throwing the rest in the bin. Then she orders a Diet Coke, something to get her through the next few hours. She clutches the can, turning her fingers slightly blue, and sips beside the bus stop until the bus finally appears.

As she climbs the steps awkwardly, with her can in her left hand and the gift resting against her right leg, she tries to find her Opal card, the drink spilling slightly.

'Yeah, you can't drink that on my bus.' It is as though the bus driver is laughing at her.

'Oh, oh, sorry. Where can I . . .' She looks for somewhere to throw it out, even though it's still three-quarters full.

'Not my problem.' He looks straight ahead.

'Um,' she spots a bin across the road, 'can I just throw it in there?' She gestures.

'And hold up this whole bus because you couldn't resist a Diet Coke?'

She doesn't know what to say, but can see her lumpy stomach and dimpled thighs. She stands still and silent.

'Go.' He signals his head to the right.

'Will you . . .'

'Just bin it and we'll sit here like we have all day,' he says flatly, crossing his arms.

Hot tears form in her eyes as she hurries off the bus, wishing he would just close the doors and continue on. But he waits, while she braces for a break in the traffic. As she darts across, a Kia Rio honks at her and shouts 'dickhead' out the window.

For the fifteen-minute bus journey, she looks at no one, staring straight ahead and feeling every second stretch by. She rids herself of thought or feeling, breathing slowly and clenching her fists in her lap. She can still taste the Diet Coke in her mouth and it makes her want to retch. Hot redness has spread up her neck and onto her jaw but she ignores it, barely blinking.

When she arrives at her stop she promptly disembarks by the front doors, whispering, 'Thank you so much,' to the man who chose to humiliate her. She turns right, feeling a twinge of relief as she watches the bus accelerate, struck by the irony that the ad on the back is for Diet Coke. It is only then she realises she's left the gift wedged between the seat and the wall, without a name on it or a card, just a badly wrapped rectangle that will make no sense to anyone but Lottie.

She cannot take another step. She sits on the grass in front of someone's brick fence, her knees up to her forehead and cries. Gutturally cries. Something about it almost feels good. The warmth of her tears and how they taste as they flow into her mouth. There is some pleasure in how the outside reflects the inside, a woman howling in the street as though she is mad because she is mad. All of it. Everything that's happened today has been her fault. A hellish day by pure design. Saliva drips from her mouth down onto her chin and she wipes everything on her stained tracksuit pants.

Eventually she stands back up, eyes misty and face pink, and walks slowly towards Lottie's place. She realises when she reaches her street that she doesn't even know if anyone will be home, but when she rings the doorbell to apartment fifteen, Lottie answers. She can tell by Lottie's exasperated tone that Clinton isn't there, and she feels a flood of relief.

'What are you doing here?' Lottie asks as she opens her door, as though she was in the middle of something very important.

'Sorry, were you in the middle of something?'

'Yeah, *Real Housewives*,' she says, pointing at the television.

'I just wanted to drop off your engagement party present.'

'You didn't have to do that,' Lottie says, shaking her head. 'I didn't expect anything from –'

'I left it on the bus.' Adella's voice is flat.

'Ah, fuck. That sucks. Sorry. Why were you on the bus?'

'Car isn't turning on.'

'Again? Did you leave the lights –'

'Yes.'

'We have jumper leads. We'll come over tonight.'

'It's fine.' She hates how Lottie now uses exclusively collective pronouns, as though she's incapable of helping her own sister independently.

Adella sits on the couch, shoulders slumped, looking at the paused television screen.

'You look . . .' Lottie begins, standing above her.

'Like shit?'

Lottie smiles.

'Are we going to talk about last night?' Lottie sits, pulling one knee up under her chin.

'What about it?' Adella feels tired.

'The fact you were really late. And stood in the corner barely speaking to anybody the whole time? I wanted you to meet Clint's family.'

'I showed up, didn't I? And I bought a present even though that doesn't count for anything.' As she delivers the words they sound childlike.

'Of course it counts for something. That's really kind of you. But it's like you turn up to places intent on having a terrible time. You weren't being forced into a fucking warzone. It was an engagement party with spring rolls and champagne.' Lottie shakes her head, baffled. 'It was the same with Mum's birthday and when we went to Lucio's for dinner. How hard is it to just talk? And engage? We've gone through this with Mum for our whole lives and now it's you too.' She's speaking faster now.

'I'm not *making* my life sad. My life is sad.' Adella tells her about what's happened so far today, the mess Jack left, the bus driver, the gift.

'It's like I'm down and everything is just kicking me and kicking me and I can't get back up because I keep being kicked . . .'

'Your life doesn't have to be this sad.' The pitch of Lottie's voice goes up. 'You've become this sad person who does sad things and lives a sad life and then wonders why they're so sad. I'd say go to the beach or go to fucking New York! But you would just somehow make that sad. You'd make everything look lonely and isolating when it's not.'

Adella swallows. She is trying. Today she tried. 'Lottie. I'm trying.'

'No you're fucking not.' Lottie is shouting now. 'I have spent my whole life trying to avoid this. Constructing my life so I don't have to see this.' She faces her palms towards Adella. 'And then you bring it with you everywhere.'

Adella looks at what's left of her nails, how they cut into her red, irritated fingertips.

Lottie isn't finished. 'You bring this perspective that I've trained myself not to see. The look on your face. Like everything is just too hard. It repels everyone. Even the people who love you. How do you think I feel about myself after I've seen you? It's like you bring in a bad smell and it catches. It's . . . it's the way you hold yourself,' spittle forms at the edges of her mouth, 'the way your shoulders lean forward and your feet are always dragging and your eyes look like the light is too fucking bright.' She looks around the room. 'What is this apparent nightmare you're living in that no one else can see?'

'If you think I don't already know I'm a piece of shit, you're wrong,' Adella says quietly. 'I don't want to be here. A day is ruined . . .' She wants to say how angry she is at herself and her inability to enjoy anything. A doughnut or a coffee. An orgasm or a TV show. Lottie can tell her to do things she enjoys all she likes, but by virtue of her doing it, it is no longer able to be enjoyed. It becomes sad and pathetic, black ink spilling onto everything. 'I want to go to sleep and never wake up. Or to wake up and be someone else. I am trapped in this, Lottie. No matter where I go or what I do.' She doesn't have the energy to finish her sentence.

'It's easy for you,' she continues after a moment. 'You've got Clinton and a job you like and things to look forward to and when you walk into a room everyone doesn't immediately want to leave.'

'Oh Jesus, this self-pity,' Lottie says, and rolls her eyes. 'Fuck you. It's "easy" for me?' she says, making air quotes. 'What a dismissive thing to say. You know why it's easy? Because I try really, really hard. You don't think I have days when I don't want to get out of bed? And when I think I'm going to end up exactly like Mum, lonely and basically mute? I feel that every fucking day. The difference between us is that I *try*. I get out of bed. I go for a run. I eat even if I don't feel like it. I think about people other than myself. I practise mindfulness which makes me want to shoot myself in the head and I manage stress and make my bed and guess what? It works. But you're just this . . . victim. Like life is harder on you than everyone else. Admit it *feels good*. Believing you're at the centre of a universe conspiring to make your specific life shit. Nothing is ever your fault. Nothing is ever within your control. You're an adult and you don't take any responsibility.' She is so full of anger her eyes are misty. 'And now I'm trying to plan a wedding with a psychopath dad, a mentally ill mum and a depressed sister. How could you do this to me?'

Adella lets out a huff she's heard her mum make and says, looking Lottie in the eye, 'You are so selfish.' With that she stands up and heads towards the door. She just wants to be curled up beneath her bed in the dark.

'I am so sorry that I can't help but spoil everyone else's lives,' she says sarcastically, although she means it.

'At least let me drive you home.' Lottie grabs her keys, but Adella is already storming down the stairs.

She catches up out the front and convinces Adella to get in, driving her home in silence.

Adella will later replay this day in her own mind, trying to recall if at any point she asked Lottie a question. How is it that she did not consider that Lottie's inner world might be just as complicated as her own? She did not imagine that in the car with them, silent and still, was something Lottie had so far told no one, a problem depriving her of sleep and focus, a decision that might just be the most significant a person – a woman – ever makes.

But that is what happens when we have been swallowed up, entirely, by our mind.

There is no space for anyone else.

31

Adella

Two weeks ago

It's Monday, the sky is grey and dark, and the word on the card-board flashcard is 'reign'.

Pauli's lips are pursed and Adella can tell from his expression that he has no idea how to say the word in front of him.

He shakes his head and she insists he try, just take a guess.

'Rine,' he says, in a way that rhymes with line.

'So close. *Reign*. Like pitter-patter . . . like it's probably about to do all day.' She glances at the window and then stops the timer.

'But that word doesn't look like that.' He points to the flashcard.

'Yes, so this has a different meaning. Have you ever heard the phrase "The king had a long reign" before?' She moves the word to the bottom of the pile.

'Yeah,' he says softly, in a way that reveals he hasn't.

They spend the rest of their session reading a passage she found about a sixteenth-century queen named Joanna of Castile. The students are studying King Henry VIII in History, and the literacy program suggests you find readings that loosely relate to their subjects. She had studied King Henry VIII and his six wives at university, and remembered that Catherine of Aragon had been her favourite wife, and so lost forty-five minutes of her life trying to remind herself why. That's when she came across Catherine's older sister Joanna of Castile, also known as Joanna the Mad, and read and read until her eyelids grew heavy.

Joanna the Mad, the passage laid out, married Philip the Handsome in 1496 when she was sixteen years old. She was highly intelligent and could speak three languages. Then, in short succession, she lost her two elder siblings. Her sister-in-law gave birth to a stillborn baby two months after her own husband died, and then Joanna's sister Isabella lost her two-year-old son. That's when her mother fell ill with a fever, and, as the story goes, Joanna started exhibiting signs of madness. In retrospect, one might wonder if they were simply signs of grief.

She stopped eating and sleeping, the story goes, and she would throw herself against the wall in despair. She would fly into jealous rages over her husband's known mistresses, and once went as far as to physically attack a woman he was sleeping with. At this point, Pauli starts laughing and singing 'Joanna gone loco' while circling his forefingers around the sides of his head. Adella smiles, not because she finds it funny, but because she hasn't yet been able to see any signs of madness.

Her mother died, and then a few years later her husband. Following his death, Joanna refused to part with his remains. He was embalmed and most of the time the coffin was closed, but he joined her on her travels and at the dinner table and by her bedside. She was known to open the coffin and check he was still there.

'Imagine how much he'd stink,' Pauli says, eyes wide. But Adella is thinking about how unnatural it had felt to watch Jake's coffin be thrust into a hearse, and to see it drive away, knowing Jake was about to be buried six feet underground. Perhaps she would have liked to lift the lid, just for a moment, and check that Jake was still there.

Joanna's late husband had declared her mad before he died, and after his death, their son Charles ensured she was functionally jailed in a royal palace for more than thirty years until her own death. Some historians think that perhaps her maternal grandmother, Isabella of Portugal, also suffered from mental illness. She too was exiled to a convent. Joanna's grandson and great-granddaughter were additionally understood to have 'gone mad' – from some condition that might have been depression or bipolar or schizophrenia. Historians are also quick to point out that the men classifying Joanna as 'crazy' – her husband and her son – had a lot to gain from such a diagnosis. She was prevented from ruling, and everything she said was roundly dismissed.

'Do you think Joanna was crazy?' she asks Pauli as he picks up his school bag, in no rush to get to Period Three.

'Obviously,' he exclaims. 'She full slept beside her dead husband and there would have been maggots and did you know that when you die you shit yourself?'

She does know that. But she also knows what 'embalming' means and that his body would not have been crawling with maggots.

'I think we should always be sceptical of men who call women crazy,' she says, opening up the spreadsheet she's been neglecting.

He looks at her blankly. 'Miss, can we play Scrabble next time?' He has spotted the box on the top shelf.

'Yes. As long as we get all this testing out of the way.' In front of her is a notepad with random numbers, times belonging to different students.

'Okay, bye, Miss,' he says, sidestepping Mr Pappas on his way out the door.

Elias sticks his head in briefly. He asks how she's going and why Shardae retold him a story about some queen who continued to have sex with her dead husband.

'Okay, well, that's not what happened. What's scarier is that Shardae thought the word "queen" started with the letter K. And then when we got to Philip the Handsome she made us Google his portrait and said he looked like a deflated ballsack.'

'Well. I think that sounds a lot like an engaged student. And "like a deflated ballsack"? Isn't that a simile?' he says, impressed.

They talk a little about the testing. The results were meant to be submitted by last Friday, but a few students have been absent so she managed to negotiate an extension until today, the second-last day of the school year. She doesn't tell Elias what, exactly, she's finding so difficult.

'You weren't at the Christmas party on Friday night,' he says, crossing his arms.

Something Bad is Going to Happen

She had, for a moment, intended to go. On Friday morning she'd assured him she'd be there. But as the day went on she was struck by a feeling that was beginning to plague her even more than usual, a returning sense that something very bad was going to happen. Sometimes in the mornings she could keep her fixation on badness at bay, but as the day went on, it leaked and it permeated every thought. She could think only of bad things that have happened and the bad things that will happen. It was as though badness was tar that ran through her veins and poisoned her bloodstream. But it was also a tumour in her chest that grew and grew and grew until traces of it could be found in her arms and legs.

As she drove home on Friday afternoon, slipping away as the women touched up their make-up and the men cracked open beers dripping with condensation, she thought about how people didn't seem to realise how distressing it was to have stopped enjoying the things that previously brought you joy. Can one even imagine a worse predicament? It's a laughable irony, an unsolvable riddle. She had moved so far past *I would be happy if* . . . Instead she had landed in the territory of *I have no capacity to be happy*. Not if she won the lottery or fell in love or buried her toes in the sandy beaches of Santorini. Her joylessness was terminal.

She fumbles through an excuse about a migraine and then he asks if she gets migraines and she has to pretend that, yes, migraines are a problem she has.

'Good luck with it all,' he says, referring to the migraines but also the testing, and turns to leave. 'Always just shout if you need a hand.'

She feels like her insides are exposed, her lie about migraines transparent. People must be able to see right through her.

It's 11.57 am and she has until the final bell to submit the results. Pauli was her last session for the day.

Spreadsheet. She has the numbers on her notepad. Pauli. Three minutes eleven seconds. Yes. But how many words had he read correctly? Where had she written that down? She flips through the notebook. Sees a number in a different-coloured pen. That must have been from Friday. Or Thursday. Then she reads the time, two minutes forty-nine, but no name. Fifty-one words, but no time. The spreadsheet blinks at her. She isn't sure she did it correctly last time. How is it possible that Pauli's last time was one minute fifty-five? Had she really gone through all the cards? Or maybe this was the idea. That the students take longer as the words get harder. She clicks the cell next to Shardae's name. Fuck it. She types three minutes. Well, that looks too neat. Three minutes and four seconds. But something gnaws at her gut. What happens if the students appear to have performed *too well* in the test? She remembers Michelle, Mrs Birmingham, saying something about how there was a waitlist for kids to do the program, so if anyone outperformed they'd be replaced. But then, she supposes, if they perform too badly it will look like the program isn't working at all. Like she is a useless teacher. She can't fudge the numbers.

She opens her emails. Reads the newsletter then checks a few homepages. She cleans her desk. Taps mindlessly on her phone under her desk in case the librarian can see her.

After an hour or so she goes for a walk to nowhere but ends up

in the staffroom making a cup of tea she has no interest in drinking. Her hands are shaking. One of her students, Angelique, is
staring at her from the noticeboard. She's one of the kids with
a peanut allergy, so her school photo hangs with instructions
about how to administer an EpiPen. She thinks about Angelique
always turning up on time, her studiousness despite how hard she
finds English. She feels light-headed. How monumentally she has
let these sixteen kids down. A job she had felt overqualified for,
harbouring an air of superiority because she had spent more years
at university than most of the people here, and she couldn't fill
out a fucking spreadsheet.

She hurries back up to her tiny room, smelling the dampness
as she enters. December has so far been humid and wet. Through
lunch, she types and deletes, types and deletes, trying to enter the
formula of time, words read correctly, and level of improvement.
She considers asking Elias for help, confessing what she's done,
but surely he would be as horrified as anyone else.

She is paid a salary to test and record results. For a year this
had been part of her PhD work, complex graphs and statistics.
The work had once been seamless.

The books on the shelf need rearranging. Maybe in alphabetical
order. As she sorts, she thinks, trying to problem-solve. Could she
pretend her computer broke? The results disappeared into the ether.
Once she's finished, she spends some time researching how her
computer might self-combust, and how this would result in losing
critical documents. Too complicated. She can't follow the instructions and the spreadsheet is shared in some drive. Impossible to lose.

As the clouds open up and the handball courts are pummelled

with rain, she holds her jacket up over her head and jogs to her car. The drops are heavy and biting, and she feels permission to cry, although the tears won't fall. As she slips into her front seat, resting her head on the wheel, she knows she won't ever see Pauli or Shardae or Angelique again. Elias will probably wonder for a day or two where she went, and then get on with his own life, forgetting a person named Adella, short with dark hair, ever worked at St Francis.

An odd thing happens as she drives in the direction of home. Pauli, doing that signal with his fingers and saying the word 'loco' plays on loop in her head. It's like she can feel Pauli's hands conducting some sort of electrical current through her temples and she can see him doing it again and then again. She sees the sky crack, lightning shattering the grey overhead, and then comes the bang, like a clap right beside her ear. It's happening out there, on the other side of her windscreen, but it's also happening inside, within her own skull.

Summer is erupting into a storm and a storm is erupting between her ears.

Inexplicable pain surges through her body and her thoughts go to places she can't follow. Just like with a storm, she thinks, this cannot get any louder. The pressure cannot increase any more. The disturbance is surely at a crescendo.

And after the storm, she hopes, a deathly quiet will finally fall.

32

Adella

A week ago

She opens her eyes. Doesn't know where she is. Too much light. She groans and closes her eyes again, but senses someone close. In the same room. Muttering. Footsteps. An unfamiliar smell.

She rolls to her left and sees a wall the colour of sick. Her back is sticky with sweat. The blanket is too heavy. She kicks it off and turns to her right. A woman, maybe in her mid-thirties, is dressed as though she's about to go to work. She is wearing tailored black pants, a white button-up shirt and black shoes that might be orthopaedic. Her hair is long and straight, hanging down the length of her spine, tied loosely at the base of her neck.

'Abigail,' the woman says, pretending she's not been staring in Adella's direction.

'I'm Adella.' Her voice is gravelly from not having used it in a while.

Abigail's bed linen looks like it was brought from home, two decorative purple pillows with suns on them, and a brand-new teddy that looks like it was purchased from downstairs. Beside her is an overflowing plastic bag, full of clothes and shoes and a few bottles of Coca-Cola.

They hear a thud.

'John,' an accented voice says faintly, full of exasperation.

'Not again,' Abigail tuts, heading towards the door.

'What happened?' Adella asks. She can hear the moans of someone in pain.

'It's John. He throws himself out of bed every morning. He'll break a hip. The man must be sixty-five. Seventy. If he breaks a hip . . .' She starts speaking under her breath again, barely audible. 'The data on patients over the age of sixty with a hip fracture . . . the mortality rates . . . and if he manages to survive, his quality of life . . .' She turns and makes her way down the hall.

Adella looks up at the off-white ceiling and tries to put together the last few days. Her memories return to her like snippets of dreams she can't quite reach. The brightness of the ambulance. Knowing she'd done something stupid. A young man who asked questions, who sat beside her stretcher. Then Emergency; a flash of the noise, of feeling claustrophobic. Nurses and doctors and clipboards and Velcro around her arm. Her mum. Pale. Pyjama pants. Half a conversation with a doctor she knew she needed to follow but couldn't. Repeating herself. But the words weren't coming out right. Slipping into disturbed sleep.

She squeezes her eyes shut, trying to remember. There are black swirls where the rest of her memory belongs. She's back in her bedroom. No chronology. The bathroom cabinet. Yes, she remembers that. Taking whatever is there. How much? She isn't counting. Gagging. They feel caught in her chest. Her body says no more but she is in a trance. Pill. Gulp. Pill. Gulp. She's shivering and retching. Just one more.

Her mouth is dry and tastes metallic, the lingering sense of something she doesn't recognise. She feels drowsy and disoriented. She strains her ears to hear the murmurings of next door.

'John, you mustn't.' It's Abigail's voice. 'Look at all these people who care about you.' She must be pointing at something. 'Don't disappoint them, John.'

He groans in response. 'All right, Abigail, that's enough. Let's just leave John to rest,' a nurse says firmly.

For the next few hours, she drifts in and out of sleep. There is some relief in lying in a hospital bed, nurses on duty, a plastic band around her right wrist, a doctor wearing a collared shirt walking down the hallway. For the first time her environment feels appropriate – it matches the gravity of what is happening to her. She is sick, with what she is not quite sure. But what right does she have to be anywhere but in this hospital bed, without car keys or access to her phone, quarantined from those whose lives she so mercilessly disrupts?

When she next wakes it is to the sound of a nurse entering her room.

She takes a seat in the chair sitting between her bed and Abigail's, and introduces herself as Cathy.

'We've had a rough few days, have we love?' she asks, leaning backwards as though to make room for Adella's response.

Adella nods. Something about this setting makes her feel like a child.

'Well, the good news is you're in the right place. And I am here for anything you need. Always just shout out. And you will feel like a different person by the time you leave, trust me on that.' She looks like she believes it.

She slaps her thighs and stands back up, but Adella finds herself with a question.

'Can I just ask,' her voice is quiet and apologetic, 'how . . .' She can't find the right way to phrase it.

Cathy sits back down.

'If I'm a sick person. How is a sick person meant to cure their own illness?' She looks desperately into the nurse's eyes, realising that that's the difference between this ward and all the others. How does one think themselves out of madness? There is no surgery to be performed or chemotherapy to be administered. She is in hospital and yet it is not like being in hospital at all.

'Oh, love.' She smiles. 'Who said anything about you curing your own illness? You're going to have so much help, and the psychiatrist, Dr Black, he is going to make sure he gets you the best medicine . . .'

'But I'm already on medication.' Her voice shakes. 'It made me sick, I vomited and I fainted and I felt worse than before. It didn't work.'

'I understand. But you know what the advantage of trying a new medication in here is?' Cathy says, moving closer as though it's a secret between the two of them. 'We monitor you. Closely. We don't let you get sick. We can tweak your dosage and give you something if you feel unwell. If one doesn't work for you – that's not a problem. We try another.' She shrugs.

Adella rubs her eyes. 'I'm so tired,' she says, holding back tears.

'Of course you're tired! You'd be exhausted.' She pauses. 'You know, I've given birth to five babies. And people will often say childbirth is the most painful thing a person can experience, which is true,' she laughs. 'But even with childbirth, there is relief between contractions, where suddenly you're yourself again and you can breathe, even though you know there's another contraction around the corner.

'I look at people in this ward, in Ward C, who have depression or anxiety or, you know, schizophrenia, even issues with addiction, and I think, *You poor things. How long has it been since you've had any relief?* Getting through the day can feel like running a goddamn marathon on a broken leg.'

Cathy stands again. 'You'll get out the other side of this. But it won't be through grit – trying to push through something that feels too heavy with gritted teeth. It will be through grace.'

Not by grit but by grace. It sounds like something from the Bible, but there is something about the sentiment Adella likes. She repeats the words in her head until she slips into a dreamless sleep.

*

When she first sits across from Dr Black, she hates him. His legs are crossed and something about his active listening seems contrived, like he is performing choreography he was explicitly taught. Her eyes are fixed on the angry blister beneath his lip.

'What's going on for you?' he asks.

She can barely hold her body upright. But she knows exactly what she wants to say. It is all she can think about in that stiff bed, with pillows that feel they're fitted with cardboard.

Is this all? Because this is nothing like I was promised.

In my parents I see the parts of myself I loathe the most. My mother is full of neuroticism and self-pity. I can see it is unattractive and yet I see it in my own reflection. My dad abandons things whenever they become hard. He is selfish and cruel and he doesn't have a single friend because he isn't deserving of one. I see that in my reflection, too.

So there is my destiny. Which one might I choose?

What is going on for me, she wants to repeat, raising her eyebrows. I am angry. The kind of anger that makes you laugh. I hate the men I wish loved me. It is all I have ever wanted. Nathan. Mike. Even Luis, after one night. Half a dozen men I've met on apps who were one person when we met, and another just a few weeks later. They have lied to me, manipulated me, hurt me, used my body as though it was soulless and made of cold, hard stone rather than soft, warm flesh. Every relationship has been built on empty promises; a reminder of my own worthlessness. You cannot tell me that dating is the same for men, she wants to say. You cannot. It is the man who decides when sex begins and when it finishes. The man who has no timeline, no sense of when this bullshit game of musical chairs should end. Their emotional unavailability is met with my own emotional desperation, made more so by a series of senseless rejections. It is enough to make anyone go mad. To be told one thing to your face by a person who might disappear. Who will probably disappear. The inhumanity of it all. What do we do when we sleep with someone or we go out on a fucking date or we swipe or we text? We ask them to love us. It is not an obligation. It is not even an expectation. But to respond to that request with silence is a form of psychological torture that I cannot resolve within my own head.

Do you think there is such thing as 'almost rape'? she wants to ask. Consent you give but don't feel? Sex that is wrong but isn't criminal? A traumatic sexual experience without a rapist? Why haven't we come up with a word for that? Perhaps because for some women, for me, it is virtually all I know of sex. A thing indistinguishable from pain and degradation.

She looks around at the sad room. Vertical blinds that look like they were once white but are now almost yellow hang from the window. A silver filing cabinet sits beside Dr Black's desk, with a plant on top that looks to be made out of plastic. She stares at the painting just to the right of his head. It's abstract, but not in a beautiful way. It reminds her of bushland, burnt to a crisp.

'I don't know,' she says. 'I feel, um. Numb. I guess.'

What is going on for me, the voice inside her asks again. I was meant to be something. I did everything I was supposed to. I've worked since I was fourteen. I worked forty-five hours in a week when most other kids went to Schoolies and spent their parents' money. I studied and I studied and I suspected I was clever but I never dared say that out loud. Not like the boys I met at university who announced it before I had even taken my seat beside them. They declared their marks and their scholarships as badges of honour whereas I had to bury mine deep in my pocket, lest anyone think I was arrogant. Arrogant. I have bitten my tongue and hidden my successes, and yet I have been called arrogant more times than I can count. People hate me because I try but I have no choice. Back then, I wanted to try.

It was my one 'gift' – a stupid word but apt because it connotes that something was magic about it. I worked hard, but I worked hard at it because it felt like magic. I won awards and scholarships and all I wanted was to work inside the walls of these prestigious academies that are full of people nothing like me.

But then. She wants to snap her fingers. Like that. *Try now*, my brain whispered. *Who are you now? What are you without this? If you are not the person who can write and win then who might you be?* I never should have had to find out who.

What's going on for me? Her jaw tenses. She watches as Dr Black scribbles something in his notebook.

I spend most of my life scrolling but barely tapping on an aluminium alloy brick designed to addict me.

I grew up on the internet where I was told by strangers that I was ugly before I thought it about myself.

What makes you an adult, exactly? Savings? A house? A husband? Kids? Stability? Purpose? Knowing how to cook? I have none of that.

What's going on for me?

Time has already started to speed up. You know how that happens. When you're five, a year is a fifth of your life. At twenty-five, it's one twenty-fifth. Christmas comes faster and summer lasts just the blink of an eye and everything goes faster and faster and faster until youth disappears and your knees are arthritic and your family has died and you live haunted by regret.

What's going on for me?

There is nothing in here. She wants to beat her chest. It is empty. I am empty. Everyone always talks about finding themselves. I think I am meant to create myself. I don't know what I like or dislike, what I value, what I stand for.

I am ambivalent to being alive.

I inherited this brain.

That is part of what is going on for me, she thinks, tired.

When we are sick, we feel something a healthy person cannot imagine. Can pain ever be understood by someone who is not currently feeling it?

'I see. Below the numbness there's often a lot going on. It can mask feelings of overwhelm . . .' he explains, trying to maintain eye contact. Her eyes dart back to the painting.

She knows he cannot understand. She swallows. And then repeats, 'Yeah. I don't know. Maybe . . . maybe I'm angry?'

The words come out like a question.

33

Adella

Present

On Tuesday the first of January she has two visitors, neither of whom she expects.

It has been twelve days since she first arrived on Ward C. Sophia has visited twice, bringing snacks Adella doesn't feel like. She doesn't know what to say, so often they sit in comfortable silence. Sometimes she asks if Adella feels tired, or if medication makes her feel weird. She occasionally asks Adella if she's starting to feel better. Sophia sees Adella's suffering, appreciating perhaps for the first time the gravity of it. Here, Adella's distress has a diagnosis.

Her mother comes every day, attempting small talk about the food or group therapy or what movies they've been watching. Lottie sometimes comes with her. She has a fractured memory of Lottie the day after her admission. Everything is hazy; she kept forgetting where she was, tormented by nightmares telling her she was in hospital, only to wake and discover they weren't nightmares at all.

Her body felt numb that day, as though it was floating above her bed. She saw Lottie, alone, moving towards her, an unreadable expression on her face. Adella wanted her to sit, or to climb into her bed beside her, but she did neither. Instead, Lottie stood with her arms crossed and spoke to her through gritted teeth.

She listed all the things she'd do to make Adella's pain go away. How she'd give all her money, trade her happiness for Adella's sadness, offer her a bed in her home, leave her fiancé, quit her job. Anything. Her voice shook with anger.

'We would do anything,' Lottie said, almost a whisper, the 'we' inferring their mother this time, rather than Clinton.

She didn't have the energy to plead with her not to be angry, to explain that Lottie's pain was precisely why she thought the best thing she could do for the people she loved was to not be here anymore. She didn't want to die, she wanted to tell Lottie. All she wanted was for the pain to stop. To rest, just for a moment.

There was something else she noticed that day with Lottie. She looked different. It wasn't just that she appeared tired, her skin grey and her hair unwashed. There was something Adella couldn't put her finger on. When Lottie finally left, her gait seemed slightly off centre. As though she too were in pain.

A few days in, she received a phone call at eight in the evening on the ward landline. She couldn't imagine who it might be, until her right hand held the receiver and she knew immediately.

'Pa?'

Since then, he has called every night. They speak about big things, like 'the desire to become oneself' as he puts it, and the small things, like how he's started receiving unusual phone calls from a bloke overseas who wants to help with his internet, but for some reason wants his bank details. Between them, their lives are just big enough to sustain a conversation. She finds herself thinking about that phone call throughout the day, making note of things she wants to tell him.

The first visitor that day is Elias. Two days before he had sent flowers along with a small card that simply read, 'Get better soon. We want to see you next year. Elias X.' She assumed 'we' included her schoolkids and it had delivered a pang of guilt deep in her gut. But by the time Elias left, it appeared the 'we' meant mostly 'I'. Perhaps what he was trying to say was, 'I want to see you next year'.

He arrives just after ten, his body moving with the energy and agility of someone who does not belong here.

'Well, look who it is!' he says as he wanders towards the couches, where she sits reading a novel Abigail lent her, with a plot she can't follow and with characters whose names she can't remember.

'Elias.' Her eyes are wide with shock and she considers immediately how awful she must look, her hair tied back tightly, her washed-out skin emphasising the dark circles beneath her eyes. She may be in a psychiatric unit, but that does not mean she isn't aware that her eyebrows need a pluck and her legs need a shave. She feels relief that today she is wearing loose, long pants.

'Is now an okay time?' he asks, as though sending him home is a choice. She feels another wave of relief that she brushed her teeth this morning. He stares at her closely for a second or two, in the way men sometimes do, perhaps realising this is the first time he has seen her without any make-up on.

'Yeah. Ah, I don't have an appointment until eleven. Shouldn't you be at work, though?' She double-checks the clock on the wall.

'Given it's New Year's Day, absolutely not,' he says, and looks at her, slightly confused. 'I thought I'd like to come and see where you're hanging out.'

She thinks about last New Year's Day. Terrible. She was mostly curled up in bed after drinking too much with Mele at some depressing house party the night before. Then two years before that, Jake. They'd spent the day in his backyard, her a blow-in at a family barbecue. Even then, he'd seemed himself.

As though reading her mind he adds, 'Your mother called the school the day after everything happened, to explain why you weren't in. She left her number and I called her back.'

She squeezes her eyes shut, mortified that the school knows.

'Are you sure it's okay that I'm here? Sorry . . . I did try to message but I'm guessing you don't have your phone.'

She notices Abigail watching from the doorway of their room, and Kirra staring at them from a table a few metres away where she has paused in doing her puzzle. Even John is eyeing them from his wheelchair.

'Can we sit outside?' She leads Elias to the courtyard, grass seared by the heat, and they sit side by side on a metal bench.

'I'm just really embarrassed,' she says slowly, staring straight ahead.

'What, why?' His expression is curious and Adella recalls that last term he was out for a day at one of those mental health courses. They probably taught him the exact spiel to give and the precise questions to ask.

'Because I'm in here?' she says, matching his confusion.

'Nah, none of that. You're not well so you're getting better. Can I just say something really selfish for a sec?' He swallows. She nods.

'I wish you'd said something on that Monday. I knew you weren't yourself. Next time, please, just say something?'

They sit in silence for a moment.

'I care more than you think I do.' He taps the side of her knee with his.

She smiles. Her lips feel dry and tight.

Before he leaves he stands with his hands in his pockets and says he wishes he could message her whenever he wanted. She likes that. When he puts his arms around her he smells like clean washing and sunscreen. She can feel his stubble against her ear, only for a second, but it signals something. This man, with his car keys and sunglasses in his pocket, his job and his lean legs, is a Grown-Up. He does not want to message her one day and then delete her number the next. He is not attempting to come across as cooler than he is.

He does not see Adella as an empty sack of flesh, worthy of being spoken to only when she's underneath him, her clothes in a bundle in the corner of the room. He doesn't want to hold her down but instead to sit beside her. What's the difference? she wonders. It might be that this person likes her, yes. But it's more than that. He respects her. Has she ever been able to say that before?

Her appointment with Dr Black that day is mostly about the medication. Her dreams are vivid, full of apocalyptic images like tsunamis wiping out whole cities and earthquakes where she falls into the cracks. She wakes dripping in sweat, she tells him. But otherwise, she is able to sleep, which is an obvious improvement. She has begun to wake and rise without a nurse having to check on her. She is eating again, a little bit, and the nausea she experienced a week ago has subsided.

After lunch there is a mindfulness session, all about alleviating anxiety with three deep breaths. She does her best, but can never seem to get the pacing right, breathing out when the instructor says to breathe in. The focus brings on discomfort, and she is overcome by the knowledge that she is not doing this right. Twice she nearly leaves the room, her hands shaking, red in the face from concentration. She is light-headed from focusing too much on her inhale and exhale, seemingly doing both at the same time. As the voice in her head shouts at itself on a loop that it must shut up, she remembers something Dr Black said about perfectionism. She is a perfectionist, and as a result she is always at war with herself.

'I'm not a perfectionist,' she corrected him. 'Perfectionists always brush their hair and make their beds.' She didn't know if she was joking anymore.

'It's not as simple as that,' he laughed.

'A perfectionist never completes anything,' he said, without knowing she has never finished her PhD.

'A perfectionist has no self-worth distinct from their external achievements,' he said, without knowing how she'd worked for awards, for the gratification of knowing who she was existed on paper.

'And perfectionists have no self-compassion. So they're angry. They're furious with themselves,' he said, without knowing how desperately she wanted to scream and punch and bite and kick and spit.

The following day Cathy coaxes her into a guided meditation session. It is run by a woman named Stacey she hasn't seen before, with a messy bun full of grey streaks. She speaks too quietly and seems to be comfortable sitting cross-legged which Adella has never understood. It makes her hips hurt. She assures herself, as she tries to get comfortable, eventually lying flat on her back, that if she is bad at this, that would be okay. It turns out she is bad. Very bad. She keeps opening her eyes and trying to solve problems and the chattering in her head is so loud she can barely hear what Stacey is saying. That makes her angry. And she realises she is very bad at being bad at this. And for a moment, that makes her smile.

When she leaves the session, a woman with shoulder-length dark hair is sitting in the common room. Adella doesn't recognise her at first. She can tell even from a distance how frail she is. A handbag sits on her lap and she is taking in the room, glancing from her left to her right, until she spots Adella behind her.

Grey hair now frames her face and the lines around her eyes

and mouth have deepened. Her cheeks are gaunt and her hands bony. Her blouse hangs from sharp shoulders. Adella knows that expression, though, a smile that leaves a dimple only on the left. It's Annie.

They speak at one of the white, square tables, where Adella usually sits at mealtimes. Sitting opposite each other, the dynamic feels a little like she is a prison inmate, being visited by someone not entirely comfortable being there. Annie's clasped hands sit on the table in front of her, and she clears her throat.

'Are you feeling any better?'

'A bit,' Adella says, not meeting her eye.

'You can't do that to your mother.' Annie speaks quickly and clearly. Her eye twitches. Rage, perhaps.

'I know. I won't do it again, I'm so sorry.' She fixes her gaze on her foot, tapping the table leg below.

'I've actually been meaning to speak to you. For a while now.' She rifles through her handbag, which is still resting in her lap. Adella wonders if she's nervous someone might steal it.

'Oh?' Adella responds. She had been waiting for the questions. For the blame she deserves. A scolding from a furious mother who wants to know why her son died, and where his best friend was.

Annie nods. Pauses before she hands over an envelope. It has already been opened, but its contents remain inside.

She rubs her lips with her thumb. 'Did you know he had applied to a university course?'

Adella's instinct is to lie. To shake her head. But she cannot find the energy. Instead, she nods silently.

'A month or so after he died, a letter came. We were so confused. No one from our family has ever been to university.' She points at the stamp in the top right-hand corner. 'We didn't know what they'd want with Jake.'

Adella pulls out the crumpled letter, folded in three.

'I didn't want to open it because it was addressed to Jake. But Sam did, in the end.'

Slowly, Adella turns it over. Unfolds the letter, an ache in her chest as she does. Her eyes find the first sentence. The shape of the word 'congratulations'. The word 'successful'. Now she draws her hand to her mouth.

'What?' Her mind tries to solve a puzzle. 'But I thought . . . It doesn't make sense.' Annie looks at her, her expression soft.

Adella continues, 'I assumed he wasn't – that he wasn't accepted and that's why it all happened. I just don't understand.' She shakes her head in bewilderment.

'He had so much to live for,' Annie says, leaning forward. She places her index finger on the letter. 'This is what happens when you stick around. This is what could be waiting around the corner. And Jake never got to learn that.'

She thinks for a moment, looking up towards the ceiling.

'When you die, Adella, you don't exist. The lights are out. No one is sending postcards saying "Wish You Were Here". Even if they were, you don't receive them. Your life,' she looks around the room, as though trying to find the words, 'does not just belong to you. That decision destroys families. They never, ever recover. It is the worst thing you can do to the people who love you.'

Adella nods, knowing that if she speaks she will cry.

'You are so, so lucky that you're here. Not everyone gets a second chance.' Annie's tone is stern but not cruel.

They sit in silence for a while.

'What do you think it meant,' Adella asks, unable to look Annie in the eye, 'that he stopped going to church?'

Annie exhales and considers the question for a moment. 'I've thought about that a lot. I tried to push it the first few times, but he was an adult who was allowed to make his own decisions. I think . . . I think he was disconnecting. It was the only thing that saved us after Malcolm died. We were so angry and deep in grief, you never get over that, but there was a sense that someone, somewhere had a plan, I suppose. As though there was some sort of larger meaning even if we didn't fully understand it.'

She looks at the wall to the right of Adella's head. 'But for him to disengage, that meant he was starting to believe that there was no one there watching him. That there was no plan. That everything that happens is random and pointless and it would've left him believing that he was it. No meaning extended beyond him. Is there a more depressing thought than that, I wonder?' It's a question, but she does not expect an answer.

'I keep having this memory of Jake as a kid. He might have been four or five and we were at that park up the road with the, what do you call it, jungle gym thing. With the ropes. It was a broken arm waiting to happen,' she smiles. 'And if he could see me watching, he'd climb and climb, craning his neck every step of the way making sure I was still there if anything went wrong. If I went to push Paul on the swing or change Sam's nappy, he would just stop. Or he'd slowly make his way back down and sit in the sand below. He could only keep climbing if he felt there was someone watching him, ready to run over if he slipped. Maybe when he stopped going to church it meant he felt no one was watching him. No one should ever have to live like that.'

After a while, Annie stands up and places her handbag over her shoulder.

'Did you want this back?' Adella holds out the letter.

'No, no. You keep that.' She smiles with that same dimple.

Annie hugs her as she leaves, whispers to her to take care of herself. As she walks through the glass doors, Adella wonders how someone like that, who has endured such loss, can wake up in the morning, and put one foot down on the floor, and then the other.

How she can get into the car, drive to a facility like this, and tell Adella what she never got to tell her son?

Some people are made of different stuff, she thinks.

Or perhaps, more terrifyingly, they're made of the same stuff. And still, they find a way to survive.

34

Adella

The night before Adella is discharged, she shakes with such intensity that Abigail notices.

Adella hears Abigail dramatically grunt before calling Cathy's name, loudly enough to wake up the rest of the ward.

Cathy appears beside her bed, her spine always straight, her eyes always cheerful.

'Hey, hey,' she says, looking towards Adella's legs trembling under her white blanket. She places a hand gently on her upper arm.

'Can you talk to me? What's going through that head, love?' she whispers.

She's panicking. She feels like she went into hospital for surgery, for some procedure that never took place. And now they're sending her home with a few Panadol and their fingers crossed. She doesn't know how to articulate any of that, so instead she says, 'What are you meant to do when you've run out of dreams?'

'As in dreams in your sleep? Sometimes we just don't remember them . . .'

'No. I mean dreams. Ambitions. The wanting of something. What are you meant to do when that disappears?' She is shaking as though she is cold, but she can feel sweat settling under her arms.

'That's okay, hey. Don't force it. You're still recovering. This isn't going to happen overnight.'

Adella wonders if saying any of this will make the staff concerned. If they might decide against sending her home. Does she want that?

'When you're sick, you know you're sick,' Adella whispers, thinking out loud. 'All you want is to get better. But this is different. Being in here,' she looks at Cathy, 'sometimes it's like sickness is the truth and health was always an illusion. Does that make sense?'

She can tell Cathy doesn't understand.

'The last six months, when things have been really bad, it's almost like I can finally see clearly. And before, everything was blurry. I might be depressed and I might be in here, but I'm still convinced I'm right. How I see things is right,' she says. 'Everyone will die. That's just the truth. There is no inherent meaning. No grand plan and there's no god looking out for us. That's all just made up by people who know that without those delusions none of us would ever do anything. We'd all just be lying here, in a bed like this.' Her voice is hushed but emphatic.

Cathy leans in, gets down onto her knees and rests her forearms on the bed.

'We had a man in here a little while ago. He had survived a suicide attempt. He was in his house, preparing to end it all, I think he was in the garage. His wife had left, taken the kids – probably for good reason – but he felt he had nothing to live for.

'So he is in his garage and he hears scratching against the door. At first he said he was irritated that anything would interrupt what he was in the middle of, you know? But for whatever reason, he opened the door. And sitting there were his two labradors, with their big brown eyes. He told me he knew exactly what they were saying. They were asking, "Why would you leave us?"

'Instead he called his brother and sat with the dogs until his brother could get there. He spent a few weeks here. Was an absolute mess when he arrived. But he saw Dr Black, got his medication sorted and started some kind of therapy. He still had work to do once he left, we all knew that.' She says the last sentence like it's an inevitability she isn't altogether comfortable with.

'I ran into him just recently and he looked like a different person. He was walking those two dogs, actually. He told me he now has shared custody of the kids. Got back into surfing, he's out there every day. Even has a new girlfriend which he was pretty excited about.'

Adella is quiet. She has been confronted with a memory her mind did not know it had stored. It's the sound of Jack's scratching. The way his nails had clawed at her closed door that night in a way he had never done before, whimpering and even daring to bark. Perhaps he had heard unusual noises. Or could sense she was just on the other side, lying on the floor, within arm's length and yet not bothering to stroke his head or rub his stomach.

'What no one bloody tells you,' Cathy whispers, leaning in closer, 'is that people get better. Every day. And you will look back on how you feel right now and not be able to believe it. Do you trust me?'

Adella nods. She trusts Cathy, even if right now she doesn't entirely believe what she says.

'You call out if you're having a rough night, okay? I'm here. I can make you a cup of tea or we can chat or just sit here together. Sometimes, you've just got to get through the night, got it?' She stands back up, groaning a little from the stiffness of her knees.

Adella tries to sleep after that. She shuts her eyes and counts backwards from one hundred. But after a few minutes she is drawn to the sound of a woman's voice, sharp and high-pitched. The sense she has that what she can hear is a scolding is confirmed by the words that begin to float into the room.

She listens to the Nurse Unit Manager, a prickly woman named Jenny, interrogate Cathy about where she's been, why her night-time rounds haven't yet been completed.

Cathy's voice is hushed, and Adella can only make out certain words. She thinks she hears 'patient in distress', but the Nurse Unit Manager interrupts. She taps away on a keyboard and explains that Cathy has more than one patient to take care of. That the ward is at capacity. Something about paperwork. How the whole ward suffers if Cathy keeps 'disappearing'.

As Adella drifts off she thinks about the nature of psychiatric care. How with medication and nightly checks they can be made to feel more like bodies than minds. While Dr Black has monitored her dosage, it is Cathy who has sat by her bedside, looked at her with tenderness and empathy, offered words that might have just saved her life. And yet Cathy is paid the same as Sal and Martina and Vlad, presumably less than Jenny, none of whom know her name and all of whom look like they'd prefer to be anywhere else. Martina visibly rolls her eyes when a patient calls for help, and spends most of her shifts telling anyone who will listen that she's doing a double and hasn't had enough sleep.

How bizarre it is, Adella thinks, that when we are ill – as she has been told she is – we are sent to institutions that smell like disinfectant and powdered eggs. We are given food that is neither appetising nor nutritious, and sleep in beds beside strangers who often can't sleep themselves, so are kept awake by screaming or tapping or footsteps wandering down the hall.

Funny, she thinks. These places are designed to make you better, but if you put a sane person in here, wouldn't it make them sick?

The next morning she wakes up groggy. At a table alone she butters herself a slice of stale, cold toast and feels relieved she has no appetite.

It is mid-morning when her mother arrives, beaming in the way a parent of a twenty-nine-year-old leaving a psychiatric unit has no right to be smiling. She helps Adella pack up her things, her pillow from home under her arm, and everything confiscated now returned.

Cathy had left a few hours before, laughing, 'I hope I don't see you again!'

The nurses on duty smile at Adella as though she is leaving because she is well enough, not simply because they need the bed.

Her mother drives them both to the house she grew up in. Some of her things are back in her childhood bedroom, while the rest sit awkwardly in the living room. She knew that her mother had spoken to Mele and Helen, offering to pay two weeks of Adella's rent, explaining that after that she'd be moving back home for a while. They understood. Her room had already been filled.

And so she returns to the home she had left, realising as she places her duffel bag down onto her bed that she was only ever cosplaying adulthood. The job she couldn't do. The rent she could barely pay. The relationships that never amounted to anything. It was all pretend adulthood, landing her back into a state of parental dependence.

In Ward C she sensed she was living on the edge of civilisation. But back at home it is like being sent to purgatory, where time elapses yet you cannot move, reduced to an eternity of adolescence.

35

Adella

Elias is the one who suggests the beach.

Thursday is set to be hot, thirty-four degrees, and most Sydneysiders have been forced back into their air-conditioned offices for the year.

She wakes just after nine and spends the morning doing what she supposes has become her new routine over the last two weeks. She stumbles into the shower. Butters some toast with Vegemite. Opens her backpack and collects her Speedos, goggles, a towel, sunscreen and a book Pa recommended called *Man's Search for Meaning*. She pulls up by the cafe on the corner for a takeaway coffee, pays with the very little money still sitting in her bank account, before driving the fifteen minutes to Crest Park Pool. There, she sits on the grass for a while, feeling the sun warm up her limbs and watching teenagers still on school holidays bomb into the shallow end, beside a big black sign that reads 'No

Bombing In Pool'. A lifeguard steps forward, a whistle between her lips, then decides it isn't worth it. The water glistens in a way it only can when the sun is unobscured, reflecting a cloudless blue sky.

She eases herself in and swims lap after lap, the first few always the hardest, then her body adopts a rhythm that feels hypnotic. Stroke. Stroke. Stroke. Breathe. Repeat. She thinks of nothing in particular, every now and then focusing on the kicking of her feet or the lift of her hips. There are moments where she feels like she is gliding, her arms and legs and neck and breath working in effortless harmony. When she feels tired or her shoulders ache, she stops for a while, enjoying the sensation of being submerged in water, her body weightless. The colourful swim flags hanging above make her think of Sophia, of the swim classes Sophia's mother used to take them to on weekday evenings in high school. Sophia could always swim slightly faster, slightly further, placing in all her races at the swimming carnival. Might I beat her now? Adella wonders, before stopping herself. That is no longer the point.

And so she swims until her lungs demand more air. She reads for a while, understanding why Pa recommended this particular book.

He quoted a poem to her over the phone last night that he'd recently come across, which he said put into words how he'd so often felt. She'd later found it online. The stanza by Akif Kichloo read:

'When I see a rat I see a rodent,
When I see a sparrow I see extinction,

When I see a lion I see death
When I see myself, I see a monster.'

She had smiled in recognition as Pa had recited the words. We
see what we see. She could no sooner train herself to see good
when there was bad, than train herself to see a yellow sky when
it was so clearly blue. For a while she thought it was just her who
only saw extinction and death and monsters. Perhaps that had
been why she'd felt so close to Jake; because he'd seen it all too.
And now there was Pa.

He was plagued by the same fears. He felt the emptiness in
his chest and at times had felt the absence of a soul, just as she
had. He knew what it was to move from pain to pain, as William
Styron had put it. To know, as much as a person can ever know
anything, that no remedy would come.

'For a long time,' he said to her one evening, reflecting on
his Christian faith and how it had at times encouraged self-
flagellation, 'I truly believed there was something virtuous in
suffering.' He spoke slowly and carefully.

'But now, now I'm not so sure. Suffering can provide insight.
But suffering without,' he searched for the right phrase, 'without
real *reason* for suffering. There is nothing virtuous about that.'

She had wondered this too. If her sadness had come with a
hint of self-importance, even arrogance. Her pain, she felt, had
meant she could see more, not less. But what rewards had that
left her with?

They spoke about her medication, which did, on the surface,
seem to be working. But did the medication make her more

herself or less? Did it numb her from feelings that were fundamental to the human experience? Was she truly getting better or was she floating above a life that warranted further examination?

Pa asked her to name another medication, painkillers, radiation, insulin or blood thinners, that changed the fundamental make-up of a person – that made them something other than what they were. There were none. But if medicine did not have the capacity to alter one's personality, then how could she explain what was happening?

She returns home after the pool, showers and eats last night's leftovers. Elias messages to say he is ten minutes away and can she bring an extra beach towel.

They drive to Gordons Bay, an hour or so's expedition across Sydney. He plays music and winds down the windows, and they spend most of the trip exchanging stories of shark attacks they'd either read about or seen videos of deep on internet forums.

It is two in the afternoon by the time they arrive, parking at the top of a rocky headland and following a winding boardwalk to the bottom. Bronzed bodies look like lizards prostrated on rust-coloured rocks, and the turquoise water is entirely transparent, the sandy bottom visible as far as the eye can see.

'How did you know about this place?' she asks, struck by how hidden it is.

'Mum and Dad used to drive us out here heaps as kids, because it reminded them of the beaches in Greece,' he says as he walks towards an unoccupied rock.

'Have you been there?'

He stops and offers her his hand. 'Greece? Yeah. Mum was

from an island called Kastellorizo and Dad is from a town just outside of Rhodes. But we've been to Crete, Corfu . . . a bunch of places where we have family. And there's something about here, with the little fishing boats and the colour of the water, that makes it feel like you're on the other side of the world.'

'I'm so jealous,' she says, watching a group of older women being buoyed by coloured pool rings.

'I'll take you one day,' he says, looking at her for a moment, before setting down his bag and pulling off his shirt.

He had made a few comments like this. Just in the car he had made a passing remark about 'when you see my place' and last time she had seen him he'd told a story about his brother and finished with 'you'll know what I mean when you meet him'. It was strange, his tone. They had never kissed. They spent time together but neither ever called it a date. He texted her most days, always replying straight away, and a few times he'd gone as far as to call her. She knows he doesn't have a girlfriend, he'd come out of a relationship about a year prior and spoke of her fondly, like she was a friend he'd grown apart from. A few times she had imagined herself asking what this was or how he felt. But then she supposed that if she was truly honest with herself, she already knew. And not since Jake had she enjoyed someone's company so much – a friendship first, although she couldn't ignore that she also found herself looking at him when his attention was elsewhere. She liked the shape of his legs and the sharpness of his jaw. As he climbs down to a rock closer to the water's edge, gesturing for her to join him, she wonders how it is possible for someone to both calm her and excite her so much at the same time. It is as though her heart speeds up but her breathing slows down. For the first time in as long as she can remember she thinks, *This is exactly where I want to be.*

They swim all afternoon, every now and then resting on the rocks, which quickly become too hot, and so they dive back in. Elias brought a snorkel for them to share, so they take turns exploring the Underwater Trail, spotting fish and a small stingray hiding beneath a stretch of seaweed. Only once the sun disappears behind the cliffs do they dry themselves and realise how hungry they are. It is well past six.

Elias drives them to a nearby fish and chip shop, and because the air is still warm, they decide to stop to eat at a park by Bronte Beach, another spot in Sydney Adella has never been to. The sky turns from yellow to a burning orange to soft pink to purple, the sensation of encroaching mosquitoes signalling that it's time to go home.

When she lies in bed hours later she can barely recall what they'd talked about. He told stories about work that had made her laugh so hard she'd got the hiccups, and she liked how excited he'd become when she asked the man at the fish and chip shop if they could please have chicken salt. Mostly she had noticed that no story she told or admission she made compelled him to look in the other direction. Instead, he just looked her in the eye, his expression full of curiosity.

The days that followed were slow and aimless. Twice a week she was visiting a clinical psychologist, a woman in her thirties named Renee. At the end of most sessions she felt depleted and worse than she had before, impatient with the return to her childhood and examination of her relationships with her mother and father. She felt like Renee was mining for trauma that wasn't there, overlooking the fact that this was just how Adella was genetically programmed, and it was her current distress she was hoping to relieve. Weeks on she still thought incessantly about death, oscillating between abject terror and intrigue.

As her sense of what had happened at the end of last year became clearer, like a mirage that was slowly coming into view, she found herself unable to look her mother in the eye. Her bedroom. The visions of how she had left her bedroom that night. Her mum had mentioned it in hospital, how difficult it had been to find anything, but Adella had rolled over in bed, wanting to hold her hands over her ears and drown out the sound of her mother's voice.

In the weeks leading up to the end of the school term she had found herself incapable of washing her clothes. Of taking a bowl to the sink. Of throwing pizza boxes in the bin. Her room had one window which remained always closed, the blind drawn. There was no patch of floor space where the cream carpet was visible, and she knew there were spots that were wet with water glasses that had spilled, half-empty soft drink cans and sopping towels that had been discarded on the floor. She no longer had a dirty washing basket; all her clothes were thrown together, clothes that stank of being worn too many days in a row, unwashed under-wear strewn across her unmade bed. She couldn't remember the last time she had changed her sheets, her pillows imprinted with the day's make-up she couldn't bring herself to wash off. The paramedics must have seen that room. Her roommates too. And then her mother, who she imagined had taken it upon herself to clean it, to pack away her things.

She spoke to Renee about the vision she had of that room, of how revolted the people around her must have felt. Renee asked about Mele and Helen, if she had heard from them since that night. Mele had messaged her. She could only reply after she left the hospital but they had texted back and forth since. Helen had reached out, too, asking how she was. Both Helen and Mele said how much they wanted to see her when she was feeling better. Their correspondence, she imagined, was very much out of a sense of obligation. But Renee did not accept that explanation, which is how seeing Mele and Helen became somewhat of an assignment for that weekend.

She had hoped they'd suggest a quiet restaurant near her old apartment. But Mele insisted they visit a new bar in Darling Harbour where her boyfriend was working and could get them discounted drinks. Adella didn't tell them she hadn't had a drink in months, how she hated the taste and how it made her dizzy and confused. What little control she did have seemed to disappear after a glass and then two, until she inevitably embarrassed herself. This, though, was about returning to normalcy. And so she agreed.

They meet at Bar 312 early on Saturday evening. She spends the hour-long train trip trying not to think about the first moment they see her, their minds envisioning that night, the state of her bedroom, the subhuman groans she was making. It occurs to her that this is likely some kind of pity catch-up, a way for the two of them to absolve themselves of any guilt they would likely feel if they never spoke to Adella again. *Just get through tonight,* she repeats to herself. *And then you can tell Renee you were right.*

The evening is not how she imagined. They order cocktails and talk about everything but that rainy night in December when she ended up in Emergency. If the subject of their new roommate comes up, they move along swiftly. Mele speaks repeatedly about how much Jack misses her. For weeks, she says, he waited by her door, sniffing under the doorframe, sitting as though if he were just more obedient Adella might appear. She wishes Mele would stop. The image overwhelms her with guilt. As though sensing her discomfort, Mele eventually moves on, assuring Adella that she can visit Jack anytime, and even take him for a sleepover if she'd like the company.

It is when they are eating fries and arancini balls and bruschetta that Adella gets the distinct sense she will see someone she knows tonight. It is difficult to explain. She used to joke with Sophia that after a couple of drinks she becomes a little bit psychic, able to see the night unfold right before it does. And tonight she is sure something is going to happen. There is a presence in the room that feels familiar.

She cannot have seen him yet, because he is sitting on the other side of the bar, buried in a corner booth with six or so friends. But when she goes to the bar and stands before the dozen or so beer taps, deep inside her own head, her gaze pauses on a familiar side profile. The way his hair is parted on the left side. The bridge of his nose is straight and small. His shoulders are broader, and his facial hair longer, but her body knows it is Nathan. And Daniel is sitting a few places down from him, telling a story that has everyone's attention. Her stomach drops. She looks down at what she's wearing, a black linen dress with a tie around the middle. Does it even suit her? She hadn't thought about it until now. Suddenly she feels visible. Conspicuous. Had she done her hair? she thinks to herself in a panic. Yes. And her make-up is simple but at least an attempt had been made. By the time she looks back up, Nathan's eyes have found her. When he sees she has recognised him too, his expression transforms into a wide grin, a subtle wave with his left hand.

She orders drinks from Angelo, Mele's boyfriend, who is working the bar, and as she lifts her phone to tap, she feels a hand on her upper back.

'Adella.' Nathan smiles at her as though he had not once ejaculated in her mouth. Choked her. Looked up at her from between her legs.

'Nathan, hi,' she says, frozen as he kisses her on the cheek.

'It's been years.' He shakes his head and runs his fingers through his hair.

She nods, unsure of what to say. Her eyes are drawn to freckles scattered across his nose and cheeks, and all she can think about is that morning in Thailand. What Sophia said.

'How's Daniel?' she asks, lost as to how to sustain this conversation.

'Yeah, great. He's just over there actually. He got engaged last week, that's why we're all out. Angelo here is in our basketball team.' He smiles and nods at Mele's boyfriend.

'Ah. And you?' The question escapes her lips without thinking.

'Me what?'

'Are you engaged?' She lifts her eyebrows, an attempt to look playful.

'Ha!' He feigns laughter. 'No. No special woman in my life at the moment.'

He insists on paying for Adella's round and adds his own order. She feels relief despite herself, knowing her bank account is about to reach single digits. After that, she has no plan. He helps carry the glasses to her table, where, as it happens, Mele recognises him from watching Angelo's basketball.

After another round, also paid for by him, the three of them find themselves at Nathan's table, Daniel asking her questions about what she's been up to all these years with wide eyes as though she hadn't once been a joke to him. Eventually he asks the question he's been waiting to, as casually as he can muster.

'How's Sophia been, by the way? Haven't spoken to her in years.' He shifts in his seat.

Funny, she thinks. How even an engagement doesn't break the curiosity we have about people we once slept with. No flesh-and-blood person can entirely fill the space of a series of ghosts, and the imagined futures that are unfolding simultaneously.

She answers how any friend would. She exaggerates Sophia's happiness. Her successes. She describes her life with Leon, how they're thinking of having a baby, looking to buy an apartment. In her rendition, Leon almost sounds desirable.

With Nathan, she shares very little. He buys her drinks and they talk about that trip to Thailand more than seven years ago that marked the end of a relationship they never had. That's not how Nathan appears to remember it, she discovers. With a beer in his hand he juts out his bottom lip and clutches his chest, recalling how he reached out to her afterwards, and she never replied.

'That's not quite how it happened,' she laughs, behaving as though she is unperturbed by the details. As though there were many Nathans throughout her twenties. As though she barely remembers him.

It is late when he squeezes her knee, in a way he used to almost ten years ago. A part of her begs him to kiss her. But Mele leans across the table and lets her know they are leaving, the last train will depart in fifteen minutes. Despite what her body wants, she retrieves her bag from the sticky floor, and slides out from the booth. Nathan walks her to the door. Asks her to stay. Says he can drive her home in the morning. There is something she likes about his tone. The desperation. How it borders on begging. She knows the most desirable thing she can do right now, the most erotic, is to walk away. With a turn of her body she can ensure he will message her tomorrow.

And as she does, Mele and Helen laughing about something beside her, she feels something unfamiliar in her belly. A stirring sensation. One she has not felt in months. Perhaps years.

Butterflies.

36

Adella

She is on the phone to Pa, just after dinner. He is in the middle of explaining how he's set up a makeshift putting green in his living room, going into details about improving his alignment and the placement of his front foot and quiet wrists.

He is in a particularly good mood and she suspects he's had a second glass of red wine.

'I was watching something on the telly the other night,' he says, 'an interview with some lady and she was talking about everything she'd been diagnosed with, all the psychologists she'd seen, and she was sharing these awful thoughts she had, banging on about awareness . . .'

'That's a good thing, though, isn't it?' She smiles as she challenges him. 'We're meant to talk about it so we know we're not the only people to have ever had those thoughts.' It is a clichéd thing to say, but sometimes she speaks in clichés to her grandfather.

'You'd think if talking about it was the answer then the problem would be getting better, not worse!' he chuckles. 'Seems to me more people have this anxiety and depression stuff, whatever we call it, these days than they did fifty years ago.

'Maybe the old-fashioned approach where we kept things to ourselves . . . maybe we were on to something,' he laughs, blind to the irony of saying so on a phone call to Adella, where neither of them keep much to themselves.

'I was thinking today, you know what the trick to it is?' He has certainly had an additional glass of wine, Adella thinks.

'When we're young, like you,' he clears his throat, 'we're meant to believe that our lives ought to chart in an upwards trajectory . . . where every day is better than the next. Does that make sense? Happiness is believing that tomorrow might be even better than today. We ought to live like that is the case, even though we know it is not.'

She thinks about growing old. How when a hip begins to creak or an ache crawls up your spine, it is not a matter of waiting for an injury to subside. Illness becomes a permanent state. Degeneration only goes in one direction. Imagine knowing, as Pa had gone some way in describing to her, that all the good life had to offer was buried in the past. The only surprises left were not the kind anyone looked forward to. When the phone rang, it was most often another friend who had died. Or a diagnosis that meant they would die soon. The only time he dressed up was to attend a funeral, where fewer and fewer people cried because death wasn't a tragedy anymore. When he noticed his roof had begun to sag, he wondered whether it was worth fixing. Did he have the energy to repair something for a world in which he didn't exist? All that humans fear: pain, illness, death, loss, that was all there was now.

'For once,' he said to her late one night, 'this melancholy I've lived with for most of my life is entirely rational.'

Tonight, though, his voice is lively, and it is only when she hears the front door open and close that she says she'd better go.

She hears Lottie's voice, and her first instinct is to worry that Lottie has come over to complain about the loan she gave her two nights ago. She hadn't wanted to ask, but she promised she'd pay her back as soon as one of these jobs came through she'd been applying for. Just five hundred dollars to cover her for the next few weeks. She couldn't bring herself to ask anything more of her mother, who she'd heard on the phone trying to cancel her Foxtel subscription, even though watching real estate shows on the Lifestyle Channel seemed to be one of the few things she truly enjoyed. But Lottie had seemed unbothered by the request, insisting there was no rush to pay her back.

By the time Adella reaches the kitchen, Lottie and her mother are sitting at the round dining table, Lottie tapping the surface with her fingertips, her legs fidgeting beneath. She asks how Pa is. Adella notices that her face looks fuller, specs of pigmentation on her cheeks from a summer generous with sunshine. A bad feeling establishes itself in her stomach. There is something about Lottie's expression that gives her a sense of unease. Might something have happened with Clinton? she wonders.

A natural pause falls between them, and neither Adella nor her mother moves to fill it.

'Okay. Well,' Lottie mumbles. 'It's been a really . . . hard few months and I haven't known what to do and I didn't think this would be it.'

Adella looks at the worried expression on her mother's face. This must be about Clinton.

'But I'm pregnant. Six months, now, actually.' She rubs her left eye.

'What the fuck?' Adella shrieks. 'You're six months? You're having a baby? In what, April? May?' She feels as though this has to be some kind of joke, but as she looks more closely at Lottie, she sees the size of her chest beneath a loose-fitting, long-sleeved shirt.

'Where's the bump, can I see the bump?' She feels a desperate urge to hold this baby, her niece or nephew, immediately. This table. A high chair. Christmas. A play mat. A pram. Pink cheeks and drool and tiny little fingers and the word 'Mama'. Lottie. A mum. Jake's half-sister Megan had had a baby when they were in Year Nine and Adella had spent school holidays for years carrying little Indi on her hip, feeding her early dinners and blowing bubbles in the backyard. If she knew Indi was at Jake's, she'd always walk a little faster, anticipating the smile that would be waiting for her, and the tiny hand that would reach for hers. At Jake's funeral she had spotted Indi from a distance. She must have been eleven or twelve. Adella had barely recognised her.

Her mother sits, covering her eyes with her hands, and when she looks up her eyes are glassy and red.

'Oh, Lottie.' The lines around her mouth deepen. 'This will be the greatest adventure of your life.'

The expression on Lottie's face, though, matches neither of theirs.

'Wait. Six months. How come you didn't tell us? Does this mean you knew at your engagement party?' Adella does the maths. The engagement party was in October, five months ago. Then they'd had that fight after she'd lost Lottie's gift. It dawns on Adella what that time must've been like for Lottie.

'Yeah, but just. I didn't want it.' Lottie looks at her now-still hands on the table. 'I don't know, maybe I still don't.'

She tells them she never wanted children. She's never felt maternal; doesn't think it is the thing that makes life meaningful. Something had happened with her Mirena that she didn't entirely understand. There was light bleeding she ignored for a while, and then when she finally saw a doctor they said it had been dislodged and had become essentially ineffective. That means she had been ovulating. And after a urine test in a doctor's office on her own, her fears were confirmed. She was pregnant.

At the engagement party not even Clinton knew yet. She planned on having the pregnancy terminated the following week. She was anxious about the discomfort; what the body would need to do. Eventually she told him, framing it almost as an apology. An apology for not being more careful. But when Clinton cried, she tells them, it was not because he was angry or overcome by her ineptitude. It was because he felt this was a miracle. He hadn't thought much about fatherhood before Lottie came along, but sitting beside her in their living room, he admitted for the first time how much he wanted a child.

Lottie felt numb. She did what she always does when something makes her feel anxious; she avoided it. Whatever she needed to do, she figured she could put it off for just another day. Until the end of the week. But then she couldn't really do much on the weekend anyway. And so weeks passed. She did not go back to the doctor or stop eating soft cheese. She just barely existed, ignoring the way her breasts were now spilling out of her bra, and the nausea that plagued her from morning well into the night.

'I didn't want to bring a baby into the world,' Lottie says, and Adella wonders for a moment if she's going to bring up climate change, and already doesn't believe her reasoning. For the first time since she arrived, Lottie puts her hands around what they can now see is a swollen belly.

'I know what it's like to worry about you,' she looks at Adella, 'and I'm not blaming you, obviously. But I don't know if I can worry about another person like that. Seeing people in that state is actually really traumatising.' Adella wonders when Lottie started using words like 'traumatising'. 'Sometimes I think it can be just as bad as being the person who's depressed or anxious or whatever because you can't do anything but watch. With Pa, and with you, Mum, what chance does this kid even have?'

They sit in silence for a moment until their mum, eyes fixed on Lottie's stomach, says under her breath, 'In terms of not having a baby,' she pulls a face that says *whoops*, 'that ship might have sailed.' Even Lottie cannot help but laugh.

'I know, but what have I done? What gives me the right to think I can do this?' The palms of Lottie's hands squeeze her temples and then pull downwards on her cheeks.

'I get irritable if I've had less than eight hours of sleep. I'm selfish and lazy. I can't cook. I've never changed a nappy. Last week I hit my shin on the coffee table and cried because it hurt so much and now I'm looking at a marathon labour where my vagina and my butthole morph into one and my bladder just fucking hangs between my knees.'

'Mum had two kids and she can't cook,' Adella reassures her. 'And you're a bitch when you don't get enough sleep, right, Mum?' Their mother dutifully nods in response.

It becomes clear as they speak that Lottie had never, really, changed her mind. She simply had not undergone a termination, and was still in shock that this thing continued to grow. She did not feel anything for 'it', as she referred to the child. They hadn't found out the gender and had only recently seen a doctor for the first time. Clinton spent more time touching her stomach than she did.

'Can I touch it?' Adella asks, as the table falls quiet.

'Yeah. It might even kick,' Lottie says, lifting up her jumper to reveal a hard, rounded stomach.

Adella doesn't expect to feel something when she places her hands as close as she can to her unborn niece or nephew. But she can sense an energy beneath the skin, a little thing so far untouched by the world around them. This thing does not know what it is to be disappointed or lost, that they might prefer to be over there than over here. This dark place is all there is. They do not know cruelty or injustice, the feeling of being in a room where you don't belong or the devastation of letting someone down. She murmurs a 'hello' and after a few seconds she feels a kick, as though confirming someone is there.

She is overcome by her capacity to love this unborn, unseen

thing, a ghost of all their ancestors. A compilation of all their imperfect genes.

Isn't it funny, she thinks. *What I want for this baby.*

She doesn't care whether they are rich or poor. Who they love. If they're attractive or plain, smart or average. None of that, it turns out, matters very much.

What does she want for this child?

To know, more than anything, how loved they are.

They speak until the early hours of the morning, until Lottie yawns and stretches, announcing that she ought to get to bed. While their mother washes up, Adella follows Lottie to the front door.

'You know that's what did this to her,' Lottie whispers, tilting her head in the direction of the kitchen.

'Did what?' Adella isn't following.

'After me, Mum was never the same. Postpartum depression. It, like, ruined her life.'

'How do you even know that?' Adella pulls a face, unconvinced.

'The way we know everything about our family. Some weird letter I found in the bottom drawer from Aunty Liz. I don't know if she was ever properly diagnosed but she couldn't get out of bed and had problems with attachment or something.'

She tries to convince Lottie that today is nothing like things were thirty-two years ago. That maybe if their mother had a partner who didn't spend almost every night at the pub, the outcome could have been different. Lottie is already seeing a psychologist, Adella discovers. One the hospital referred her to.

'When they think a mum is maybe gonna hurt their baby,'

Lottie says with intentionally wild eyes, '*that's* when they really care about women's mental health.'

Just before she leaves, Lottie's expression turns earnest.

'You'll help me, right? With this?'

'Of course. I'll probably kidnap it. And Mum . . . it won't be long until she retires and you can go back to work or whatever.' She is certain, for reasons she can't articulate, that Lottie is going to be okay.

'What if we don't vibe? Like, what if this baby is one of those kids who calls me by my first name and asks if this restaurant has corkage?'

As kids, they had been out to dinner with family visiting from Adelaide, and were seated either side of a cousin named Harry who was roughly their age. Ten or eleven. When the waiter ('waiter' was a stretch, the restaurant had plastic tablecloths) asked what they'd like to drink, Lottie and Adella had shouted 'Coke' at the same time this floppy-haired blond kid asked the waiter if they charged for corkage. His mother had laughed and said he always asked questions like that, but it was all they could talk about on the car trip home. After their mother explained what corkage actually meant, she conceded 'that boy was very pretentious', and they'd taken turns doing impersonations of him.

'Dickheads don't happen by accident. Dickheads are made. If the kid asks about corkage then that's your deal-breaker. That's why there are two parents. So one can tap out.' Adella shrugs.

She crawls into bed that night, her body coursing with excitement. She instinctively messages Elias. Lying on her left side, she thinks about this little person. How she thinks it will be a girl.

She entertains the possibility that this baby does carry the same genetics that had infected her. Her mother. Her grandfather. *Why am I not afraid?* she asks herself. And then it occurs to her. She knows enough about Clinton, quiet and loyal, to be sure that he will not walk out on his family. Not on New Year's Eve, like their father did, when his daughters were six and eight. Not with his breath smelling of Tooheys New and cigarette smoke, another woman waiting for him a few suburbs over, who wouldn't yet nag him about when he'd be home or how much money he'd spent at the pub. Clinton was not a man who would improve himself for his next wife. And by 'improve' she means become a more functional alcoholic, who somehow earned a decent salary as, would you believe it, the manager of a thriving pub.

Men always seem to be able to find a woman who asks less of them, she thinks. *Yes*, they must say to themselves. *That's more like it.*

Clinton didn't want a woman who asked less of him. He wasn't a man who life simply happened to, waking up one day wondering where these kids came from and why his house was a mess. How lucky this baby would be to have the parents who were waiting for them.

When she turns to her right, hoping to sleep, her phone lights up. It's Elias. Most of the message is exclamation marks and she smiles. But as her mind turns to tomorrow, her stomach whirls with guilt. It will, in one way or another, be significant.

She's going out to dinner with Nathan.

37

Adella

When Elias asks what she's doing tonight, she delivers a lie immediately.

'Applying for jobs,' she says, before taking a sip of her cappuccino. They're at Cafe Luxe. She had joked about it every time they'd driven past for weeks, so finally Elias demanded she take him there.

'It's a Saturday night. That's so depressing.' He places a forkful of scrambled eggs and sourdough into his mouth.

Adella shrugs. He is going to a gig in Newtown tonight with a bunch of friends.

'I'll say it one more time,' he says, swallowing. 'Just come back to St Francis. There's no way they've replaced you yet and the staff will get it.'

She shakes her head even as he's speaking. Her boss knows she will not be returning. This year she needs a fresh start. To begin somewhere new.

Elias will return to work on Monday, which means she'll no longer have company on weekdays. She feels pre-emptively home-sick, overcome by a sense of longing she can't quite articulate. If she thinks about it too much, she finds herself wading into the territory of resentment, like a petulant child begging their parent not to go into work.

Whatever this is, their brunches and their trips to the beach and their walks through the parklands that Elias hyperbolically calls 'hiking' will necessarily change after Monday. He will work long hours, his weekends full of commitments, and their messages will fizzle from daily to a few times a week, to sporadically, when something comes up that reminds one of the other. While she had been sure only a few weeks ago that Elias felt something for her, her sense had shifted. There had not yet been an invite to his place. When they went to the drive-in cinema a few nights ago, he dropped her straight home afterwards, without so much as a sideways glance when he pulled up. There hadn't been a fancy dinner or drinks, a compliment that might be interpreted as flirtatious, or a late-night drunk text confessing everything. He might enjoy her company, she figured, but he found it offensively easy to keep his hands off her.

That's why she is so surprised when he says, 'We could hang out after the gig, if you're still awake.'

'Won't it be late?' She hopes she doesn't sound dismissive.

'Nah, not that late. Finishes at maybe ten or eleven. I could come to yours and we could actually start *Parks and Rec.*' He'd been talking about watching the TV show with her since she was in hospital, joking that it cured his depression one winter while he was at uni.

She says she'll see how she goes. She has a big night ahead of her, looking for a job she doesn't want. 'But text me when you're done,' she says.

For the rest of the afternoon she feels twitchy and uneasy, unable to sit in the same spot for more than a few minutes. She scrolls through jobs online, partly to make her lie to Elias true, but only catches every second word. Instead she is pulled towards thoughts of Nathan, a nervousness brewing in her gut. Just as she begins to believe that tonight might not happen, Nathan messages and double-checks she can make a six o'clock booking. He even adds he's looking forward to seeing her. Did he speak to women like this all along? she wonders. Was it just her he ignored or rescheduled, not even checking his messages for spelling errors? To be the focus of a person who only ever looked at her peripherally is intoxicating. Perhaps she did it. She became the person he always wanted.

They meet at a local Italian restaurant with white tablecloths and linen napkins, the closest to her he has ever travelled. She is dressed as herself, in denim jeans and a shirt she's been wearing all summer. He stands up as she walks in, kissing her on the cheek as though she is precious. He orders them cocktails, and remembers that she is somewhat of a picky eater, uninterested in seafood. She can't even recall telling him that.

'I remember seeing Sophia after that trip to Thailand,' he says over a plate of cacio e pepe. 'She said something had happened between you two but never told us what.' He twirls his pasta. It's clear he's curious.

'She really never told you?' Part of her is surprised. If the roles were reversed, she thinks she probably would have told them everything.

He shakes his head. 'I remember Daniel even egging her on, you know he can be a wanker. And she was always so defensive. She left a party once because he wouldn't drop it. Actually I think that might have been the final time they broke up . . . a few weeks after that trip.'

The room suddenly feels hotter. While she's struck by Sophia's loyalty, she is also confronted by the knowledge that Sophia saw them at all after their trip. It might have been nine years ago, but her heart pounds as though it were yesterday.

'We were both interested in the same guy. It was stupid.' She waves her hand, sipping at her second cocktail. 'I do remember, though,' she smiles, buying herself time, 'she told me what you guys used to say about me. How you'd make fun of my messages. And you were seeing other girls, which I had absolutely no idea about, by the way.' She isn't sure if she achieves the playful tone she's going for.

He places his forearms on the table and fixes his gaze on some abstract point above her head.

'Yeah. I've thought about that a lot since,' he says slowly. 'I'm pretty embarrassed, to be honest. I don't know what to say other than I was immature. I wasn't ready for a relationship. And I think I was scared of how much I liked you.' He is looking her in the eye now. 'You were so smart . . .'

Adella rolls her eyes.

'You were! I'm sure still are. I felt a bit out of my depth, I think.' He leans back, his hands cradling the back of his head.

'I'm sorry, is what I'm trying to say. I couldn't believe you'd even speak to me at that bar the other night after how I behaved back then. I've changed, though. A lot. I wouldn't ask you out, properly, if I hadn't.' His eyes look pleading.

She can smell his cologne from across the table, strong and fresh. In some ways, she notices he has become less confident rather than more. He shifts in his seat. If she were on any other date she would assume this person was nervous. But she'd never known Nathan to feel nervous, especially not around her.

They have a third cocktail and talk about their jobs, where he's living, the people they'd known back then and lost contact with. She tells him about Lottie, and he pulls out his phone to show her pictures of his two nieces and a nephew, who he can't talk about without laughing. At one point she swears she hears him say under his breath, 'I can't wait to be a dad,' but then he locks his phone, and slides it back into his pocket.

When she's in a taxi, on the way to Nathan's house, his hand rubbing the inner thigh of her jeans, she quickly checks the time. There are two messages from Elias lit up on her screen. She doesn't open them, but can see they're asking if she's still up. If she wants to hang out tonight. One even ends with an 'X'. He's never done that before. But before her body can generate a feeling, she feels Nathan's lips on her neck. He whispers into her ear, his breath hot.

She turns, and kisses him back.

38

Adella

The buzzer for apartment thirteen sounds, and she steps back, waiting to hear a familiar voice.

She places her handbag down beside her right leg, rolling out her shoulders. Inside are the things she picked up on the drive over here.

Something about this building smells faintly of hospital. Maybe someone is just cooking mashed potato. She studies the intercom system; the kind where the names of former tenants are written on pieces of paper covered by a layer of plastic. The closer she looks, the more unsure she is that the doorbell even works.

'Hey,' a muffled voice says. 'Come up, level three.'

The corridor is dark and the stairs sunken. She had expected something more modern. There are kids' bikes outside doors and several pairs of shoes lined up. By the time she gets to the top of the stairs, she's out of breath.

Before she knocks, the doorknob twists.

'Finally you get to see the place.' A cat wanders up the hall, and rubs itself up against Sophia's bare ankles.

In Sophia's kitchen, Adella finds two red wine glasses, and fills them with the bottle of Diet Coke she bought on the way here. Then she presents her bag of M&Ms. Peanut. 'We're grown-ups now. And these seemed more mature,' she explains to Sophia.

They sit on Sophia's couch, sipping their Diet Cokes, and talk for hours. Every time they press play on *The OC*, one of them says, 'Oh, pause it, pause it, I meant to show you,' retrieving something like a photo of a confronting newborn baby a girl from their year just gave birth to.

'You'd tell me, wouldn't you?' Sophia asks, holding up the picture of the newborn with so much hair it's been swept into a side fringe.

'Okay, honestly,' Adella studies the picture, 'I would tell you to just hold off posting a picture for a week or maybe a few months. Until the baby grew into its skin. Because you'd be too jacked on hormones to even know that that baby isn't remotely cute.'

'I would never say out loud that a baby needs Botox,' Sophia says, shaking her head. 'But that baby . . .'

Then they press play, and some other question would come up about Leon – he is on night shift – or Lottie or Elias.

They speak about Nathan, Sophia entirely without judgement. Her expression remains neutral as Adella tells her about the date, the sex, the messages since. She verbalises for the first time how she feels. How he makes her feel alive and seen and wanted. The sex had been like a build-up, years of desire brought to a boiling point.

315

She had felt young again, which she knows sounds ridiculous given she is not yet thirty. But he reminded her of the newness of sex – real, adult sex – at twenty. How her mind was not yet able to anticipate every touch. There was such novelty in going home with someone. What might they say or do? By now, she felt she could almost write the script. It was formulaic. Everyone, it seemed, was having the same sex. What a depressing discovery.

If she is honest with herself, dating Nathan is also about proving something to the person she was at twenty, as though living out some adolescent dream. She has developed an affection for who she was then, ten years ago, thinner but more awkward. She could see now she wasn't as repulsive as she'd thought.

Did she want Nathan? she wonders. Or did Adella at twenty want Nathan? And what is the difference?

'I did get home this morning,' she confesses to Sophia, 'and find myself scrolling through his profile to see if there's anything I should know about. So far so good.'

Sophia smiles, as though happening upon a memory. 'So the question is, he might have changed,' her expression suggests she isn't entirely convinced, 'but have you?'

They watch another fifteen minutes of *The OC* until Sandy pops up and Sophia pauses to ask how her dad is going. Adella shrugs. He'd been in Queensland over Christmas when she was hospitalised, and they hadn't told him until she was about to be discharged. He had shouted down the phone line at her mum a few times, but then moved on, calling Adella a little more frequently than usual to enquire about her 'health'.

'And how are you feeling now? You look like a different

person,' Sophia says, clearly uncertain about whether that's the right thing to say.

Adella pauses, and thinks about the last two months. It is as though, very slowly, a fog has lifted. The fog is not gone. She is still aware of it and sometimes it obscures her vision. But she can see through it. Everything is a little louder. A little clearer. 'I feel like I've fallen into my life again. And last year, it was honestly like I'd been ripped from it, floating above my life wondering how to change things when I couldn't even touch it.'

She pauses and brings a knee up under her chin. 'The medication has made a big difference. It's meant that I can sleep and have the energy to exercise and talk to people. And that's the stuff you get told to do but sort of can't when things are bad. It's kind of like,' she tries to find the right metaphor, 'riding a bike. It's like I tried to ride a bike one day and couldn't even find the pedals. The wheels were glued to the ground. And the more you think about doing this thing that should be instinctive, the harder it gets.' Sophia nods.

'And now I'm back on the bike, and it's wobbly or whatever, but my legs are doing something without me having to consciously think about it. That might be a weird way to explain it.'

'No, I think it makes perfect sense,' Sophia says. 'I'm just glad you're –'

'Nope,' Adella says, raising her voice. 'Nup, we are not going full Mel.'

'I had forgotten about Mel!' Sophia laughs, remembering the girl from high school who used to narrate the depth and quality of their friendship.

'If our friendship ever becomes all about us declaring how much we mean to each other, I'm out.' Adella shudders in disgust.

'Yuck,' they say at the same time, right before Adella burps louder than she intended.

'That's better.'

She asks about Leon and Sophia does that thing where she says how great everything is, before providing more details that reveal things are not, in fact, great. He went out with his friends last weekend and didn't get home until five am, not really answering when she asked where they'd all been. He's territorial over his phone and doesn't make much of an effort with her mum.

'It's still good though. All just normal stuff, I guess,' she says. 'And Elias? What's happening with him? I like him . . .'

Adella laughs. 'Yes, I know you do. So do I.'

'He's hot.'

'You've never even met him!'

'But I've spent a lot of time stalking his photos.' Sophia takes a sip of her Diet Coke.

'I feel very . . . safe with him. Like, comfortable and like myself. But I'm not sure what it is. I don't feel nervous or . . . fireworks or whatever. Things are very different with Nathan.'

Sophia nods and looks at her inquisitively. 'Fireworks are over-rated,' she says, pressing play.

After a few minutes, while still staring at the television, Sophia says quietly, 'So does that mean we're never going to talk about Thailand?'

'I'd rather not,' Adella replies, her gaze also fixed on the screen. She scratches the side of her head without really feeling it. She sighs. 'Obviously I'm just really sorry. I'm embarrassed and I hate myself.'

Sophia reaches for her empty wine glass. 'I hate myself a little bit too,' she says, cheersing Adella's glass without looking her in the eye.

On the drive home, her mind wanders again to Nathan. His hands. The way he looks at her. The nights she didn't sleep almost ten years ago, imagining how their conversations would unfold, what she might say to impress him. A song comes on the radio, years old by Justin Timberlake, that always reminds her of Jake. She has a memory of being in a dark club; in her recollection it's just them even though it wouldn't have been, and he is dancing to it. Half as a joke, the other half knowing he was actually a great dancer, much better than she ever was. He's laughing and he knows all the words and there was a whole year where this seemed like the only song that played on the radio. She sees him driving, this song turned up too loud. Him visiting her at the pub towards the end of her shift. Was this song playing then too? They are twenty-two again. And she asks him what she should do. She tells him, as though he is in the passenger seat, but she doesn't have to open her mouth, about Nathan and how much he has changed. How we are all different people at thirty than we are at twenty. You wouldn't know that though, would you, Jake, she adds. She is more honest with him about how she feels than she ever was; that she wants to be in love just as much as she wants a career – a thing she knows she shouldn't say out loud. She tells him she wants a best friend, an equal, who wants to road trip around

Australia with her just as much as he wants to have sex with her. She wants someone who doesn't leave.

He talks back. Not quite in his voice, but imbues within her his answers. He reasons with her. Articulates what she, deep down, knows to be true.

By the time she arrives home, she knows what she is going to do.

As she turns off the ignition and flicks off the lights, she whispers, 'Thanks, Jake.'

39

Adella

Ten months later

When Adella woke up today, the morning of her thirtieth birthday, everyone she had ever met was pregnant.

That sounds like an exaggeration. It is, but not by much. Girls from school. Two friends from work. Four of Lottie's friends just had a combined baby shower. How ridiculous.

She might not have noticed if it hadn't prompted a gnawing in her gut, as though for the first time in her life she can explicitly feel the emptiness of her own womb. As she pulled on a dress before dinner, she noticed the width of her hips and the layer of fat coating her stomach that she has always so despised. Is something meant to be in there? she wondered. Is she truly no more than an animal, made up of organs and blood, hormones and unfertilised eggs?

321

Sometimes she wishes she were, she thinks now, lying in bed. How much simpler everything would be. She knows she wants children. She is fairly certain she wants children with the man lying beside her. But biological impulses have a funny way of arriving at precisely the wrong time.

For six months she has been employed at the University of Western Sydney as a research assistant. She enjoys it more than she thought was possible. She works for the School of Psychiatry, researching physical treatments for depression and a variety of other psychiatric disorders. Specifically, their studies include electroconvulsive therapy, novel brain stimulation treatments, and ketamine. Finally she has something that resembles a career, that has the potential to lead to even more interesting places.

Lottie gave birth to a little girl on the last day of April. Her name is Chloe. When Adella arrived at the hospital, and was passed this tiny newborn with her pink face and eyes scrunched closed, she believed she had never seen anything so perfect. Lottie and Clinton kept bursting into tears, while her mother fussed about food and if anyone needed anything from the shop.

In the time since, she had been routinely surprised that it was somehow possible for Chloe to grow cuter every day. She smiles with pink gums, often rocking back and forth in fits of laughter as though she cannot control herself. She remains the happiest baby any of them have ever come across.

Chloe, it seems, takes after Clinton.

The first few months had been difficult for Lottie. Every time Adella came over she would exclaim, 'What the fuck is this?' and expose another part of her body. A soft belly. Nipples that now took up most of the real estate on her breasts, dark and blistered, like just the two of them had been on a tropical holiday while the rest of her body stayed behind.

Abandoning breastfeeding had been the best thing for Lottie. It meant they could all take turns feeding Chloe the bottle, her little fingers clutching at the sides.

Other than to work, Clinton barely goes anywhere without Chloe. He straps her to his chest as he heads out to drinks with friends, and often takes her for solo trips to the park or for a drive if she refuses to sleep. Adella's mother has never seen anything like it.

Their dad sees Chloe rarely but posts about her on social media often. In the early days he bought her a onesie that didn't fit yet with 'Grandpa's little girl' written on the front, and then demanded pictures. They find complaining about the performance of it all helps, Chloe sometimes nodding along as though she can understand exactly what they're saying.

Adella thinks about the past year or so. How much has changed. She shakes off memories of St Francis, the school she'd left. Still, she is overcome by guilt and shame about how she had let people down. She wonders if that will ever pass. In the aftermath, Elias had been so kind to her. She won't ever forget that.

She still swims. Still eats too much sugar and spends too much time on her phone. Still dresses as though she was running five minutes late and pulled something from a coathanger, not having the time to iron it. She loves her mother from a distance and finds her irritating up close.

She hears a sigh from beside her and pulls the sheet up to below her chin. This life she has created, everything in its place, feels like it is made of glass. It's as though she's tiptoeing around to ensure nothing falls off its ledge, terrified that at any moment everything might shatter.

And yet. Tonight as she lies beside a warm and safe body, it still feels as though something is missing.

In her early twenties, the world had felt so big. Suffocating in its limitlessness. But now, at the dawn of her thirties, life feels the opposite. There are parameters. The career path is set. The person chosen. The rent automatically paid. Those parameters make her feel protected. But in another breath, those limits can also make her feel as though she is trapped inside a cage.

Is life better when some of the doors have closed? When some of the branches on Sylvia Plath's metaphorical fig tree, each their own distinct path, have shrivelled up and died?

Maybe.

Here she is. Beside him. Being in her late twenties had felt like being in the middle of a game of musical chairs. She was sick of the game. A game she'd been playing for almost a decade. The music had begun to grind. Then, suddenly, it stopped. And she was sitting on a seat. She's lucky. She'd seen friends miss out. Her chair is sturdy and comfortable. She can't fault it. But the part of her that yearns for excitement continues to ask, *Is this all there is?* Should she play another round, and see where she ends up? How do you even know when you've won? When life is as good as it gets? That would take an awful lot of self-confidence, to be sure you've got it right. It would be pathological to not constantly ask the question.

Something Bad is Going to Happen

Is a better life waiting for me in the next chair?

Or is it worse?

Does she like her chair more than I like my chair?

The uncertainty, surely, is a part of it all.

Just as she decides to go to sleep, as though he can read her mind, he rolls over and puts an arm around her middle, kissing the back of her neck. He mumbles, 'I love you.'

She pulls his arm closer.

'Love you, Elias.'

Acknowledgements

I devour the acknowledgements of every book I read because whenever I finish I think, *How did they do that?*

Perhaps you're not thinking that and in fact you're just relieved it's over, but either way I'm going to attempt to answer the question of how anyone writes a novel – an endeavour I've been in awe of since I was a child.

Firstly, thank you to everyone who helped me think out loud. In particular my mum, Anne Stephens, my dad, Peter Stephens, and my twin sister Clare Stephens, who was the only person allowed to read anything. Thank you to Tai Luani and Hugh Baulderstone for their invaluable insights into the mental health system, and to the psychologists and psychiatric nurses who spoke to me for this project. A very special thank you to the dozens of women who generously shared their own experience in mental health facilities. Without your insights, this book would never have been written.

I want to acknowledge my grandfather, Philip, whose relationship with happiness has been complicated despite a lifetime of trying to work it out. My brothers Jack Stephens and Nicholas Stephens who are the wisest minds I've ever come across on this subject, even if they too are still looking for answers.

Thank you to the people who shaped my twenties and heavily inspired this book. Tai, Luke, Andi, and of course my now

327

husband Luca Lavigne, whose kindness, encouragement and unwavering belief in me is beyond anything I deserve.

Chilli, my dog, gets her own paragraph, because she never offers criticism, only cuddles, and does not care even a little bit if this book is any good.

Luckily, I've got Cate Blake, my brilliant publisher at Pan Macmillan, and Pippa Mason, my literary agent at Curtis Brown for that. Their investment in this book and faith in my vision is something I cannot thank them enough for. This is an infinitely better book because of their direction. Thank you to Cate for the chats and weird questions and for the invaluable edits. Unfortunately, every piece of feedback Cate offers is correct.

The same goes for the entire team at Pan Macmillan, from Brianne Collins who made this book make sense (timelines are not my forte) to Elena Gomez who picked up millions of errors.

Thank you to my team at Mamamia who inspire me and keep my mind full of ideas every single day. I am so lucky to have a workplace that supports my independent pursuits and works around the chaos that is my day-to-day life. Thank you especially to my *Mamamia Out Loud* co-hosts Mia Freedman and Holly Wainwright who challenge how I think, always send helpful links and know when not to ask how the book is going.

Finally, to my baby girl who has been growing in my tummy for the last nine months of writing this book. The second trimester energy boost really helped me meet my deadline, although her contribution at other stages needs to be addressed. For generations our family has struggled with happiness. My only wish is that for you it is a little bit easier.